# Devil Black

## by

## Laura Strickland

**Devil Black**

COPYRIGHT © 2013 by Laura Strickland

Cover Art by *Tina Lynn Stout*

The Wild Rose Press, Inc.
PO Box 708
Adams Basin, NY 14410-0708
Visit us at www.thewildrosepress.com

Publishing History
First English Tea Rose Edition, 2013
Print ISBN 978-1-61217-693-2
Digital ISBN 978-1-61217-694-9

Published in the United States of America

**He pulled her hard against him, into his arms.** His mouth plundered hers, battered it open, and he felt her terror spike. Yet it subsided as swiftly as did his desire to handle her roughly. Sweetness met passion and broke over them both like a shower of fire. He felt her hesitate, and his lips softened, began to woo hers, coax and persuade them further apart. Greed washed through him in a staggering tide that left him feeling all at once weak and powerful. Surely he would sell his soul for the taste of her.

She raised both her hands and planted them flat against his chest. He expected to feel her push him away; instead her fingers curled into the fabric of his tunic and pulled him closer.

The motion went straight to his head. He contemplated pushing her down there before the hearth but dismissed the notion. Not before they saw the priest. He would stand accused of raping no woman.

He broke the kiss, and a sound came from her throat, a sigh of protest. They gazed deeply into one another's eyes, and Dougal's heart began to pound the way it did before a battle, when his sword cried for blood.

She still had her fingers fastened in his tunic, and they stood barely a breath apart. Every inch of him could feel every inch of her—some more than others.

"So, lady," he said, allowing one corner of his mouth to turn up, "will you wed wi' me?"

## Dedication

For my friends of the
fanstory online writing community
with gratitude for
your encouragement and enthusiasm.
A hundred thousand thanks!

Chapter One

*Central Scotland, 1608*

"Do you know what they call you? The monster without conscience; the destroyer; he who ruins whatever he touches. They call you the Devil Black: *Diabhal Dubh*."

The words hissed through the hush of midnight, competing with the voice of the wind rising outside. Dougal MacRae—the Black Devil—narrowed his eyes and propped one booted foot on the hob, reaching for comfort he did not expect to find. The wet night, foul and chill, had cast a pall upon the hour and unsettled him. He had no desire for his companion's wild opinions, smiting his ears.

But no one had ever convinced Lachlan MacElwain to keep his opinions to himself. Lachy had been Dougal's closest friend—his one friend, would Dougal admit it—for as long as either of them could remember, and the sole person Dougal had not succeeded in driving away. Truly, Dougal had tried. Heedlessly and persistently, he had banished whatever good feeling anyone in his world harbored for him: his sister, his raggedy slew of cousins, his father's men at arms, and the other companions of his childhood. Aye, well, the clansmen still stood with him. Had they any choice?

"They are saying," Lachlan went on in a tone halfway between enjoyment and condemnation, "your soul is damned and even God has washed His hands of you."

"God?" Dougal repeated the word in a harsh tone, and snorted. "Where is He, then? Busy playing chess with the Devil, no doubt." He inclined his head toward Lachlan. "The real Devil, I am meaning. Never doubt he exists, Lachy. And he has been far more active in my life than any God."

"Heresy," Lachlan muttered.

Dougal drank deep from his cup of raw whisky, savored the bite as the liquor went down his throat, and shrugged. "I say only the truth. And who are 'they,' who speak so ill of me?"

Lachlan raised thoughtful eyes to meet Dougal's. Lachlan, Dougal admitted, looked mild and harmless, the bonny sort of man with whom the lassies might get up to dance at the parties to which Dougal himself no longer received invitations. Lachy's honey-brown hair brushed the shoulders of the leather jerkin he wore, and his blue eyes looked almost serene in the dim candlelight.

"'They,'" he said concisely, "are the neighbors you have been busy robbing these last eight years, the clans you have battled, the many women you have wronged, the very government of Scotland itself. They would hang you if they could."

Dougal crooked a brow. "I cannot deny those charges." Whatever else he might do, he strove always for honesty. "If these folk feel better for calling me by a foolish name, so be it."

"Do you not care?" Lachlan asked, only partly

feigning his surprise. "I recall a time when you did."

"Long ago—almost beyond memory." Dougal slanted his gaze so the firelight reflected from his eyes in a fiendish manner. He knew he looked the part of a Black Devil, with the dark curls spilling down his neck and eyes so deeply grey they might as well be black.

He knew, too, what the clans folk whispered—that Satan himself had marked Dougal MacRae with the scar that marred his right cheek in the shape of a claw or talon.

Dougal alone knew the true origin of that scar, and he would not tell.

"I care for naught now, Lachy," he finished in a hard voice. "You know that." Naught but revenge.

"They would hunt you down like a rabid fox, did your father's reputation not still stand," Lachy mused on, "even now, after his death."

"Only let them try," Dougal said carelessly. He had confidence in his ability to protect himself and his own. The keep he had inherited from his father, not far west of Stirling, and from which he terrorized much of Central Scotland, stood strong. He could take down any man who challenged him with sword or bare fists. As for the rest of it, he'd been clever enough to preserve at least a suggestion of innocence. "There is no proof."

Lachlan drank from his cup. "Make a man angry enough, as you well know, and he will dispense with the requirement for proof. Revenge is a fine thing, Dougal, but not if it begets the desire for more revenge."

"Bah," Dougal said dismissively. "You tire me, Lachy. When did you become such a cautious old woman?"

"Perhaps when the King got involved. No less than five of your neighbors have applied to him for relief from you—not the least of whom, MacNab, is a particular favorite of the King's. What will you do if James calls you to Stirling and decides to make a judgment?"

Dougal's lips curled in an unpleasant smile. "I suppose I will need to appear before him—he is my Lord and King. Yet you know James is busy in England and comes to Stirling quite rarely." And the King could be bought, Dougal added to himself—sometimes with stolen gold.

"He cannot ignore his subjects' complaints forever," Lachlan asserted uncomfortably. "And I do not think you can accuse me of being an old woman for warning you."

"Is that what you are doing, then?" Dougal asked with mock surprise. "Warning me?"

"Aye, for my sins. I do not know why I bother."

"Nor do I," Dougal agreed readily, and drank again. Sometimes his very veins seemed to crave the fire in the cup. It brought forgetting and, if he was lucky, even oblivion.

Lachlan shifted in his chair uncomfortably. "Perhaps it is Meg about whom I am worried," he admitted.

"My accursed sister?" Dougal narrowly avoided snorting. "That harridan? I assure you, Lachy, Meg can look after herself."

"Aye, so," Lachlan agreed, looking unhappy. "Yet, does she not concern you?"

"Only so much as she threatens to usurp my title as the black sheep of Clan MacRae. Truth be told, I curse the day she ever came home. How long has it been, now?"

"Eight months," Lachlan supplied in a low voice.

"Eight long months since she murdered her husband and returned to the family bosom."

"There is no proof she murdered MacDonald," Lachlan objected, without much conviction. "Not but the bastard deserved it."

Dougal scowled. "I do not argue that. If the rumors are correct, I might have crossed the Highland Line and settled him myself. Not that Meg needed my assistance. She poisoned him, Lachlan, and he died in agony. Never say you worry for such a creature?"

Lachlan shrugged.

Dougal went on with a hint of humor in his voice. "If I am a black devil, then she is a witch—the old sort, whose path men would do well to avoid crossing. She may live here, Lachy, but I do my very best to avoid her."

"Perhaps that is your mistake."

"I am certainly not going to coddle her. Might just as well coddle an adder. My sister hates me, Lachy. Far more than my neighbors do."

Lachlan said nothing but stared at the fire moodily.

Dougal slopped more whisky into his cup. "A fine bit of drink here," he said, after a moment. "Remind me—from whom did we steal it, again?"

"Robertson, over near Kippen," Lachlan said gloomily. "You tied up himself and all his family before looting the place, remember? I thought his wife would succumb to apoplexy."

Dougal laughed harshly. "Oh, aye. He has a bonny daughter, though, I recall."

Lachlan rolled his eyes. "A daughter you saw fit to kiss and fondle before we left. You had your tongue well down her throat and your hands up her skirt."

"Aye, and a sweet bit of female she was." Dougal grinned wolfishly. "She enjoyed it, Lachy. Do not doubt that."

"Perhaps you should offer for her," Lachlan suggested a bit spitefully.

"Me?" Again Dougal crooked an eyebrow. "Why would I do that?"

"Because the King has virtually decreed it. Do not say you fail to remember the message that arrived from London last month?"

"London is a long way off."

"Maybe so, but that letter was nothing save a veiled threat. He implied if you do not settle seriously into running your father's estate, take a wife, and begin a family, he will have to consider confiscating your lands."

"MacRae lands! We have held these hills since the time of Christ. No one will take them from me now."

"He can do as he pleases—he is King."

"On these lands, Lachy, I am king."

Lachlan muttered, "There lies your problem, I am thinking."

Ignoring his friend, Dougal tossed his head and laughed. "Besides, can you imagine me, with bairns? Now, there's an unholy prospect—the Devil's spawn!"

Lachlan scowled and said nothing. A brief silence fell, during which the fire popped and the wind heightened its wail around the stones of the keep until it sounded like droning bagpipes.

"What will you do," Lachlan asked then, "if the

King does require you to wed, if he issues a decree?"

Dougal MacRae's teeth flashed white in an unholy smile. "Well, then, if it comes to that, I suppose I shall just have to steal myself a suitable wife."

Chapter Two

"It is unacceptable," Isobel Maitland said bitterly, much aggrieved. "Father, you cannot send Catherine away to marry. She is second born."

"Fourth born, in truth," said Gerald Maitland tersely. "Are you forgetting I had two sons? The fact that both have predeceased me does not make them any less significant."

"I did not mean to imply that." Isobel frowned. The wounds her father bore following the loss of his sons were raw and likely to remain so. The elder, John, had perished fighting valiantly for the Crown, and James scarcely a year later in a fall from a horse maddened by a bee sting. Isobel had watched her father sour thereafter, turning from a reasonably considerate man to one who cared little for anyone's opinion save his own.

He now had no heirs save his two daughters, Isobel, nineteen, and Catherine, two years younger. Precedent existed for the lands to pass down the female line—the estate had, after all, come to Gerald Maitland through marriage. Isobel's mother, a strong-minded Scottish heiress, had not lived long enough to see her daughters grown.

With that thought in mind, Isobel now spoke as perhaps wisdom dictated she should not. "Mother would not approve this marriage, not with Catherine's heart so set against it."

The look in her father's blue eyes—the one feature Isobel had inherited—chilled. "Will you cite your mother's will to me? What do you know of it, girl? For that matter, what does Catherine know about an advantageous union? She is but a child."

"If you think her a child," Isobel retorted heatedly, "you have no business sending her off like a bundle of high-priced goods."

She could see her father struggle to keep his patience. "The MacNabs are a fine family, with ample lands. It is a grand match for her, secure and stable. Randal MacNab is an old friend of mine, and his son, Bertram, a worthy husband."

"Catherine does not even know him!"

"She met him years ago. Lord Randal and Bertram both came to your mother's burial service."

"When Catherine was seven and Bertram nearly twenty. He is too old for her, Father."

"Nonsense. She is of an age to wed, and men often take brides younger than themselves."

"His first wife—"

"Bertram's first wife was a delicate specimen who did not survive childbed. I have promised that whatever else my daughters are—wild-headed and hasty-tongued at times—they are strong women able to bear many sons. I am hoping the MacNabs, being themselves Scottish, will overlook the heedless tendencies your mother's Scots blood has lent both of you. All my children have suffered for their heedlessness: John, too impetuous in battle, James insisting upon riding that half-broken stallion, you—"

Gerald broke off and fixed Isobel with a hard stare. "You complain to me, daughter, of the fact that your sister will be wed before yourself, when it is you who ruined your own chances?"

Heat raced to Isobel's cheeks, yet she met her father's eyes unflinchingly. "I have accepted blame for my sins, Father, and paid for them."

"Have you? I dare say you will continue to pay, all your life. MacNab wished his son to wed you, and not your sister. I had to put him off with Catherine—hinting at, though not admitting, the truth. Should I admit your shame to even so dear a friend?"

"Is it such a shame?" Isobel could not help but challenge.

Now Gerald's gaunt face flushed. "I am surprised you can ask that, and it proves, perhaps, what a woeful job I made of your upbringing in your mother's absence. I should have married again, given you and your sister a gentling influence. Your downfall—"

Isobel bit her lip in an effort to contain her simmering anger. "My downfall, as you call it, cannot be laid solely at my feet, Father. John's friend was seven years older. He seduced me—"

"You allowed yourself to be seduced! And by the kind of man to whom no sane father would see his daughter wed. A rapscallion, a ne'er-do-well. John, God rest him, should never have brought the blighter here. But make no mistake, my girl. It is your fault you fell victim to him."

Such had always been his opinion. Isobel sought words to refute without angering him. She had meant to speak on Catherine's behalf, not her own.

"Send me to MacNab in Catherine's place," she asked.

"Do you not think I would, if I could? MacNab

wants a virgin. Daughter, must I speak more plainly than that?"

"Bertram MacNab need not know that I...that I am damaged goods. Once we are wed—"

"Marriage is a contract. And the man is no fool—it will be his second wedding night. He knows full well what to expect. Catherine must go."

"And what of me?" Isobel asked, miserable and humiliated. "Am I to live out my days here as a spinster, unloved and unwanted?"

Her father's expression softened slightly. "Not unloved, Daughter, nor unwanted. You will make yourself of help to me running our household."

"And the lands? Will those go to MacNab, with Catherine's hand?"

"We shall see. I may see fit to settle the estates on Catherine's son, should she have one. For now, I do not plan on surrendering them to anyone."

"Of course not." Isobel looked ahead through years that suddenly seemed stunted and blighted as a barley field after the frost. Was her life as good as over, at nineteen?

Making one last bid, she lowered her voice to something approaching meekness. "Father, I beg you— Catherine and I have been so close since Mother died. Inseparable! Do not send her away from me."

"It is not like you to be sentimental, Isobel. It will do Catherine good to be away on her own, taking up the life of a woman grown. Were you not always trying to defy me, you would see that. I am, as always, doing my best for my children. This is a good match for her, within the safety of a good family."

"The MacNabs? I hear they are engaged in clan

feuds half the time, virtually at war with their neighbors."

Gerald shrugged. "What Scot refrains from raiding and feuding? My old friend Randal assures me Catherine will be the gem of their household. Now go and speak to your sister, Isobel. It will make things easier for her in the long run if she makes up her mind to this match."

"Yes, Father," Isobel murmured as she turned away and left the room. But beneath her breath she muttered, "Make her mind up to it? Never!"

## Chapter Three

"Never!" Catherine Maitland wailed like a she-raven crowing on the battlefield. "I will never wed Bertram MacNab, Isobel! Will not! Cannot!"

No surprise there, Isobel thought ruefully, sprawled upon her sister's bed while Catherine paced the room. Neither Isobel nor her sister had made a habit of meek obedience, and at the moment Catherine looked like a wild woman—chestnut hair flying, blue eyes wide and desperate.

She looks like me, Isobel reflected with grudging admiration.

"Father's mind is set," she warned. "I offered to go in your place, but he would not hear of it."

That made Catherine quit pacing and stare at her sister. "You would sacrifice yourself so, for me?"

Isobel, suddenly unable to face the look in her sister's eyes, stared at the embroidered counterpane that covered the bed. "In an instant."

"Oh, Issie!" Isobel suddenly found herself enveloped in a hard hug. From earliest youth she remembered such embraces, Catherine's strong arms clutching at her in gratitude, fear, or pure love.

Tears rushed to her eyes, and in order to combat them she said wryly, "It is no good. MacNab insists on a virgin."

Catherine released her and sat back on the bed. The

strangest look Isobel had ever seen came to her face.

"Ah, well," she said ruefully, "then the fine Bertram MacNab will not want me, either." She concluded in a whisper, "I gave myself to Thomas three months ago."

Isobel gasped. Her sister had been childhood playmates with the son of their father's bailiff, and over the past year, seeing each other secretly, their friendship must have grown into love. Gerald Maitland disapproved the friendship, saying quite openly he did not feel it appropriate. He relied heavily on his bailiff, John Hewett, but none of the man's five sons could be considered a suitable match for either of his daughters.

I should have seen this coming, Isobel told herself now, should have stepped in and done more to protect her, dissuade her. Though how did anyone reason with a lass so headstrong as Catherine?

Reading Isobel's expression, Catherine said, "There is nothing wrong in it. I love him! Should I rather save myself for some man—a stranger—I despise?"

"Father will go mad. His reputation rides on this. And I have already let him down in this regard."

"Not your fault," Catherine began, but Isobel cut her off.

"You promised me, Cat, this relationship between you and Thomas was platonic. I confess, I expected better of him—he seems a young man of high scruples and considerable restraint."

"He is. In most regards." Catherine had the grace to lower her glowing eyes. "But, Issie, we are in love!" Catherine's flawless complexion grew rosy. "I suppose it is a blessing in disguise. Once I tell Father, that will be the last I hear of marriage with Bertram MacNab."

"Tell Father?" Now it was Isobel who jumped up and began pacing. "And what do you expect him to do then? Make excuses to his good friend Lord Randal? Swallow his humiliation and wish you and Thomas well? He will have the skin off Thomas's back, for starters. I would not be surprised if he has him killed."

The color drained from Catherine's face as swiftly as it had come. "No!"

"Oh, yes, my girl. If you think Father is not serious about this match, you are much mistaken. At the very least he will deprive Thomas's father of his living, send them away—"

"I cannot live without Thomas! We wish to wed."

Isobel stared at her sister with a mixture of pain and aggravation. "I am sure you do." John Hewett's youngest son had been blessed with the kind of good looks not unusual here in the borders, a direct legacy of Viking settlers many years gone. Long of limb, knit with slender strength, Thomas had hair the color of ripe corn and a smile of singular sweetness. He even possessed a sense of humor. Isobel could not say she disliked him, but that, she feared, lacked relevance in the present situation.

"You are mad," she told her sister in a steady whisper. "Father will send him away and ruin his family. You have to end it."

Defiant tears flooded Catherine's eyes. "I cannot!"

"My darling, I know you fancy yourself in love—"

"It is no fancy! I cannot go to MacNab!"

"I agree it will be difficult—"

"More than that, it is impossible. I am carrying Thomas's child."

That set Isobel back on her heels. She felt the breath rush from her lungs and a chill fill her limbs. "You cannot be. Catherine, you must be mistaken."

"No. I believe it happened the first time we lay together, for my visitor has not arrived three months running," Catherine confessed in a whisper. "I do not think there can be any mistake."

"My God! What shall you do? Father will go wild. Nothing will keep him from flaying Thomas alive."

"I will keep him from it! Listen to me, Issie. Thomas and I mean to run off together. We will go north, across the border to Gretna Green, and be wed. For weeks we have talked of it. We wish to wed anyhow. The babe will just force us to act more quickly than planned."

"You cannot tell Father." Gerald Maitland possessed a temper of considerable intensity. In truth, his daughters had inherited the trait, Isobel more so than Catherine. Gerald seldom unleashed his ire on his children, and when their mother was alive she had acted as a buffer between them. Yet a few incidents stood out in Isobel's mind, youthful misdeeds Gerald had punished with a heavy hand.

And this—this was no small misdeed. Catherine might well lose her child before Gerald finished with her.

Isobel's protective instincts rose in a rush. Catherine might be wrong in this, and mad to think she could get away with it, yet Isobel had to take her part.

"And what do you suppose you will do after you are wed?" she asked incredulously. "How will you live? Certainly there is no room in the Hewetts' little cottage."

"Thomas has written to his cousin in Bristol, who has just taken over his father's shipping office and is in need of a clerk. It is a good opportunity and a real chance for us."

"Bristol!" Isobel's eyes widened. It might as well be the far side of the moon instead of the far side of the country. And yes, it might be a fine opportunity for Thomas, a rare one, but scarcely the station in life that Gerald Maitland demanded for his daughter. "And you think Father will accept that?"

"I think, by the time he catches up with us, it will be too late. Time will make it obvious I am carrying Thomas's child. His anger will fade."

It would not, Isobel knew, no more than had his grief over the loss of his wife and sons.

Catherine went on, her firm voice belying her desperate expression, "You see, this whole business of a match with MacNab has precipitated things. Thomas has been trying to save for the journey. We had hoped to go the month after next, when my condition became evident. But if Father insists I go to MacNab at once—"

"He does." Isobel thought furiously. "The whole of your plan will fall apart, I fear, before you ever begin—unless we are very clever."

Catherine's eyes lit. "You have a plan?"

Isobel scowled. No more than a half plan struggled into formation in her mind. Suicidally dangerous, it nevertheless might just give Catherine time to be away and wed before Gerald Maitland even knew.

She put her head close to her sister's. "Listen now to me—"

\*\*\*\*

Some time later, Catherine Maitland took herself

17

before her father with submissively bowed head and defiant eyes and agreed to travel to Scotland in order to become the wife of Bertram MacNab. Gerald Maitland should, perhaps, have been more suspicious about his daughter's sudden acquiescence. But, preoccupied with matters of his estate, he proved well satisfied to have the matter settled.

"I am glad your sister succeeded in talking you round to a sensible point of view," he declared. "This is a very good union that will see you well set for life. The situation in Scotland is, aye, unsettled at present, but I have faith decent landowners like MacNab will outlast the unrest and prevail against the rabble that presently infests the north."

"Will you travel with me to Scotland, Father?" Catherine peered at him from beneath her lashes.

Sir Gerald grunted. "I regret I cannot. Affairs here demand my presence. But we will arrange a visit for the New Year, perhaps in the spring. By then you may have glad news to share with me. MacNab is very eager for an heir."

"Yes, Father." It was now October, and the idea of a six-month separation should have been devastating. Catherine tried to look crushed.

"As I say, Daughter, you will be in good hands. Your husband will inherit a significant holding in Central Scotland and is a favorite of the King. You should be grateful."

"I do realize that, Father. When will I be sent?"

"You will leave a week hence. You must begin your preparations."

"Yes, Father, I will."

"Good girl." Such praise, rare enough from

Gerald's lips, should have made Catherine smile. Strangely, her lips turned down instead.

"May I go now, Father?"

"Certainly."

Catherine padded away in her soft slippers and climbed the stone stairs to the room she and Isobel would share this night.

"Well?" Isobel asked as Catherine climbed into the bed.

"You were right." Swiftly, Catherine burrowed into the warmth of her sister's presence. "Father professes himself too busy to accompany me on my wedding journey."

Isobel snorted. "When has he not been too busy for us, since Mother died? All to the good. When do you leave?"

"A week, only."

"Ah, it is short time for planning. Never mind. He will send his most trusted retainers for the journey, and they know us very well. This will take some care. I am thinking you shall have to affect a cold and remain swathed in your wraps the while."

"He will send a maid."

"He will. Bethan, most like. She can be bought."

"Think you so?"

"Bought and kept in Scotland, after. She need not return to face Father's wrath."

Catherine shivered. "Can we fool the MacNabs?"

"I see no difficulty there. Bertram and his father have not laid eyes on us since we were children, and besides, we are as like as may be in appearance. And it does not matter, does it? If the ruse is discovered, it will be too late for them to do much about it. You and

Thomas will be long gone."

"And you will take the brunt of everyone's anger, all round." Catherine threw a protective arm over her sister. "It is too much! I cannot let you!"

Isobel lay silent in her sister's fierce embrace a long moment and then said, "Cat, you are closer to me than anyone in this world. Dearer to me! I would give my very life for you. Besides, do you know what my future will be, if I stay here, a fixture of Father's house, always shamed and shunned?"

"Never say you wish to go and wed MacNab?"

"I am not eager to wed him, no. But to go from here might be a fine thing. By the time our ruse is discovered, Bertram MacNab and I may well have come to terms." She breathed softly into the darkness of the room. "There is scarcely a man on this earth I cannot tame."

"I believe you are right. And I almost feel sorry for Bertram MacNab."

## Chapter Four

"I almost feel sorry for Bertram MacNab," said the Devil Black in a tone that indicated he felt no such thing, "finding his bonny bride stolen away beneath his long, skinny nose."

"You are assuming she will be bonny," said Lachlan MacElwain, hiking his coat up round his ears. Another foul night full of snaking wind and wet surrounded them, containing demons that played on the mind.

But Dougal MacRae rarely suffered from those kinds of demons.

He laughed. "You must admit, Lachy, 'twill be worth a bit to see his reaction when the news reaches him that his betrothed has been snatched on the road not ten miles from his door."

"This plan is accursed," Lachlan stated dolefully, "and you are mad. I always suspected it. Now I am sure."

Dougal laughed, and his laughter contained genuine mirth. "Come, Lachy! Was it not yourself told me to obey the King's command and find myself a bride?"

"Not like this. And not some milk-white, simpering miss of MacNab's choosing."

"You underestimate the fine Bertram. She is no doubt an heiress."

"No doubt." Lachy agreed. "And well bred. She will swoon at the sight of your black countenance."

"Do you think so?" Dougal smiled, amused.

"Tell me this is but a wicked game—you will hold her a while and then leave it be."

"Release her to MacNab, you mean?"

"Aye, so." A particularly fierce gust of wind buffeted them where they sat their horses by the side of the dark road. "Or do you mean to extract a ransom from him? That is your plan, eh?"

"And what of the King's desires for my future? Am I to thumb my nose at our lord and liege?"

Lachlan snorted.

"I suppose I shall just have to make my mind up after I see the wench. If she proves a beauty, or not too hideous, I may need to sample her before sending her on to him."

"Ruin her, do you mean? A pallid, fragile, English maiden? You would not."

"It could be she is no maiden."

"No chance of that. Highborn lords who deal in wives insist upon their purity. MacNab will have your head."

"I would like to see him try."

"By any road, she is doubtless ugly as the bottom of an empty tankard. Such brides usually are."

"True. A beautiful bride is a rare enough thing." The thought cast Dougal into a mood blacker than the night.

He remained silent until Lachlan spoke again. "They are late. I thought your man said they left the inn at three this afternoon?"

"Our roads are not what English coachmen are

used to. Hark, now!" Dougal cocked his head. "Don your mask, Lachy. And go canny."

Borne on the gusts of wind, and intermittent, came the sound of a carriage climbing up the hill. Dougal MacRae eased his sword from its scabbard, feeling a surge of energy flood his veins.

He had done this a hundred times—played bandit, a role that was, aye, in his blood—waylaid travelers on the road and neighbors in their own drawing rooms. But never for such stakes as this. He'd stolen his share of cattle and horses, but a bride? Never.

An unholy grin split his dark face as he eased his horse out into the road and raised the sword high.

No need for shouted commands—the silhouette of him there in the road, stark and threatening, had the coachman hauling on the reins almost before Lachy took the place at Dougal's side.

Everything went abruptly silent. The creaking of the coach springs ceased; the horses rolled their eyes but held their ground. Only the coachman's soft, heartfelt curse competed with the gusting wind.

"Drop it," Dougal said, his casual tone belying the excitement racing through him. The second man on the box had drawn a sword. "Throw it into the road!"

Neither the coachman nor the guard moved. Dougal urged his horse closer and poised the point of his blade at the coachman's throat. "Now."

The guard's sword clattered as it hit the road.

"Come now," Dougal urged. "Any other weapons as well, if you value your lives."

Lachlan, well enough versed in his role by now, rode round to the back of the coach, where Dougal heard him order a second guard to surrender his weapons. "Welcome to the festivities! Divest yourself of any weapons, and your life shall be spared." A knife and dagger followed the man's sword into the road.

The coach door flew open and a lass, only dimly seen in the weak light, leaned out. "Daniel? What is going on? Why have we stopped? Are we—? Oh!" She caught sight of Dougal, black as sin, sitting his equally black horse. He heard the breath catch in her throat. For a score of heartbeats he waited for her to scream, wail, sob, or perhaps swoon, which in her present position would deposit her in the road. She was, after all, a gently born English miss.

Instead, she swung the door wide. He saw her skirts thrash as she scrambled down, without benefit of steps or assistance, to face him.

"What is the meaning of this?"

She looked tall standing in the road, and he could not see her face clearly in the gloom. Her voice surprised him. It shared little with those of any English ladies he had encountered in the past and held a strange lilt, as well as an edge that might slice granite. Her coach had been halted on a strange road at dusk by two armed bandits but, by all that was holy, she did not sound afraid.

Dougal's lips curved in a grudging smile. "This, lady, is a robbery."

"Yes?" She glanced over her shoulder into the coach, where someone had begun to shriek. "Well, I must say you have terrible judgment. We have virtually nothing to steal."

"Is that so?"

"It is. I really hate to disappoint you, Sir Bandit, but I am on a wedding journey, and my dowry was sent ahead last week. You should have intercepted that courier."

"I see," said Dougal, feeling amusement race through him in the wake of the excitement, a strange sensation.

"I do have a few pieces of jewelry on my person that I am willing to hand over—not terribly valuable, I fear, and I have no emotional attachment to them."

"Why do you not keep them for the moment?" Dougal suggested.

"Keep them? Why?" She turned her head again. The shrieks inside the coach had risen to an alarmingly shrill level. "Oh, Bethan, do get hold of yourself."

"Might I ask, lady, who is in the coach?"

"My maid, a bit disconcerted at present."

"Tell her she has naught to fear. She shall remain unharmed. I mean to steal but one object this evening."

"Oh? What might that be?"

Dougal bowed low from the back of his horse. For answer, he edged the beast nearer the coach, closer to her. He longed to see her face, the color of her eyes. He suspected she must be homely as the back end of a sow. No woman could possess such courage and beauty besides.

She stiffened when he looped his arm around her and scooped her up effortlessly out of the road. He felt indignation flood her and—was it fear, at last? He had no opportunity to tell, because she turned immediately into a wildcat, twisting, hissing in fury, and beating against him with both hands.

One blow landed on his chin, a respectable thump. Others rained down on his forearms and battered his chest. She made a soft, tempestuous armful, all right, and to his surprise he felt himself grow aroused. Ah, and he had not even seen the wench's face.

The shrieks of the maid, apparently watching from the open door of the coach, doubled. All three coach attendants started up.

"Ah, ah!" Lachy cautioned them and waved his sword. "Is she truly worth your lives?"

"Miss Catherine!" one of the men bleated.

Ah, so that was the firebrand's name. He restrained her, forcing her against his body using but one arm; the other still employed his sword. He enjoyed using his strength and clearly felt it the moment she decided she had no hope of escape.

She swore bitterly under her breath, causing him to smile again. "Hush," he bade her with his mouth against her hair. "I will not hurt you—much."

"Who are you?" At last she sounded shaken. Not terrified, he would give her that.

"Now, lady, you canno' expect me to tell you that, here before your maid and your attendants." He gestured with his sword. "All of you, inside the coach."

They obliged, albeit reluctantly, and Lachlan shut the door and then turned the coach, with some difficulty, in the narrow road. The coach now pointed back down the hill. Dougal had chosen his spot well.

"What are you going to do?" his captive demanded. She had gone very still, watching the scene. He could feel her breathing, though, and he could smell her—a bouquet of pure woman that made his senses swim.

"If they are lucky, they will not be hurt," he said into her ear, and felt her shudder.

Lachy rode to the front of the coach, took up the coachman's flail, and hollered at the already spooked team of horses. They tossed their heads and took off at a dead run, the coach bouncing and clattering behind. Dougal could still hear the maid shrieking as it disappeared down the hill.

Catherine made a strange sound in her throat. "They will wreck and be killed!"

"Perhaps not. But they will be a long way distant from here when they stop."

Lachy had dismounted and was gathering the weapons from the road. Dougal nodded to him, sheathed his sword, and lifted his horse's reins. He and Lachlan would see no more of one another this night.

"What happens now?" Catherine demanded.

With an unwarranted feeling of possession, Dougal shifted the arm that pinned her so his hand splayed over her breast. Her body pressed against his so fiercely, he could feel every breath she dragged into her lungs, and he wanted to enter her, so badly it hurt.

"Now? Now you come with me."

Chapter Five

"Welcome, Lady Catherine, to my abode."

Isobel blinked up at the stones of the structure as the black horse thundered through the gate. Night had now truly fallen; she had seen very little of the countryside during the ride hence and had been almost wholly distracted by the presence of the man pressed to her back, but here torches flared and fear stuttered over her senses. She could not guess where she might be, but the place breathed age.

A keep of some sort, not large, though it gave that impression. The black horse's hooves clattered on stone, making echoes off the face of the building proper. Tiny windows stared down at Isobel, and her heart struggled within her breast. She did not know for what she had hoped during the long, captive ride, but not this. The grim place offered little hope of escape.

And, of course, escape possessed her mind—escape and gratitude that, at least, Catherine was not here in her place. By now Catherine should be far away from home, perhaps even wed with her Thomas and out of this nightmare.

A lone retainer ran out when the horse entered the courtyard. He wore a rough kilt and leather jerkin, and he hurried to shut the gate against the darkness before catching the black horse's bridle.

"Well, now," he growled, peering up at Isobel from

beneath a wrinkled brow.

"Give him a good rubdown, will you?" her captor returned. "He's run hard and carried double."

"Never bothered him afore," the man said.

Afore? How often did this monster who had hold of her seize women? Ah, Isobel had heard of such men, in tales told of Scotland's depravities, yet had never quite believed. Neither, apparently, had her father, or surely he would have sent a stouter escort.

Her captor's hand, which for miles had splayed across her left breast, at last shifted. She felt the play of muscles in his body as he swung her across the saddle effortlessly and dismounted with her still in his grasp.

Isobel's feet hit the courtyard and refused to hold her; the long, rough ride had robbed her legs of strength. Her captor grunted. Without a word, he swung her up and over his shoulder. Before she had the breath to protest, he carried her through the door of the keep.

The place smelled of wood smoke and clammy stone, and something that might be wet dog. Isobel could see little enough besides the floor passing beneath her, until they entered a chamber and her captor kicked the door shut behind them, then set her down quite carefully.

They looked at one another.

The light here came from a fire that burned steadily on the hearth and from a few tapers set about the room. A rough place it seemed, but Isobel, holding hard to her wits, had no eyes for it.

"Who are you?" she demanded, reaching for her courage. "What is the meaning of this? You cannot just snatch women from the road—"

"Can I not?" he returned swiftly, his voice pricked

with humor. "Imagine that!"

I am in trouble, Isobel thought clearly, far more trouble than I have ever seen. He must be a bandit, one of the rapscallions for which Scotland was famed. He looked like a devil, one who happened to possess a lean, clever face and a long, lean body to match. Isobel weighed him as she might any adversary, looking for strengths and possible weaknesses. The process, made difficult by terror, won her a disparate number of facts: terrifying aspect, clothing as rough as that of the retainer outside, black hair tumbling down his back like the mane of his horse, and an air that virtually oozed confidence. He oozed something more, as well: a blatant maleness that, even in these circumstances, made Isobel's senses stammer.

She could not let herself think about that now. She needed all her energy to fathom the level of intelligence behind those eyes, narrowed between lashes black as ink, and to guess his intentions.

He did not look stupid, which would have benefited her much, since she had confidence in her own wit. And he looked as dangerous as an adder.

"Who are you?" she asked again, wishing she sounded less shaken. "Why am I here?"

He took his time completing his examination of her before deigning to reply. His hard gaze, invasive as a touch, seemed to strip the clothing from her, lingered long on her hair, which had come unbound during the ride, and even longer on her bosom. Reading that look, Isobel very much feared she knew his intentions, and the breath caught hard in her throat.

Thank heaven she was no virgin, if he meant to rape her.

But he gave her a graceful bow before saying, "My lady, you are here because the King has decreed I find a bride."

That stole every coherent thought from Isobel's mind. The King? A bride? And, in Scotland, were men in the habit of snatching those from the road?

"I..." She struggled to speak. "I am the intended bride of another. Sir Bertram MacNab."

Her captor inclined his head. "I know the man, villain that he is. You would do better with me."

"That is scarcely the point. My father has entered into an agreement with Lord Randal as to a marriage between our families. You cannot just seize another man's betrothed wife."

"Aye, you keep saying that. Yet you are here, are you not, Lady Catherine?"

"You mean to hold me for ransom, is that it?" Isobel asked, calming a bit. Ransom was reasonable, at least in this environment, and Lord Randal would pay. She could be out of here inside a day.

His gaze played over her again, slowly, and something that might be a smile quirked one corner of his mouth. "And, what of the King's decree? If I am a good and obedient subject, I must wed you myself." Wed, and bed, his tone implied—possibly not in that order.

"I doubt very much you are a 'good and obedient' subject," Isobel remarked.

"You have barely made my acquaintance, yet you judge me so harshly?"

"I have not made your acquaintance at all. You abduct me from my carriage at sword point on a dark road and send my maid and attendants to their possible deaths. At least tell me your name."

He smiled, a real smile this time, and it was not pretty. "They call me Devil," he told her. "Devil Black."

Isobel shivered. Standing there in the leaping firelight and with the wind gusting outside, her superstitious Celtic side surged to the fore, leaving the practical Yorkshire half of her nature in the lurch.

"I requested your true name," she said. "Or are you too much the coward to give it to me?"

He frowned, and at that moment the chamber door flew open and a woman rushed in, a raw, avid look on her face.

"I do no' believe it, Dougal!" Her eyes raked Isobel where she stood. "Have you gone mad entirely?"

Dougal, Isobel thought, Dougal the Devil. Oh, how it suited! Yet hope leaped in Isobel's heart. Here was a woman, surely a merciful, gentling influence…the man's lover, perhaps? But no, the resemblance between them was uncanny, and she looked as wild as he.

Black hair, worn loose, spun in a glossy curtain down her back, and she carried the energy of a western gale. Her face—undeniably beautiful—held an element of cruelty, as well, and when her eyes met Isobel's, the hope in Isobel's heart abruptly died.

"Who is she, and how did you come by her?"

"Calm yourself, Meg. This has naught to do with you."

"You can say that?" The woman's eyes flashed what looked like hatred. "Do no' tell me this is MacNab's bride?"

"He snatched me from the road," Isobel said quickly. "He endangered my attendants. It is a violation of every rule of decency."

The woman—Meg—laughed. The sound carried real humor and a hint of mockery. "If you expect decency from him, miss, you are sorely mistaken."

"And yourself, mistress?" Isobel returned swiftly. "Have you no proper feeling either? Is this Scotland, or wild America?"

The woman smiled, and her resemblance to Isobel's captor became rampant. "You might be safer in America just now," she pronounced, and turned on the man.

"'Tis a mad stunt, Dougal. Do you want MacNab and his army at the door?"

Dougal walked to a side table, where he poured himself a drink of amber liquor—whisky, perhaps.

"I welcome a visit from our erstwhile neighbor at any time; I and my men will meet him with drawn swords. But MacNab will have no way of knowing who has snatched his fine son's bride till he finds and interviews her servants, and no proof I have her even then."

Scathingly, Meg said, "The man may be stupid, but not an utter fool."

Dougal drank deeply. "They saw little—not enough to identify me. 'Twas dark and, suspect what he may, he will not dare accuse."

Isobel's blood chilled in her veins. No one had seen this man's face, nor that of his now vanished accomplice—no one, save herself. But she had seen both him and his presumed sister. He seemed a ruthless man; would he prevent her from telling? Was she fated to die here, in this unknown place?

"You think not?" Meg demanded, with another

look at Isobel. "You think the abduction of a virgin bride insufficient to rouse all MacNab's boldest instincts? I think you may have overstepped yourself this time."

Dougal shrugged, displaying no apparent concern. He too eyed Isobel—with speculation. "I may have other plans for her."

"Rape?" Meg asked. "Surely not."

Isobel's heart leaped into her throat. What sort of folk were these, who could discuss such an abomination so calmly?

But Dougal answered, echoing, "Surely not." He crossed the room until he stood so close to Isobel she could smell the damp on his clothes, and the slight tang of whisky on his breath. Isobel fought not to shrink away. The man gave off an aura like that of a stalking wolf: power tinged with the threat of destruction.

She gazed into his eyes and saw they were not black, after all, but a dark, smoky grey that seemed to smolder like a banked fire.

He reached out and captured her chin between long fingers that felt like steel. "You are a beauty, I will give you that," he crooned. "And you have spirit. A bit too fine for MacNab, I am thinking."

Heat flooded Isobel's skin, and she struggled to meet his eyes, defying the fear inside. Of all the terrible moments in her life, this competed for worst, yet she must be grateful, yes—at least Catherine did not stand here in her place. The thought sent a rush of courage through her, and she jerked herself free of his grasp.

"I understand, sir, you are no gentleman, and you play some evil game I am not at liberty to understand. But I demand you impart your intentions toward me."

"You demand, do you?" A curious look invaded his eyes, half annoyance and half admiration. He withdrew just far enough to make her a mocking parody of a bow. "Why, my lady, I intend to make you my wife."

Chapter Six

"I shall escape from here," Isobel vowed to herself, a promise muttered under her breath. She could not, however, imagine how. She surveyed her surroundings and felt desperation arise and threaten to choke her.

She had been given a sleeping chamber in the monster's keep. Shortly after his outrageous declaration, his threat of marriage, the woman—his sister—had cursed him, employing words no decent woman might utter, and marched from the room.

Dougal had then called a servant, an ancient man wearing a filthy kilt, and instructed him to make their guest comfortable in the "best bedchamber."

The "best" proved rough, indeed. The room, though spacious and lofty, contained few comforts. The stone walls seemed to radiate damp; the furnishings consisted of a wardrobe with warped doors, an ancient chest, and a bed, about which Isobel barely dared think. The servant kindled a pitifully small fire in the hearth and abandoned Isobel to her doubts and fears.

As soon as she found herself alone, she began to tremble, the remnants of her courage deserting her abruptly. Panic filled her heart as she struggled to make sense of her situation.

The MacNabs awaited her arrival: that one truth nothing could change. Someone would discover the wreckage of the coach containing her attendants—

injured or dead. Her fate would eventually become evident.

She paced the chilly room, trying to remember what her father had said about this region of Scotland. Lawless, infested with bandits, yet he had been confident MacNab, advantaged by his connections with the King, could protect Catherine. Obviously, even her father had misjudged the temerity of a bandit who would snatch a woman supposedly under MacNab's protection.

Isobel cursed her father for his careless arrogance. It was typical of his high-handed tendency to assume no one would interfere with him, or his. He should have sent a small army rather than a coachman and a pair of attendants. Or MacNab—curse him also!—should have sent an escort, since presumably he knew the dangers of these roads.

But none of that would help Isobel now. She must deal with what lay in her hands, and it did not look pretty.

She knew nothing about her captor, save his first name. She knew little enough of where he had brought her after leaving the road, through rough country, much of it, and incipient darkness. He possessed this keep, which argued some measure of wealth, yet this place was shabby, ill kept, and possibly ill staffed. She knew a guard stood outside the door of her chamber, for she had heard the exchange between him and her captor after she had been shut in.

"She goes nowhere, Geordie, understand?"

The guard replied with a grunt that needed no interpretation.

The only windows in the room were two slits so

high Isobel doubted she could reach them even if she climbed onto the chest. She found herself caught and fairly, like a trout in a net.

But…why? Her captor—this lawless, terrifying man—said he meant to wed with her, but that was illegal without her consent or that of her father, and it made no sense. What sane man would snatch a stranger for a bride?

Chances were he was not sane. That thought caused Isobel's knees to wobble; she sat down abruptly on the edge of the bed. She knew madness when she saw it. Despite her father's platitudes and praise, neither of her brothers had been completely sane. For that matter, her father possessed a streak of madness, come on since her mother's death, that made him cold and unreasonable.

Isobel considered herself capable of dealing with difficult people, but not in this case, not when the stakes promised confinement and forced marriage.

Which, to be truthful, did not differ so terribly from what Father had planned for Catherine. This chamber might as well be located in MacNab's house, and Catherine could be sitting here awaiting her fate, to be bedded by a stranger.

Isobel closed her eyes for a moment, grateful she had at least been able to spare her sister that.

And what would happen now? That question dominated her mind. Presumably the coach had wrecked at the bottom of the hill. And, presumably, MacNab would eventually go searching for his son's missing bride. Should any of her attendants survive the wreck, he or she would tell of the bandit on the dark road.

Only Bethan, though, knew Isobel's true identity, that she had taken her sister's place. The odds of rescue coming—finding her here—were so slight, it made Isobel feel ill.

The Black Devil, he called himself. She shivered again; the name seemed all too apt.

\*\*\*\*

"Of course you will not actually marry her," said Meg, her eyes narrowed to slits. "This is another of your games, a particularly vile one. You are doing this to get at MacNab."

Dougal made no answer. He shot his sister an unfriendly look and poured himself another tall whisky.

"This will rebound on you," Meg predicted. "You have done a fair bit of thieving in your time—cattle, aye, ponies, jewels, silver, even whisky. But a woman? And from MacNab, of all men. You know full well he shall run, at once, to the King."

Dougal shrugged carelessly.

"And," Meg seethed on, "how will you collect the ransom without telling the world of your guilt?"

"I do not mean to ask ransom," Dougal replied. He slumped into his customary seat by the fire and stared into the flames. All he could see, though, was the rage in the eyes of his captive. Not what he had expected—not at all—and far too good for MacNab. The wench had courage and defiance. She also possessed a rare beauty that relied not at all on golden curls and simpering smiles. The very thought of bedding her had him hard as a length of iron.

He wondered who she was. MacNab would choose no peasant for his precious son. Catherine, of no surname. English, though she did not look it with that fire in her hair. He had seen his share of English misses, though he had not yet had one. This one must be a virgin, and overdue for splaying.

Meg laughed, never a reassuring sound. "The King will have your head for this. Is that what you want? Folk hereabouts have just been awaiting the chance to see that."

She came and squatted beside him, in order to look into his face. "Brother, I long since gave up hope for your soul—"

"'Tis in no greater jeopardy than your own."

"True. This is about revenge, is it not? You wish to bring MacNab to his knees."

Dougal felt a grimace pull his lips awry. "MacNab—the grand gentleman," he sneered. "The man of purported means who can do no wrong."

"This is about Aisla, is it not?" Meg asked softly, gazing hard into his face.

"Do not speak her name!"

Unexpectedly, Meg's expression softened. "Do you think I do not understand? She was my friend."

"I warn you, Sister, I do not wish to speak of this."

"Can the wound be still so deep, after so long?"

Dougal surged to his feet, nearly sending Meg sprawling. "The wound, as you call it, has no chance of so much as scabbing over—not while that bastard enjoys any measure of success in this world. Do not begin to suppose you understand."

"You loved her."

Savagely, Dougal turned on his sister. "What do you know of love? You, who murdered your husband."

"He betrayed me." Meg got to her feet and stood, tall and composed as a queen.

"With another woman?" Dougal laughed cruelly. "I am surprised he dared."

"So am I. He knew what I would do, should he ever prove unfaithful. I told him full well, on our wedding night."

Dougal stared at her. "I believed the poor sod enamored of you. He never left off talking of your beauty and the poetry of your eyes."

Meg looked thoughtful. "One cannot trust the tongue of a man. I, myself, would not have believed it, had I not seen the evidence with these poetic eyes."

"You caught him?" Dougal asked, interested despite himself.

"In the stable, with the young sister of a groom. The lass, no more than twelve, was sobbing. An ugly scene."

"What did you do to her?" Dougal almost hated to ask.

"Her? Helped her to her feet, dried her tears, and sent her home. She was a child, and one in no fit state for punishment. He, on the other hand..."

The rage in her eyes took Dougal aback.

"Upon inquiring about my household, it proved my husband had long been intent on deflowering every female with whom he came into contact. As time passed, the females became, by necessity, younger and younger. The staff knew, of course—and were afraid to tell me."

Dougal fully understood why. Even the echo of his sister's rage daunted strong men.

"Only imagine," she seethed, "him preferring some unseasoned wench, when he had me in his bed."

"You felt insulted," Dougal marveled. "Not

broken-hearted?"

"Do not be foolish. You know I have no heart to break. I am like you, in that regard." Meg's eyes flashed. "My husband deserved to die, if just for his fecklessness. He knew what I was—what I am."

"A witch?" Dougal suggested against his better judgment.

"A dangerous woman, one to be reckoned with. But we were speaking, Brother, of your dilemma."

"I see no dilemma."

"Oh, I think you do. The wench can identify you. How can you suppose to let her go?"

"Aye, how can I?"

"Yet you cannot keep her captive forever. You have backed yourself into an untenable position."

"And what do you care, Meg, about my fate? You never tire of saying how you hate me."

Meg scowled. "I hate the things you have done— and failed to do. However, you do, at present, represent my personal security. Should you find yourself beheaded, with all these lands forfeit, what will become of me?"

Dougal shrugged. "Why not wed Lachlan? He wants you badly enough, poor fool."

Unexpected color rushed to Meg's face. "Lachlan?"

"Do not tell me you failed to notice his worshipful glances?"

Meg's chin lifted. "All men look at me that way."

Dougal laughed harshly. "Do they, so? What a wonder."

"I cannot help it. 'Tis easy enough to attract a man. Finding one who will stay honorable and true presents the difficulty."

"Honorable and true?" Dougal spoke the words with incredulous disbelief. "For the likes of us? Aye, Sister—you must, indeed, be mad."

Chapter Seven

"Come." The guard spoke the word in a grunt that even Isobel could not fail to understand, the first command she had received in a day and a half.

It had seemed longer, trapped in the barren room with her food and drink presented at the door by yet another shabby retainer—the only person she saw. She had availed herself of the "necessary" and paced until she wore holes in the threadbare carpet, unable to sleep, and she now felt half mad with worry and distress.

At least, as she told herself repeatedly, Catherine was safe, off away with her new husband. And so what did Isobel's fate matter? She had possessed no prospect of a happy life anyway, trapped at her father's house. Was this so very much worse? At least Catherine, carrying her lover's babe, could claim a future.

She told herself all this and even, on an intellectual level, believed it. Yet when the taciturn guard at last ordered her from the room, her heart plunged to her feet.

Had the monster who held her in his power made up his mind about what to do with her? Had he, perhaps, sent a ransom demand to MacNab, her future father-in-law? Did MacNab wait for her, below?

Her footsteps echoed on the dusty stones of the corridor and stairs as she followed the guard to the rough hall she had seen before. She could hear rain pounding the outside of the keep—for a day and night, continuously, it had rained, the weather worsening Isobel's mood.

Her captor, alone, awaited her, standing before a fire that leaped and danced. He turned to survey her as she entered the chamber, and Isobel wondered what he saw. She had not been able to wash herself properly, and her hair hung loose down her back. She possessed not so much as a comb with which to put it up again. She felt like a wild woman, heedless in her impatience.

She spoke before he could. "It is full well time you addressed my presence here. Sir, this is intolerable! You cannot hold me trapped against my will without comforts or recourse. Am I a prisoner, to so languish without benefit of the law?"

"No comforts?" He quirked an eyebrow. "Are you not in out of the rain, in your chamber? Is there not a fire? Were you not given food and drink?"

Rage rose like a bubble to Isobel's head. She distinctly felt it take hold of her mind. "You understand very well what I mean."

"Had I known you would spout only complaints, I would not have had you brought hence. Sit, please, Lady Catherine."

Isobel remained standing, stiff with anger.

"By God," he said, eyeing her scathingly, "I may have done MacNab a service. I doubt you are the meek English maiden he envisioned as marrying his son."

Indeed, Isobel thought, she differed in every way from that image, being but half English, certainly no maid. And her name was not even Catherine. She felt a small smile of satisfaction curl her lips.

Her captor narrowed his eyes. "Now, what does

that look denote, I wonder? I will have you know, Lady Catherine, beneath this roof I am the law. Your fate rests squarely in these two hands."

"And what of your fate? Can you steal a woman's freedom with impunity, even in lawless Scotland?"

"Is that what they tell you back in England, that we Scots are lawless? Fools! Our laws are far older than any constructed by their foolish king."

"The King is a Scotsman!"

"And our clan law predates his advent by a thousand years. I am Laird, here. My authority is absolute."

"How very convenient for you. I hope the knowledge will comfort you when the King separates your head from your shoulders."

He evinced no reaction to her words.

"Please sit, Catherine. I wish only to speak with you. But if you prefer, I will send you back to your room."

"My prison, you mean? Before we speak of anything, you will answer my questions. Is there news of my attendants? Are they alive or dead? Has word come from MacNab? Will he ransom me soon? When shall I be released?"

"Sit! Can I offer you a drink? I regret there is no tea. We do not bother with it here. But I have some fine whisky."

"Stolen, no doubt."

He blinked at her.

"Oh," Isobel seethed, "I know what you are—nothing more than a bandit, who has set himself up as some sort of laird. Did you thieve these lands, as well?"

He looked annoyed, and Isobel congratulated

herself. It might not be wise to poke a rabid dog with a stick, yet she could not help herself.

"My family's ties to this land are ancient," he spat.

"Oh, yes? If you had any pride in your family, you would at least tell me your name."

He drew himself up to his considerable height and executed a respectable bow. "Dougal MacRae, also known as Devil Black, at your service, my lady."

Isobel's eyes flew wide. "Devil Black?"

A wry smile twisted his lips, lending him a dark attractiveness. "I am told 'tis the name whispered by the locals when they speak of me."

"And you are proud of that, I warrant? I do not doubt your forefathers would be ashamed—"

"My lady, my forefathers spent their time stealing their neighbors' cattle and women, and hiring out their swords in battle. 'Tis an old tradition in these parts."

"I see." Isobel struggled to think clearly and failed. "So what do you mean to do with me?"

"Seat yourself, my lady, and we will discuss it."

Slowly, Isobel lowered herself onto the settle that fronted the fire.

"Aye, so." He poured a glass of whisky and placed it in her hand; his fingers brushed hers and she experienced a shock, like the kiss of a lightning bolt. "Drink."

Isobel raised the glass to her lips, but then hesitated. She needed to keep a clear head.

Devil Black MacRae began to pace in front of her. His rough, hide boots emphasized the length of his legs, and he moved like a padding wolf.

"I am at war with my neighbor, Randal MacNab. It is a moral war, and I will carry it out at any cost to myself."

A moral war? Before Isobel could speak, he went on.

"There is naught I would not do to injure him. That, lady, is why you find yourself in my hands. You were sent here to become the bride of his son Bertram, were you not, Lady Catherine?"

Isobel opened her mouth to deny it.

"Do not bother to lie," he bade her. "Word gets round concerning MacNab's intentions, and I have informants in his household."

He looked Isobel up and down, from her hair to her toes. "It is an arranged marriage, aye?"

"MacNab is friend to my father, so you see you shall not get away with this. As soon as word of what you have done reaches my home—"

"Och, 'twill not take so long as that. I dare say MacNab has missed you by now and has already gone looking."

"Abduction is a crime, even in Scotland."

"So says the fine English miss. And what sin did you commit, to earn the terrible fate of marriage with young Bertram? Do you know him?"

"We met long ago."

"How long ago?"

"Years."

"Then you will know nothing of the self-entitled, humorless, and brutally cruel prick he has become. I dare say you would be better with me."

"I doubt that."

"Do not doubt it, Lady Catherine. At least I have red blood in my veins, not poison."

"And he has, no doubt, a modicum of decency."

"You think so? You would be wrong, then. He abuses his servants—and I do no' speak of forcing them to work long hours. He is known to have whipped two men to death."

"A worse failing," Isobel asked tersely, "than thievery and abduction?"

"At least I am honest about what I am." He leaned toward her slightly. "I am, always, honest. Young Bertram presents one face to the world and another to those unfortunate enough to meet him on intimate terms. What happens behind closed doors would make your hair stand on end."

"Why do you tell me this?"

Dougal shrugged. "To reassure you, perhaps, that the absolute worst has not yet happened to you. You could be in Bertram MacNab's hands, instead of mine. Indeed, you have had a narrow escape."

"You will not convince me of that. I demand you release me, Dougal MacRae. Better done now than when the law demands it."

"Aye, well, there is another option, I am thinking."

"There is?"

Once more he inspected her in a way that sent heat stealing over her skin. "I cannot release you, lady, because you can and will identify me."

"I will promise—"

He shook his head in feigned sorrow. "I trust not the promises of women. I cannot send you home, since your erstwhile sire would no doubt have you escorted once more to MacNab, under heavy guard. I will not see you sold in marriage to him."

"Because he is your enemy?"

"Because even an Englishwoman deserves better."

"So," Isobel struggled to keep from revealing her despair, "what is to be done?"

He approached her where she sat on the edge of the settle. The force of his presence preceded him like the front of a storm—intimidation coupled with a strain of male attractiveness such as Isobel had never before encountered. It felt dangerous as a bog of quicksand and sharp as an axe blade. Instinctively she caught her breath.

Softly, he said, "I believe I shall have to marry you myself."

## Chapter Eight

"You are a madman!"

Dougal watched the emotions leap like firelight in his captive's eyes—beautiful eyes, deep blue as the sea at sunset and, he did not doubt, nearly as treacherous. The sea lured men to their deaths; this beauty might lure him to depths he could not fathom.

He had known—and plundered—his share of maidens, but never one like this, with intelligence that fairly shone from her, and courage to match. She fired his blood like whisky, so he had trouble concentrating.

Aye, she thought him mad, and evil, and any number of despicable things. He could see as much in those eyes. But he might tame her like a headstrong pony and revel in the doing.

"Folk hereabouts have long speculated as to my sanity," he conceded. "I assure you, I am quite rational."

She laughed incredulously, and he found himself further inflamed by the sound. He wanted to hear it in his ear whilst he held her down on a bed and entered her, wanted her passion to meet his own—quick and savage. He wanted to lose himself in her eyes, tangle his naked flesh in those wild, red tresses, and make her weep for him.

Could she tell how hard he was? But no—her eyes clung to his, as if she searched his soul.

"I have decided you must wed with me." The words, repeated, sounded almost brutal, and her eyes widened. Dougal had not meant to speak them that way; he wanted her to want him.

She sprang to her feet. Tall for a woman, the top of her head reached his eyes, which put their bodies nearly heart to heart. He could smell a fragrance coming off her skin—that of pure woman.

He heard the breath rush into her lungs. "No! Your one course of action, if you would keep your head, is to release me unharmed."

"My one course of action is to forge you to me, so you cannot speak against me." Giving in to temptation, he reached out and seized her arm. "I can avail myself of a priest. It shall be done this night."

"Against my will?" Her head came up and her nostrils flared. "You would force me? So, you are a bully as well as a bandit."

"There will be no forcing, lady. When I get you in my bed, you will want what I have to give."

He pulled her hard against him, into his arms. His mouth plundered hers, battered it open, and he felt her terror spike. Yet it subsided as swiftly as did his desire to handle her roughly. Sweetness met passion and broke over them both like a shower of fire. He felt her hesitate, and his lips softened, began to woo hers, coax and persuade them further apart. Greed washed through him in a staggering tide that left him feeling all at once weak and powerful. Surely he would sell his soul for the taste of her.

She raised both her hands and planted them flat against his chest. He expected to feel her push him away; instead her fingers curled into the fabric of his tunic and pulled him closer.

The motion went straight to his head. He contemplated pushing her down there before the hearth but dismissed the notion. Not before they saw the priest. He would stand accused of raping no woman.

He broke the kiss, and a sound came from her throat, a sigh of protest. They gazed deeply into one another's eyes, and Dougal's heart began to pound the way it did before a battle, when his sword cried for blood.

She still had her fingers fastened in his tunic, and they stood barely a breath apart. Every inch of him could feel every inch of her—some more than others.

"So, lady," he said, allowing one corner of his mouth to turn up, "will you wed wi' me?"

\*\*\*\*

Isobel fought to retain the few shreds of reason which she assumed must still lurk somewhere in her mind. She did not know what this man might be— monster, villain—but her attraction to him was prodigious. Just touching him had the power to suspend her common sense and native caution, both.

She forced her fingers to release him and then drew back one hand deliberately, intending to slap his face. He caught her wrist before she completed the motion.

"No," he said, the passion flaring in his eyes again, "you will not! You were a willing participant in that. Do not lie to yourself."

Heat rushed to Isobel's face. She wanted to evade the brutal honesty in his eyes but could not. She struggled for breath.

"Very well," she said then. "I participated. What of it?"

He smiled, and she felt the effects all the way to her toes.

Hastily, she said, "What now?"

"I think we had better wed, and swiftly, do you not?"

"I do not."

"So, would you rather be bedded on the wrong side of the blanket? Honestly, now!"

"You do not deserve honesty."

"Nay, but we have established you do. By any road, contrary to what you may believe, there is honor among thieves—and bandits. We shall have the priest this night."

Swiftly he released her and went to the door, where he bellowed. Isobel, feeling strangely bereft, wrapped her arms about herself.

A man came in response to MacRae's call—not the same one Isobel had seen before. This man looked younger and, if possible, even rougher. He wore a sword buckled at his side.

"Aye?" he said with barely a modicum of courtesy.

"Go fetch O'Rourke. Bring him here at once."

"He will be drunk."

"Aye, so. Bring him anyway."

The man swept Isobel with a brilliant glance and went.

"O'Rourke?" Isobel questioned.

MacRae splashed more whisky into his cup. "The priest."

"The priest is drunk?"

"Most of the time. It prevents him making moral judgments. As a consequence, he is a friend of mine— much as can be said of anyone. I do not truly have any friends."

Isobel contemplated this for an instant. "Is this terrible priest not defrocked?"

"No. He is able to perform the marriage service, and 'twill stand even before your father—and the King. We will need witnesses, mind. Likely not my sister. Her reputation in the district is woefully lacking."

"You discuss this as if you dream I will agree."

That caused him to turn those eyes—the color of a stormy sky—upon her again. "Must I kiss you once more?"

"No! I believe, as I said before, you should release me."

"I cannot do that. I do not wish MacNab to have benefit of you, you see. It is an old quarrel, but a sharp one."

"Then just send me home. Send me with a safe escort, and I will tell my father you treated me well. I will tell him you rescued me from my abductor."

MacRae's eyes narrowed.

Isobel rushed on. "I shall describe my abductor as some vile lout who thought to hold me for ransom. You came along and rescued me at sword point. You will look the hero, I swear it."

"You are a clever wench, I will give you that." He actually seemed to consider the proposal, and Isobel's heart quivered with hope. She just might talk her way out of this.

"Sit," he bade her again. He came and sat beside her, the cup of whisky in his hand. "What of the fact that, should I send you home, your father would turn about and ferry you to MacNab once more—under escort of an army, no doubt?"

"He will not," Isobel lied. "I can talk him round."

MacRae drank from his cup, and Isobel watched him closely. Those lips of his—they would taste like whisky now. A part of her—a wicked part—focused intently on the pleasures and possibilities of sampling them.

Almost carelessly, he said, "Yet I have already sent for the priest."

"That is easily undone." Isobel leaned toward him. "All this is easily solved. It is a mad blunder from which we can agree to extricate ourselves."

"I must confess, lady, you are no' what I expected to be delivered to Bertram MacNab, and far too good for him, I am thinking. Randal MacNab is a clever man. His mother was a Campbell and bequeathed him a crooked, scheming mind. He always covers his back, is in well with the King, curse him, and he will do aught he must to keep the world from discovering his true nature. His son, Bertram, has inherited that nature in full. What do you know of him?"

Isobel shrugged. "Very little. Randal MacNab and my father are old friends—I am not sure how that relationship originated. Both Randal and Bertram came to England for my mother's funeral service. That is the only time I met them."

"Aye? And how long ago was this?"

"Ten years."

He studied her moodily and tossed back the contents of his cup. In what looked like an unconscious gesture, he lifted his hand and rubbed at the small scar that disfigured his left cheek, just below the eye.

"You ask me to play at having rescued you, lady, and I say I have already done so in truth. You know me not, and have no reason in the world to trust me, but believe it when I say you have had a narrow escape. You would no' wish to find yourself in Bertram MacNab's hands, nor in his bed."

"Fine, then." A surge of desperation raced through Isobel. "You have rescued me, now send me home."

Slowly, he shook his head. "I regret, but I have told you I cannot. I will not take the chance on losing you to MacNab, anon."

"I am no bone to be fought for among hounds."

"Are you not? Yet so many women find they are exactly that. No wonder some of them fight back." His gaze seemed to caress her. "I do not see you submitting meekly to MacNab, with his twisted desires."

"Nor to you!" Isobel flared.

"Ah, but the thing is, lady, that I am able to imagine." He leaned toward her and his eyes kindled until flame leaped within their grey mist. "Need I prove it to you again?"

God help her, Isobel wanted him to. A wanton part of her wished to ravage that mouth of his, throw herself, shameless, into his arms, expose the side she had kept strictly in check ever since she had been deflowered. Ah, what would it be to find herself in this man's bed this very night?

A shiver traveled down her spine. She could have this, she could claim it—the danger, the risk, the immediate pleasure. For she knew, in every part of her, there would be pleasure in abundance. What he offered, in his backhanded fashion, provided escape from MacNab, escape from living beneath her father's roof and under his dictates, and perhaps even escape from the mistakes of her past.

And entrance into a far greater blunder?

She had made a dire mistake once—she could not allow another. She knew that with every practical thought in her mind.

Yet rather than give the man a denial, she heard herself say, "Well, so long as you have summoned the priest, I suppose we should be wed."

## Chapter Nine

"I shall summon the witnesses."

Dougal MacRae did not know when he had felt so enflamed. Certainly, he had never lived the life of a monk. He enjoyed the act of coupling. Even more did he revel in his ability to bring a woman pleasure. He gloried in the power of it, the control, and having a woman quite literally in the palm of his hand.

In his experience women—most women—liked to pretend themselves immune to arousal, a product of how they were raised, he supposed. But once he got his hand up a skirt or down a bodice, his efforts were well repaid.

This woman, he sensed, would need little such coaxing. Her veneer of modesty lay very thin over a momentous fire. And it kept him so hard, he somewhat doubted he could wait for the priest.

He smiled wryly to himself as he returned to the door and bellowed for another servant. He always kept control, even in the direst circumstances. Indeed, he prided himself on his steely composure. How could he falter now?

He stole a look over his shoulder at his captive. There she sat with her auburn hair fallen, loose about her shoulders, and that look in her eyes—half knowing and half speculation—that drove him wild. He must have her this night, witnesses or no.

When Ranald—another of his guards—appeared, Dougal told him, "Go fetch Lachlan.

"That is one witness accounted for," he said, turning back to his captive, once the man had gone. "The hour being what it is, I suppose my sister will have to serve after all." Because he could not wait.

"Who is Lachlan?"

"An acquaintance, and a gentleman of the district. Do not fash yourself, lady, he will come." Dougal poured himself more whisky, then went to the door and bellowed a third time. "Meg!"

His sister must have been lurking in the vicinity, pretend otherwise as she might—she arrived far too swiftly, in response to his call, to have been far distant.

Without preamble, Dougal commanded, "You will stand witness for me. We are to wed this night."

Meg bent a look on him before sweeping his captive with an incredulous glance. "What new madness is this?"

"No madness."

"Aye, so—perhaps it is, rather, revenge. You want her because she was to be MacNab's?"

He wanted her because the blood in his veins demanded it. He said, "O'Rourke is on his way. Take our guest to her room, send her your maid, and help her—" he waved a hand, "prepare."

"Prepare?" One of Meg's eyebrows ascended. "For you?"

"Just do it, Meg. I mean to accomplish this respectably."

Meg laughed harshly. "You snatch her off the road, another man's bride, and then speak of acting respectably?"

Dougal met her stare with one of iron and, miraculously, she backed down.

"Come," she said to his captive, who shot to her feet, strung tight and trembling, and followed Meg out.

Damnation, Dougal thought when they had gone, and splashed more whisky into his cup. He felt keen as a knife's edge and had to fight to find the patience that had stood him in such good stead these last years. All would come in time, revenge and pleasure. He had never dreamed they might be so intertwined.

\*\*\*\*

In silence, Isobel followed the beautiful woman—Meg—back to her room, where Meg brushed past the guard as if he did not exist.

Once inside, Meg closed the door and turned to regard Isobel carefully.

"This is a bad night's work," she said. "I tell you now, I cannot influence my brother. Even God—whom Dougal refuses to acknowledge—cannot influence him once he has something in his head. But I swear, if he is forcing you to this, I will do my utmost to stop him."

Isobel heard no sympathy in Meg's voice, no softness—just the same savage certainty that emanated from Dougal MacRae.

"I appreciate that," she said.

"Oh, I do naught for you—and I stopped fretting for his soul long ago. But he is taking you to further a dangerous feud, and if he winds up on the losing end, it shall benefit me not at all."

*I have landed in a nest of vipers*, Isobel thought, *each more selfish than the other.*

Cautiously, she said, "This feud of which you speak is with MacNab?"

Emotion sparked in Meg's eyes. "My brother may be many things—hot tempered, hard-headed, misguided—but his memory is long and his mind set on revenge. You find yourself, now, a pawn in his game."

"For what does he seek revenge?"

Meg shook her head. "That is not for me to tell. But know MacNab once took something that was Dougal's alone. He has waited long to strike back."

Isobel's mind raced, trying to make sense of disjointed thoughts and emotions. "And I am the means of striking back?"

"So it would appear—at least for the present. What he may do anon, even the devil cannot say."

"Can you get me out of here?" Isobel asked frankly. "Persuade him to send me home?"

Meg shook her head. "I might convince him to ransom you, though quite frankly I doubt it. If you ask me, woman to woman, I will try."

And there lay the dilemma, thought Isobel, in the starkest of terms: marriage to Bertram MacNab, for which she had already steeled herself for Catherine's sake, or to this man who turned her bones to water with a single glance. A choice—at last.

She must go to the bed of one man. Which would it be?

She drew a ragged breath and took a turn about the barren room. If she honored her agreement with MacRae, faced the priest with him, would he lie with her in her bed this night? So had he vowed. She found the prospect as thrilling, and terrifying, as that of an approaching storm.

Meg waited, impatience radiating from her.

This, Isobel thought, may be the only choice I am

given to make in my entire life. If she went to MacNab, at least she had hope of seeing her father again, perhaps even Catherine, some day, and Catherine's child. If she threw her lot in with MacRae, she chose unknown danger and darkness. And passion, curse it—there was the passion, as well.

"Send me your tire woman," she said, looking at Meg again. "I have nothing to wear for a wedding. All my luggage was lost."

She heard Meg draw a breath, sharp with surprise. "You choose him? You are certain? I warn you, once the choice is made, I abandon you to your fate."

As I have long been abandoned, Isobel thought, and nodded. "Send your woman."

Without another word, Meg went out. Isobel stood where she was, wondering at herself. Surely she had gone mad, in this place of madness. But her soul—at least that would be her own.

Meg's woman, who arrived soon after, proved nothing Isobel expected. A virtual child, with pale hair and fey eyes, she wore a cap and a dove grey gown. She carried an armload of clothing, and she cast a measuring glance over Isobel as she entered.

"My lady sent me, Lady Catherine," she said softly.

And Isobel thought—Catherine. They think me Catherine. When the drunken priest arrived, when he performed the ceremony, he would marry Catherine Maitland to Dougal MacRae. Would that be binding, would it stand?

"Shall you bathe?" the maid asked, and Isobel considered it. In a manner completely unanticipated, she went to her marriage bed this night. Unprecedented intimacies would open her to that man downstairs.

She looked at the maid. "Tell me your name."

"Nell, lady."

"Nell, I am ill prepared for this. I have no belongings, I am not sure—"

Briskly, Nell dumped the clothing on the bed. "My lady sent some things of her own that you may borrow." She pulled out a gown of pale green, embroidered all over with patterns of leaves. "I will tell the men to bring hot water."

Nell turned away, and Isobel examined the gown, stroking it with numb fingers. Her wedding finery.

Sudden tears filled her eyes. Seldom had she felt more alone, nor, if she admitted it, more frightened. She could not let herself give in to the fear. It would avail her nothing. She told herself she did this, too, for Catherine's sake. She knew she lied.

The tears, she promised herself, were tears of anger. Life had not dealt fairly with her, so far—did not deal fairly with her now—but she wanted this one thing, this one man.

She wanted the feelings he had aroused in her with that kiss, and all the desire that accompanied them. Yet if he came to her bed this night, he would discover the truth—she was no tender virgin—and something about the hard honesty she had seen in his eyes made her wish to be honest with him, as well. She did not wish to begin her marriage—sham as it might be—on the basis of a lie. He needed the truth, and he needed to know her name.

"Isobel Maitland," she whispered under her breath. "Nay—Isobel MacRae."

## Chapter Ten

"Dougal MacRae, you vile sinner!" O'Rourke exclaimed as he entered the hall. "What need has a devil like yourself for a man of God?"

"God does not come into it," Dougal returned swiftly. The argument, an old one between them, had no end and no meaning. O'Rourke was clearly in his cups, so drunk he could barely stand.

Dougal felt inflamed, fabulously alive, strung so tight he barely knew himself. More than half his attention remained with the woman upstairs who prepared for their wedding.

"You will perform the marriage service here this night," he tossed at O'Rourke.

The priest, who Dougal knew from experience could handle prodigious amounts of drink, remained sober enough to look surprised. "A marriage, man? Whose?"

"Mine."

"That is what your man said, but I doubted it. We have not read the bans—"

Dougal glared at him. "You will perform the marriage and swear it true, either at your own behest or at sword point."

"Ah 'tis like that, is it? Get me a drink."

"I do not doubt you have had your fill," Dougal said, but filled a cup with whisky anyway and put it in

O'Rourke's hand. He had known the priest three years, since the fellow appeared in the district without warning or explanation, apparently banished from Ireland for deeds better left unspoken. O'Rourke looked like a leprechaun and had the mind of a lecher.

"Who is the lass?" he inquired. "And why the great rush?"

An interruption occurred then in the form of Lachlan hurrying into the room, his color high and his cravat askew. "Dougal, what in high hell is going on? Is it somewhat to do with—" He broke off abruptly when he noticed the priest. "O'Rourke?"

"Good evening to you, Laird MacElwain. We are here for a wedding, it seems."

Lachlan's mouth fell open, and he stared at Dougal. "You are not!"

"I am that. My bride prepares herself as we speak." Dougal poured more whisky and drank deep. Quite possibly he himself was no longer quite sober.

Lachlan began to laugh, which explained in a nutshell his relationship with Dougal, or so Dougal thought. "Aye, so?"

"You are to serve as witness, you and Meg."

"I believe I begin to enjoy myself." Lachlan grinned, then spun about as Meg entered the room. He made her a bow. "Mistress."

"Oh, aye, just what this farce needed," Meg said tightly. "A fool."

"Where is my bride?" Dougal demanded, drinking deep. "I am waiting."

"She is on her way, and you will wait." Meg gave O'Rourke a disparaging look and then said to Lachlan, "I do not suppose you can talk sense to my brother?"

Lachy bowed again. "Evidently I am a fool, lady. I speak no sense."

Dougal drawled, "Does what I do not fit with the King's decree?"

"The King?" O'Rourke's eyes widened. "What has that bastard to do with it?"

"Careful, O'Rourke—you could lose your head for such talk. The King, hearing complaint of me, has decided I should wed and settle."

O'Rourke snorted. "As if any woman alive could make you settle, man."

At that moment, the bride entered the room. Everyone turned to stare, and Dougal lost all the breath in his body.

Meg and her woman had wrought magic. From out of nowhere they had produced a gown of soft green that clothed the woman's body like a caress, showing to advantage her breasts and the length of her legs. She came with her head high, the auburn hair piled atop it like a crown, and pride in her eyes. At the sight of her, Dougal felt something strike him, sharp as pain.

Lachlan swore softly. Dougal stood where he was, afraid to move and break the spell.

She approached him, moving like a queen, her eyes clinging to his. Dougal MacRae, devil that he was and never at a loss for composure, nevertheless could find no words.

O'Rourke cleared his throat and spoke up. "My good lady, I have been brought here to wed you with this man. I must ask if you come to the marriage freely and in good faith, of your own will."

A flush stole up her cheeks. Her glance strayed to O'Rourke, then returned to Dougal's. "I do."

"Well, then." O'Rourke swayed slightly. "The witnesses stand ready, as do I. I need only know your name."

"Catherine," Dougal said. "Catherine—"

"Maitland," she supplied. Her chin lifted still higher. "But it is Isobel. Isobel Maitland."

Had she said she was the daughter of Lucifer, Dougal would not have cared, at that moment. He experienced one flash of surprise, sure that her servants had called her "Lady Catherine," and then he stepped forward and offered her his arm. When she laid her fingers on it, he could feel the heat clear through his sleeve.

He wondered how many bridegrooms had taken the holy vows with a length of iron between their legs. He saw little holy about this rite anyway, and he was so hard for her he ached. He remembered nothing of the vows, later, only that standing beside her intoxicated him as much as whisky and he burned to take her upstairs.

Afterwards, the witnesses, the bride, and the groom all signed the parchment O'Rourke produced. Dougal stared at her name—Isobel Maitland—and thought, with a staggering wave of possessiveness: Isobel MacRae now. She is mine.

By the time all was finished, the hour ran late. Meg retired, and Lachy began plying O'Rourke with whisky. Dougal knew they would sit by the fire till dawn.

Upstairs, a bed waited. He turned to his wife. "It is done."

She nodded. All the color had flown from her face, but her eyes burned.

He said, "Shall we complete the night's work?"

She looked at him with something like wonder. Did it only now occur to her, the step she had taken? Would she whine and weep?

But she nodded again. He offered her his arm, and they climbed the stone stairs to her chamber. No need of a guard, this night.

He closed the door and stood, trying to control his desire.

She turned and looked at him. "We must speak."

"Aye, later. After."

"That will be too late."

He saw her bosom rise as she struggled to breathe. Aye, well, most women about to be plundered experienced some fear, especially those gently bred. He would get her past it.

He unlaced his tunic, shrugged out of it, shot his sleeves and hauled open his shirt. Her eyes widened.

"You said you would not force me."

"And I shall not." He approached her carefully, as one might a skittish pony, reached out, and captured her face between his hands. He could see her pulse stir the lace at her throat.

His eyes swept her for an instant before he bent his head and kissed her, intending to keep it gentle and ease her into offering herself to him. He—they both—had felt the heat that simmered. He need only tap into that, then ride her till dawn.

Aye, he meant to be gentle, but the instant his lips met hers that fire came leaping. His mouth turned savage on hers and all the sense in his head burned away.

A fire like this could consume them both.

For a glorious instant, they both hung on the point

of flame. Then she drew away and uttered one word: "Please!"

His hands, already at work, had slid beneath the collar of the green gown, pushing it from her shoulders. He craved the taste of her skin and, lovely as the gown was, wanted it off her. With difficulty, he focused on her face.

"Aye, Lady Wife?"

She appeared to struggle with some emotion of her own. "I must tell you—before we... You do need to know."

"Then speak. I am impatient for you." And there was a braw understatement. Impatient did not begin to describe his state. Surely she could feel the truth through his kilt and her gown?

Doubt flickered in her beautiful, dark blue eyes— or perhaps it was fear. "I am not what you think."

"No? Are you not beautiful and desirable, and my wife? I care for naught else now."

"Is it so? You care not you have married a woman who—"

"Speak, Wife!"

Her gaze fell to his lips, then further still, and she paled. "You will discover the truth when we lie together. I am no virgin."

Despite his state of double intoxication with whisky and lust, Dougal felt a rush of surprise. Was it so? Would Randal MacNab accept such a bride for his son and heir?

For an instant he froze, his hands still against the silken skin of her shoulders, his desire raging, yet curiosity whispered to him.

"How is it, then, MacNab accepted you as

suitable?"

She lifted her eyes to his once more, and he saw pain there, and shame, and hard pride as well. "He did not know. It is a long story."

"And no time for it now."

"I just thought you should—" She cast a despairing look at the bed.

Dougal felt a crooked smile tug at his lips. Probably just as well, he thought through the haze that possessed his mind. The way he felt, he had little of the restraint required to pluck a tender virgin.

"I thank you for your honesty."

She drew a breath he felt shudder through her. "It is my hope we will always be honest with each other."

"A worthy hope."

"So you—" Her lips worked, seeking to form the words. "You do not mean to cast me off for this reason?"

For one, sober moment Dougal gazed at her. He did not think he could cast her off now even had he learned she had been plucked by the devil himself.

His hands finished their work, pushed the green gown from her shoulders. The fabric fell to her waist, revealing all that lay beneath.

"Lady Wife," he said, "I have many desires at this moment, but none to cast you off. Come to the bed and let me show you."

Chapter Eleven

"Kiss me," the Black Devil bade Isobel, and obediently she turned to him, parted her lips, and felt the languorous passion pour through her again. For many hours now she—who usually never embraced obedience—had complied with Dougal's every request, placing her body, her lips, where he instructed, kissing, licking, biting, with the most astonishing results. She had never dreamed such acts, performed together, constituted coupling. It felt surprisingly like magic—black magic, probably—and bore absolutely no relation to what had passed between herself and he who had ruined her, back in her father's stable.

Dougal MacRae, she decided, using what shreds of wit she still possessed, must be a master at the art of lovemaking. He had only to touch her with his long-fingered, rough-palmed hands and she lost all inhibition—all decency—and caught fire with heedless delight. His fingers wooed her body in places she barely knew existed, coaxing from her responses she had never imagined.

After many hours in the great, canopied bed, she no longer felt her body was entirely her own, but she did not mind. Were she to give herself, body and soul, to any man, it would be him.

He spoke in whispers that filled her ears, his Scots burr, in moments of intense pleasure, becoming a buzz of sensuality. The scent of him filled and seduced her, as did the feel of his glossy, black hair trailing across her bare skin when he bent to fondle her breast with his mouth. The first time he did that, Isobel nearly flew from the bed, so sharp was the pleasure.

His hands and that weapon between his legs—ever at the ready, it seemed—had claimed her, but it was into his eyes she fell: bottomless eyes the color of a wild mist, spiked with black lashes. The eyes of a devil, or a saint?

Did she care? Not at this moment. She stretched her naked limbs as he kissed her and felt his hand slide down her body and slip between her legs once again.

He broke the kiss to whisper, "I should let you sleep, Lady Wife. Are you not weary? It is nearly dawn."

Isobel made a sound of protest deep in her throat and opened her eyes just enough to see him. By God, he was a beautiful creature, naked save for the black hair flowing over his shoulders, every muscle sculpted and defined. She now knew him to be incredibly strong, agile and skillful.

She could think of things she would rather do than sleep.

He must have seen those things in her eyes, for he gave a small, wicked smile. "Ah, 'tis that way, is it?" Gently, his fingers parted her thighs and entered her, even while his gaze held hers. "Only tell me, Isobel, what you want."

Isobel's thoughts stuttered. Until a few hours ago she had no idea her body could break apart at a man's touch, fly away beyond her control, and dissolve in racking waves of pleasure. She had thought coupling a quick, ultimately painful act that resulted in shame.

She supposed she should be ashamed, now—cavorting, naked, as she was, begging inwardly for inconceivable things. But when he touched her, she lost all reason.

"I want—" But she had no words for it.

The wicked smile invaded his eyes. He needed no words. He cupped her breast, bent his mouth to it, and his fingers, inside her, played her as a master harper might his instrument.

"I wish, Wife," he said when at last the waves of pleasure subsided, "I might always find you thus—with your beautiful breasts bare and your body ready to welcome me."

"Do you?" she whispered, striving to regain her wits and her composure.

"Oh, aye. But I suppose such a thing would shock even my hardened warriors, or dissolve them in jealousy." He tangled his fingers in her hair. "You are a bonny thing—for an English flower."

"Only half English," she confessed. "My mother was a Scotswoman."

"Is it so? That explains much, including the beauty of your red hair."

He calls me beautiful, Isobel thought with a rush of dazed amazement. Either he thinks it also, or he is a damn fine liar.

The door of the chamber flew open. Isobel, lying brazenly naked atop the blanket with only select parts of her husband's body covering her, stiffened in alarm and then tried to hide herself.

A man appeared in the doorway, likely one of those rough individuals Isobel had seen the day before.

He stared his fill at the scene on the bed.

Dougal, rounding on him, snarled, "What is it? Have you no more sense than to interrupt a man on his bridal night?"

"'Tis no longer night," the man replied insolently. "And MacNab's agent is downstairs. They are scouring the country round about for his son's lost bride."

Dougal laughed. "And they came to me?"

"They are asking everyone." The man still plundered Isobel with his eyes. "A wrecked coach has been discovered and dead servants found."

Dead? For the first time in hours, Isobel's thoughts strayed beyond the confines of the bed.

Dougal got to his feet, utterly careless of his nakedness. He reached for his sword before his clothing, and Isobel was struck by the picture he made, wild and graceful, with the bare blade in his hand.

"They search for Mistress Catherine Maitland?" he asked, with a wicked glance at Isobel. "Certainly I shall help them search, for she is not here. Only my wife resides beneath this roof. Now, Dermott, get your filthy eyes off my woman!"

The man withdrew. Dougal dressed quickly, the smile still hovering about his lips. When he finished, he turned back to Isobel.

"Wait for me," he bade. He leaned down, kissed her fiercely, and marched from the room.

Isobel sat where she was in the bed, her head clearing slowly. She began to shiver uncontrollably, as if with shock, and drew the blanket about herself.

What now? The man had gone from the room, apparently taking his magic spell with him. She felt released from a kind of madness. What had she been thinking these hours past—marrying a stranger, indulging in round after round of wild pleasures with him. Now she found herself clothed only in her hair, every inch of her body tingling and, were she honest, still crying out for him.

He must, truly, be some sort of devil. Only such could possess his masculine beauty, his skill, and the ability to make her forget her past and consign her future to the unknown.

She drew a breath and then scrambled from the bed, went to the washstand, and poured from the ewer of water, which was cold. She deserved cold water, she told herself, and a bed of nails. She washed and then climbed into a crumpled morning gown. She still struggled to put up her hair when another knock sounded at the door. Before she could reply, it opened.

MacRae's sister, Meg, stood there. She bore a tray and entered the room without invitation.

"I brought you breakfast," she announced. "No doubt you need it."

No one could ever question Meg was Dougal's sister, Isobel reflected. They shared the same black hair, the same almost shocking beauty, and the identical air of self-possession. Isobel found it difficult to believe Meg came to her now out of charity. Her expression looked too cold and her eyes, moving to examine Isobel, the room, and the bed, too merciless.

"So," she said, setting down the tray. "You survived your night with the Devil Black, then? I will confess, I had some concerns. He has a reputation for charming women of every ilk, yet I could but wonder about a tender English maiden."

Not knowing how to reply, Isobel kept silent.

"I see no wounds," Meg said. "If you wish to complain of him to me, I will listen. I may even sympathize. But remember, you chose this course for yourself and made your bed, as they say."

"I have no complaints."

That caused Meg's eyebrows to fly up. "No? You find yourself wed to the worst outlaw in all Central Scotland, a man so heinous even the King despairs of him, yet you make no complaint? Are you foolish as well as heedless?"

"I am heedless, am I?"

"Sit down. Allow me to tell you a few things about my brother."

The fire in the hearth had long since burned out; the room felt cold. But they sat on the low bench facing the hearth and regarded one another like civilized women.

Meg looked thoughtful. "Let me begin by saying my brother has few redeeming qualities. He is intelligent—but his mind is twisted, and he uses his wits unwisely. He is, aye, confident, but he abuses his power and puts his clan at risk. He knows nothing of kindness or mercy—and so say I, who have, myself, been accused of cruelty. He flouts convention, custom, and the King's law with equal enthusiasm and, I believe, will one day end either by hanging or by losing his head. And I will not mourn, when that day comes."

Isobel's eyes widened. "It is a harsh thing to say of your brother."

Meg's expression became tight with fury or pain. "I hate him. I cannot wait to see him get what he deserves."

"What does he deserve? And why—"

Meg laughed harshly. "Believe it or not, we were close once, as children. We had a wild raising, just the two of us running these hills like pups, after our mother died. He was everything to me then. I thought his schemes clever and his escapades brave. I did not see his selfishness. But be warned, Mistress Isobel—my brother is utterly selfish. He sees only his own welfare, thinks only of his own hide."

"I am wed to him now," Isobel said as steadily as she could. "Surely I can expect some consideration?"

Meg's lips twisted. Abandoning her role of confidante, she got to her feet. "Be warned—those about whom he is supposed to care, he treats the worst of all. I will tell you, woman to woman: whatever you do, do not fall in love with him. 'Tis a fate that I would not wish upon my worst enemy."

## Chapter Twelve

"I bade you wait for me."

Cold to the bones, wet and unaccustomedly anxious, Dougal MacRae slipped into his wife's bedchamber. For hours without end, with a small band of men at his back, he had played at searching the roadways, hills, and braes for a woman he knew to be elsewhere, while his body ached for her. And his mind had dealt sorely with him, imagining just this moment over and over again: himself reaching the place where she waited, to find her clothed only in her hair and in one of the glorious positions to which he had introduced her last night, either on or off the bed.

Instead he found her sitting sedately by the fire, fully clothed—sewing, by all appearances.

She gave him a cool lock and lifted an eyebrow. He felt his pulse leap. One of the things—the many things—that attracted him to her was her self composure.

"I *am* waiting," she said.

He approached her, shedding clothing as he came—his sopping cloak came off first, then the clammy tunic beneath. Leaving a trail of clothing from the door to the welcome heat of the fire, he ended before the flames, clad only in his kilt.

"And did you find the young lady for whom you searched?" she inquired.

He shot her an appreciative look. "You speak of Catherine Maitland? We did not. I fear some dire fate has befallen her. To be sure, though, she is not here. The only woman in this chamber is the Mistress Isobel MacRae."

His wife made no answer to that, but continued to ply her needle, her bosom rising a bit faster than was called for by the activity.

"Has the search been called off, the night?"

He grinned. "Called for darkness. MacNab is beside himself with fury and suspicion. He would like to accuse me of something. He would also like to keep searching, but the weather is vile—snow, mixed with sleet and rain. All his helpers withdrew from him."

"I see."

She laid her sewing aside at last, and Dougal felt her looking at him, her gaze a virtual touch on his bare torso, arms, and the sopping hair down his back.

"You will be chilled, Husband, and hungry for your supper. Shall I ask for it to be brought here?"

Dougal allowed his desire to show. "I confess to being hungry, Wife, but not for food." He saw the color flood her cheek. "Did I not," he repeated himself, "tell you to wait for me?"

"And have I not?" Her eyes challenged him. "Would you have me wait naked on the bed?"

"Aye. Oh, aye!" Without thought, he unfastened his kilt and let it join the rest of his clothing on the floor. "Come, Wife, and only let me show you."

\*\*\*\*

Some time deep in the night, while the wind still gusted about the stones of the keep and the sleet drove hard, Dougal MacRae found himself spent—or nearly so. He lay in the big bed with his wife naked in his arms and his hand splayed on her breast. She breathed softly, and he thought she slept, though he could not be sure. His own mind felt wonderfully empty of thought or conflict—for once he knew no anger, spite or desire for revenge. This woman had successfully relieved him of everything but satisfaction.

Aye, and she proved clever and well adept, for a virtually untried, half-English woman, presumably gently raised. Curiosity prodded his mind as he wondered how, and in what circumstances, she had lost her virginity. He wondered, but it did not really matter. She proved passionate, open to try whatever challenge he set her between the sheets. And she tasted better than the sweetest honey wine.

Curse it, just the thought made him want her again. He opened his eyes and caught her watching him.

Surprised, he touched the hair clustered on her neck. "Wife, I thought you slept."

Unexpectedly, she said, "Your sister, Meg, warned me about you, today."

"Did she, so? Interfering bitch!"

"There is no love lost between you, it seems."

"None at all."

"And why is that?"

Dougal drew a breath that tasted of pain. "'Tis a long and ugly tale, that. Not suitable for your ears."

Her blue eyes narrowed. "You do know, eventually someone is going to have to tell me the truth. If I am to live here, your past and present cannot remain unknown to me."

"Aye so, but 'tis a tale for another time."

"Why does Meg hate you?"

Dougal felt his heart grow heavy as a stone. "Let it just be said she has good reason. You have wed wi' a devil, after all."

Isobel said nothing, though her eyes held his. He found himself breathless at such daring—not many women would face him so.

"Is this, then, the devil's mark?" She raised one finger to trace the scar on his cheek, and he shivered, affected by so simple a touch from her.

"The devil's mark, aye," he breathed.

"And this? And this?" She caressed with soft fingers the scars on his shoulders, chest, stomach, arms, some of them twisted and livid, seams on his skin. "How did you acquire so many blemishes? In hard battle?"

"Hard battle, aye." He captured her fingers in his and raised them to his lips. "Tell me, Wife, do these blemishes ruin me in your eyes?"

"They do not," she admitted steadily. "But I confess myself curious. Did you fight for the King?"

"No."

"Against him?"

"I am my own man, and fight only for my own causes."

"So many? You must indeed be a fierce warrior."

Not fierce enough. He felt grief flash through him again.

"So, Wife, my sister has warned you against me— yet here you are still, available to my bed."

"Yes." She gave a small smile that heated his blood dangerously. "It seems I cannot help myself."

"A fine thing, that." He added, surprised to find it true. "Yet I would not have you regret the choice you made, to wed with me."

"Then satisfy my curiosity." Her gaze challenged him. "Surely so fierce a warrior cannot fear speaking plainly to his wife?"

"Time may come for that. Not now." He captured her chin between his fingers and kissed her deeply, feeling the fire leap again. She was so hot in his arms, so pliable and willing. Yet his mind could not quite let him slide away into passion.

"I admit, Wife, I am curious, also, about your circumstances. Will you confess to me how a delicate English flower came to be plucked before her time?"

Again her eyebrow quivered. "I am a delicate English flower?"

To Dougal's own surprise, he smiled.

"I have told you," she said, "I am but half English."

"I stand corrected. You are but half English, and not so delicate as to wilt in my arms." Dougal drew a breath. "And, Wife, it matters not that I did not find you whole, last night. That is the truth. Neither of us is without a past. Yet," he traced the curve of her cheek with rough fingers, "I would not be a man, did I not wonder."

For the first time her gaze avoided his. "Husband, I have already opened myself to you completely. Will you allow me no private sin?"

He snorted rudely. "Sin? Is that what you call it?"

"Others have. Lying with a man outside of wedlock—"

"Wife. Isobel." Deliberately he used her name. "I am the not the man to condemn anyone. I believe not in sin. I do not even believe in God."

That brought her wide eyes back to his. "How can

you fail to believe in God?"

"Quite easily. He has, in turn, failed to believe in me enough to convince me He exists. The point is, a man—or woman—cannot earn the damnation of a nonexistent deity."

He watched the thoughts move in her eyes—such beautiful eyes. At last she whispered, "Well, then, if you believe not in sin, why would you hear the circumstances of my downfall?"

Why, indeed? It was a legitimate question. And Dougal's native honesty required him to answer it. With his hand hovering over her flesh, longing to touch her again, he admitted, "I would know what he meant to you, this unknown man who first enjoyed your favors." And that, he acknowledged to himself, was a dangerous desire, indicative of the need for possession. He wanted to know this woman and so to own her, body and soul.

She looked surprised. "What he meant to me? Pain and betrayal, nothing more. He was my brother's friend, who came to stay with us that summer, a handsome wretch who paid me more attention than I deserved. He poured compliments and lies into my ears and tricked me into meeting him alone."

"He seduced you."

Color flooded her face. "It was my fault. My father made that quite clear to me after we were discovered. His actions may not have been right, but I bear full responsibility for my ruin, and I must live with the consequences."

"And he? This rascal who led you astray? What befell him?"

"Naught. He returned to the army."

"Your father did not call him to task?"

"Oh, yes, but he was betrothed to another; nothing could be done. I—I would not have wished to wed with him anyway. Once we lay together, I saw him for what he was, an empty-headed charmer with no morals and no substance."

"Had I been your father, I would have whipped him within a hair of his death."

That made her lips part and her eyes cling to his. "I believe you. But he and my brother, John, went back to their posts soon after—they were comrades in arms, you see—and almost immediately John fell in battle. My father could think of nothing else then but the loss of his son and heir."

And so she, Dougal thought bitterly, had no justice. No more so than he.

"You did not pine in his absence? You did not miss him—love him?"

Distaste and a hint of horror filled her eyes. "Love him? That craven, spineless deceiver? Yes, I pined once he had gone—with regret for the fool I had been, with remorse and grief for all I had given away."

"Grieve no more, Wife." Dougal touched her at last, buried his fingers in the wild glory of her hair. "For have you not made a fine match with one of the most important—and infamous—landholders in all Scotland?"

She whispered breathlessly, "It seems I have."

"I will never lie to you," he vowed, "or deceive you—whatever my sins."

"Then surely our futures are cast together," she said.

## Chapter Thirteen

"Husband—Husband, you had best come awake!"

Dougal opened his eyes to weak, morning light and a staggering rush of emotion he identified, with some surprise, as contentment. For an instant he savored it, along with the warmth of the bed and his delectable awareness of the woman who lay, utterly naked, within his reach.

He could not remember the last time he had experienced anything besides anger, bitterness, or the desire to strike out, to hurt and maim. Surely this strange, soft emotion came of being utterly spent on a sexual level—he had lost count of the number of times they had coupled last night. For he knew naught of happiness, did not deserve it, and certainly did not hope for it.

Yet for this brief instant, it seemed his.

The sleet had, at last, stopped dashing against the stones of the keep, and the wind had died. His wife summoned him from sleep.

He turned his head on the pillow and looked at her. A vision, a queen from a wild, ancient tale, with her auburn hair tangled about her naked shoulders, her lips—and her nipples—swollen from his kisses, and a fathomless look in her eyes. She looked like the war goddess who came to sleep with warriors and to bless them. Yet surely he was beyond blessings?

He smiled at her and felt desire rush through him. Damn, if he did not want her again. He reached for her, and she planted both palms against his chest.

"They call for you," she informed him. "Someone waits, outside the door."

"Let them wait."

A dull pounding erupted at the door, and Dougal heard the voice of his man, Dermott.

"My Laird? The search party waits without. Laird Randal's men—"

Dougal groaned as reality returned in a dark wave. Aye, he had a ruse to play. He must go and search for his neighbor's, his enemy's, missing bride—the woman who lay beside him. His bride, now, and truly tried. Had he not, these two nights past, had her every way a man could have a woman?

Aye, and he wanted her all over again.

He bellowed to Dermott, "I will be right there." And then he kissed his wife, even as he heard Dermott's steps trail away.

"I suppose you must go," she said with regret.

"I must play at this game a little while."

"Eventually MacNab will discover I am here—and your wife. What will happen then? Can he not complain of you to the King?"

Dougal sat up in the bed and shrugged his hair back over his shoulders. "What, again? The King will be tired of hearing about me. And 'twas the King who bade me wed."

"But he did not bid you capture and marry your neighbor's intended bride."

"I have not, in actual fact, wed his bride, as he was contracted to your sister, Catherine Maitland. 'Tis she for whom we search, to be accurate about it. She whom he believes was in the wrecked coach."

"A fine enough point." Isobel—his Isobel—looked worried. Could she truly be concerned for him? His heart, which he thought had solidified to stone, gave a twinge at the prospect.

And that, in turn, was enough to get him up and into his still-damp clothing. He might enjoy bedding her and relish defying MacNab, but he had no room for soft emotions such as concern.

"Let me worry about my own affairs, Wife," he said shortly.

She sat up in the bed, her hair swirling around her, not even bothering to cover her naked breasts. The sight of her, so, caught at him and stole his breath away.

"You cannot expect to keep me hidden forever," she pointed out.

"Nor do I so intend. Your presence in my household will be revealed at the most strategic moment."

Her chin tipped up. "So, I am nothing to you but a weapon?"

And he answered carelessly, "A hidden weapon, at present. Aye, Wife, what more could you be?"

****

That day proved interminable. Though the sleet had ceased to fall, the weather remained sharp and cold, the roads sodden and mucky, and Dougal quickly tired of his private deception. Lachlan, bored and unconcerned as always, rode at his side, armed with a continuous stream of barbed conversation.

They rode in company with Randal MacNab himself. The erstwhile bridegroom, Bertram, headed yet another search party. Randal trusted Dougal not at all and had decided the best place for him was under MacNab's own eye.

But the old man was clearly half distracted with worry and desperate to find his charge. His hands shook on the reins, and he pushed on through the day and the vile weather like a man possessed.

At one point, Dougal heard him say to one of his companions, "I will need to send word to her father concerning what has occurred. He entrusted his daughter's care and welfare to me, and he is an old friend."

Dougal smiled to himself in satisfaction. *How does it feel, old man? How, to see someone stolen away and moved beyond your best efforts to protect her?*

"It is no use, MacNab," he told Randal when night once more began to draw down. "You might as well call off the search—you will no' find her."

Laird Randal glared at him, the hate visible in his eyes. "I will search as long as I choose, MacRae, and take no advice from the likes of you!"

"Aye so, but I withdraw then, from the search. 'Tis a lost cause."

"Do as you will," MacNab spat at him. "But if I find you had a hand in this, MacRae, the King himself will hear of it!"

"I?" Dougal gave him his best smile. "Have I not been out here helping to search for this Catherine Maitland, like any worthy neighbor?"

"I trust not your protestations of blamelessness, MacRae. This is a tender, young, innocent maid for whom we search—shame to any who takes advantage of that."

The words made Dougal's face—and heart—darken. MacNab dared speak to him about the protection of tender innocence? Aye, and the man deserved to be flayed for his hypocrisy.

Riding home with Lachlan at his side, Dougal was silent.

"So," said Lachy at last, obviously enjoying himself as always, "when will the ruse end?"

"Eh?"

"When will you reveal the existence of your new wife, along with her identity?"

The same question Isobel had asked.

"Soon." He wanted to flaunt her in MacNab's face, wanted MacNab to know this meant partial settlement of that old debt. And he wanted MacNab to see that his wife wanted to be with him. Even if it meant war.

Lachlan gave him a sharp look. "You do realize it will bring a load of trouble?"

"I am eager for trouble, Lachy. I have longed these years for a good, fair battle. The devil can bring justice, you ken, and I mean to bring it to MacNab."

"Aye. But Randal has the King in his pocket, do not forget."

"Oh, I will not forget." Dougal rubbed the scar on his cheek. "His power served him well once, but I was a young man then, and too impetuous for my own good."

"You are still too impetuous. Will you invite me to dinner this night, so I might make your wife's acquaintance?"

"You have made her acquaintance—out on the road, and at our wedding, as well."

"Aye, but I want a chance to speak with her. I am curious about the woman who agreed to take you on."

Dougal glared at his friend. "You will treat her respectfully, mind. None of your insolent tricks."

"Tricks? Me?" Lachy widened his eyes. "I know not of what you speak."

Dougal returned the look in full. "You have a talent for charming the ladies."

"Are you worried, my Laird, about retaining your wife's affections? And does that not smack of a budding attachment?"

"I have no illusions, Lachy, about my wife's affections. She has thrown in her lot wi' me—to her own benefit, did she but know it. I would not wish to see even a half-Englishwoman in MacNab's hands."

"No." Lachlan abruptly sobered. "Half English?"

"She tells me her mother was Scots."

"And how goes she between the sheets? Sweetly?"

"We will not speak of that."

"Aye, but, Dougal, you are the Devil Black—your exploits round the district are well recounted. Besides, do I not tell you about the ladies I entertain?"

"Aye, often, in nauseating detail. This is different. She is my wife."

"Aye, so?" Lachlan lifted his brows. "And can you imagine I would so much as look at another woman, with your sister in the same room?"

"Just behave yourself."

Miraculously, Lachlan did. The ensuing dinner, so Dougal later thought, proved among the more ordinary he could ever recall taking place beneath that roof. Meg, dressed for the occasion, looked bonny enough to strike Lachlan silent for the first half of the meal. Meg and Isobel made conversation, and O'Rourke, still in residence, enlivened the proceedings by becoming richly drunk. Both his brogue and his wit thickened, which Lachlan, predictably, found amusing.

Not until the end of the meal, when Meg and Lachlan began arguing over some nonsense O'Rourke introduced, did Isobel lean toward Dougal and say, "Well, Husband—you are very silent. How went the search for Catherine Maitland?"

Dougal raised moody eyes to her face. "Not well. 'Twas a long, cold trail, and no trace to be seen of that particular lady."

Isobel's eyes glinted blue fire. She had piled her russet hair into a knot atop her head, and managed to look both dignified and fetching. The hair, too heavy to stay up, now slid down the back of her neck and made Dougal's fingers itch. He wanted to touch her, so badly it hurt.

"I do not doubt," she murmured, "the lady in question is miles away from here and will never be found."

"And what of any sister of hers who might be in the district? Do you think she would want rescue from her present predicament?"

"I am sure not. I warrant she is enjoying her present predicament immensely."

"Oh, aye?" Dougal paused, a cup of whisky halfway to his lips, in order to eye her. Was she saying what he thought? His eyes lingered on her lips before dropping to the neck of her gown, where he could see her pulse throbbing. "Enjoying it? Is that so?"

"There is so much of interest to occupy a lively mind."

"Is it your mind needs occupying?"

"Among other things. Only look—" She nodded

toward where Meg and Lachlan still squabbled. "Is that not a fascinating display of emotion?"

Dougal nearly choked on his whisky. "Lachlan pants after my sister like a dog, but she has no interest in him."

"You think not? And I supposed you a clever man."

"So I am."

"Well, but you cannot read women. She bothers to argue with him because he attracts her."

"I fear you are wrong, Wife. She bears no soft feeling for him, nor any man."

"A lack of soft feeling does not argue indifference. Do you, my Laird, ever wager?"

"A bet, you mean?"

"I bet she will have him in her bed before month's end."

Dougal struggled to conceal his surprise. What manner of woman was this, who discussed such exploits and wagered like a man?

"Meg would eat him alive," he said dismissively.

"Perhaps, but she will do so in her bed."

"Wicked!"

"Sir, are you afraid to bet?"

He raked her with his gaze. "Hardly, given you are wrong. But what is the wager? Have you jewels, or gold?"

"I have not, but perhaps something better. The loser shall—" She leaned close and whispered in his ear, words that sent a rush of heat through him and caused all the blood in his body to pool between his legs.

He could not keep from shooting her another

incredulous look. "You are not in earnest!"

"Am I not? Do you consider the prize unworthy?"

"I do not." His honesty made him add, "Indeed, you will have me hoping to lose that bet."

She laughed, and the sound further enflamed him. He glanced at the big case clock in the corner. Barely eight of the evening, and too soon to retire, he supposed. But by the devil's own flail, she made him eager for it.

Her eyes met his and, almost as if she could read his mind, she said, "You have had a long and wearisome day, Husband. Do you think our guests would mind if we withdraw soon?"

"The devil take what they mind," Dougal replied, and meant it.

Chapter Fourteen

"So, I am nothing more than a weapon to you, am I?" Isobel murmured. "Something to be used cruelly and then put aside again?"

Her husband made no answer. He slept deeply, like a man struck between the eyes with a length of cold iron—as he should, following his exertions. Isobel, herself, felt weary to her bones, yet her tangled emotions kept her awake.

There was much her new husband did not yet know about her—they had so far been intimate in every possible physical way, but he remained largely unacquainted with the woman she was. Over the years in her father's house she had become adept at hiding and pretending, producing smiles to protect herself from her father's disapproval, and sometimes to cover Catherine's misdeeds.

Tonight at dinner, she had pretended that Dougal's words, earlier, had not hurt her, that his casual dismissal of her importance had not cut deep. He told her he was an honest man, which only made it worse. For he'd spent two nights making generous, wild, and demanding love to her—three nights, now—only to admit she meant nothing to him beyond a weapon to use against his enemy, MacNab.

It stung. Her careless, slightly naughty demeanor at dinner had been difficult to maintain, and when they were alone in the bedchamber, her promises still fresh in his ears, she had expected to feel some lingering resentment.

But all that flew from her when he touched her, stripped her clothing away gently, and lifted her onto the bed. There a kind of madness ensued, from which she only now surfaced, while he slept.

And even now all she wished was to look at him in the dying light of the fire. She should be exhausted and hurt, she should feel used, yet she knew only this desire to drink him in.

What sort of man had she married? Angry, clever, intent, devious, honest, incredibly talented with his hands and other parts of his body, and carrying some secret burden that virtually obsessed him. All these things contributed to Devil Black MacRae. He had taken her to wife in order to further some agenda of his own; she could not expect his consideration or concern. The attraction, she supposed, was a side benefit he would not allow to affect his plans.

He wanted to harm MacNab; it was the only reason Isobel found herself here with him.

And that hurt. The woman in her, the part of her he brought so successfully to the fore, wanted him to want her for herself. Her grasp of reality argued that would not happen.

While he rode out, today, with the other searchers, she had toyed with the idea of refusing him when he came back to her bed, of seeking to punish him the only way she had. She told herself to be cleverer than that, though. Her physical hold on him was the only one she possessed. She needed to further that, not curtail it.

Never mind the sheer pleasure of doing so—the

way her fingers craved touching his hot, naked flesh and her innermost senses cried out for the taste of him. She reminded herself it was all a game, one he had set, at which two could play.

Still, he made a glorious sight lying there in sleep with his black hair streaming across the pillow, one naked arm flung out toward her, and a half smile curving his lips—oh, those clever lips! Portions of her body still tingled from their touch. She did not doubt him the devil he claimed to be. Only a devil could prompt her to such excesses. Only a devil could be so beautiful. Surely only a devil would possess mist-grey eyes in which she wanted to lose herself, and black lashes longer than her own.

And one did not fall in love with a devil, not if one had a scrap of self-preservation. Isobel, a survivor from way back, had more than a scrap. She had wed him in order to survive. She would find a way, in this madhouse, to make circumstances work for her. If he used her, then, yes, she could use him as well. And pleasure might be a side benefit for her also. But she must guard herself fiercely.

He stirred then, his eyes came open, and he caught her looking at him. The lazy smile on his lips deepened, and he reached for her.

"Come here, Wife."

Isobel did not move. Her entire body responded to the temptation, yet she remained where she was, propped on one elbow.

"The hour is late, Husband, and surely you are weary."

"I begin to think weariness loses all meaning in your presence." He paused, reading her expression with those quick, clever eyes. "Never say you are sated with me?"

She was not, but now made as good a time as any to pretend. "And if I am? Have you, sir, only the one use for your wife?"

No fool, he. He withdrew his hand, and she could almost see him thinking over all that had passed between them.

"Have I implied it?" he asked then, diffidently.

"Do you not know?"

"Ah." The grey eyes darkened with caution. "You are upset with me. And, like any woman, you decide to withhold pleasure."

"Withhold it?" Isobel could not keep back an incredulous stare. "Do you forget what happened before you slept, and before that?"

"I could forget naught of what happens when you touch me."

"Then do not accuse me of being stingy with you."

"Fair enough." He folded his arms behind his head and regarded her in a new way. "Why do you not tell me what troubles you?"

So, he meant to listen? She scarcely believed it. Heatedly, she said, "A score of things trouble me. Yet all you care for is pleasure."

"'Tis not all I care for, Wife, 'tis what happens whenever we are alone together."

"You could prevent it, if you chose."

"So could you. In fact, you just have done. Do you claim you have had enough of me? 'Twas a short honeymoon."

"I say, concern for other things pushes desire from me. I wonder what will happen when Randal MacNab tells my father that I—that Catherine is lost. He will already be half mad with anger because I am missing from home."

"Anger?" the Devil questioned. "Not worry?"

"You do not know my father. Worry translates to anger, most times. It has been his foremost emotion, anyway, since my brothers died."

"How is it the servants in your coach thought they were escorting Lady Catherine Maitland to wed wi' MacNab, and I got Lady Isobel instead?"

"It is a long tale."

"Since we have suspended the pursuit of pleasure, I have naught to do but listen."

"You would do better sleeping."

"If you will not relieve the ache in my flesh, will you not at least satisfy my curiosity?"

She cast him a withering look. "I cannot imagine how you yet retain any ache at all."

"Then you can imagine little. I would guess, knowing you these three days, you came to Scotland in an attempt to protect your sister."

That made her stare at him. Did he begin to know her, after all?

"Randal MacNab and my father have long been friends," she began. "I do not know how or when the association began—it was founded before I was born."

"Both King's men, no doubt. Such men do band together."

"After his son Bertram's first wife died, MacNab decided Bertram should wed my father's daughter."

She sensed that Dougal stiffened where he lay, but intent on her story, she hurried on. "He requested me, the elder sister. But my father knew me to be…shamed, and convincing MacNab I had other faults, he contracted Catherine to Bertram, instead."

"What faults?" Dougal's eyes examined her frankly. "I can, myself, declare you without flaw."

"Save my overbearing lack of virginity."

Dougal waved a dismissive hand. "Your father did not tell him that?"

"I believe he mentioned an incident while riding that brought into question my ability to bear children. MacNab wants many sons."

Dougal's eyes moved over her again, more slowly. "And, is it true?

"It is not. The women in our family conceive and bear easily."

He nodded. "Go on."

"Catherine did not wish for the marriage, did not want to come to Scotland. She had formed an attachment with the youngest son of our bailiff and wished to marry him."

"A doomed romance. Surely your father would insist on better for her."

"Yes. But, you see, Catherine found herself in dire straits indeed, carrying her lover's child."

"The penniless bailiff's son? Aye, so. Did she tell your father?"

"No. She told me, and I…I hatched a scheme for us to trade places. I would come to Scotland, while she ran off with Thomas."

"Ah. So you sacrificed yourself for your sister."

Isobel dropped her eyes. "It was no great sacrifice. My life was in ruins."

"And, now? Do you sacrifice yourself to me, on her behalf?"

She did not lift her eyes and felt him capture her chin in his long, strong fingers and force her to meet his eyes.

"Well, Wife?"

"I do everything I do for Catherine." Isobel's color mounted with the lie. "Just as you do all you do for anger."

The expression in his eyes changed, grew more distant. "Just so long as we understand one another."

He released her, and she turned her face away.

"So," he resumed after a moment, "how did you deceive your father's servants, who believed themselves to be accompanying one Catherine Maitland?"

"Our maid—Bethan—knew the truth. I bought her off with a ruby necklace that belonged to my mother."

Dougal raised his eyebrows. "Enterprising."

"The scheme would not have worked at all, had Father decided to accompany us. But, as usual, he professed himself too busy with the estate. Catherine and I are as like in appearance as may be."

"Aye? Which, I presume, explains the indiscretions of the bailiff's son."

"I beg your pardon?"

Once more, his eyes examined her. "You must know how lovely you are."

"There is no need, sir, to flatter me. You have me already where you wish."

"I do not flatter, no more than I lie. You are temptation on two legs. If your sister does resemble you, the poor sod had no chance."

Again Isobel looked away from him. "We told the servants, and Father, Catherine had taken a cold. She went into the coach well swathed—or, rather, I did. Soon after I departed, Catherine met with her Thomas and eloped. They are long away."

"Your father will be livid."

"He will. Of course, he may believe it was I who fled with Thomas. So he may think himself well rid of the problem I represented."

"Is he truly so cold?"

"Yes." Isobel reflected upon it and added, "I believe so."

"And where have your sister and her lover fled?"

"Bristol, where he is promised a position."

"Bristol! The netherlands of hell."

"Why is that?"

"Anywhere is hell, that is no' Scotland—and especially this little piece of it."

"You love your home right well."

"It goes, Wife, beyond love. The roots of my heart run deep in this place, my ancestors' blood soaks the ground. I have hope of it—" his gaze swept her body, "for my sons. I will do what I must to retain it."

"Could the King take it from you?"

"The King can take anything from anyone."

"I am surprised, then, that you defy him."

"Do I? Have I not married, as he decreed? Do I not dutifully and diligently plant my seed?"

"Diligently?"

"And with great pleasure. Tell me, Wife, what did you plan to do when Bertram MacNab discovered he had the elder sister after all—the one who, presumably, could not give him his much desired sons?"

"I planned to seduce him, and then it would be too late. I would prove myself by getting, almost at once, with child. What could he do then?"

"What, indeed? A complete sacrifice, then?"

"Yes."

"So," he said softly and with particular intensity, "you thought of everything?"

"Almost everything," Isobel allowed. She had not considered endangering her heart to the man she married. And she had not dreamed of a man like Devil Black MacRae.

"And what, Wife," he asked, leaning close, so close his lips almost brushed hers, "did you overlook?"

"The bandit of Central Scotland," Isobel replied, and turned her face away.

Chapter Fifteen

"He is a bandit, a man without honor or scruples," Meg said of her brother, impatiently. "I do not know why the King—or you, for that matter, Isobel—expect any better of him."

Isobel gave her new sister-in-law a searching look. Meg seemed unusually irascible today, and that said a great deal of a woman who spent her days in an ill temper. She seemed edgy, and though part of that could be laid at the door of the continued vile weather, Isobel suspected yet another cause.

Two weeks had passed since Isobel's marriage with the Devil Black MacRae. The search for Bertram MacNab's missing bride had been suspended, yet Dougal still spent much of his time abroad on the roads—doing the good God only knew what. Isobel and Meg, the only two women in a household of rough warriors, had perforce struck up a relationship of sorts.

Isobel held no illusion that Meg liked or even approved of her. Obviously, Meg liked no one. But, Dougal's sister came to tolerate her, merely because there was no one else.

"I expect nothing of your brother," she replied now. The two women shared a room called the solar, a small, intimate chamber meant for sewing and conversation. A shabby place, it nevertheless always boasted a decent fire.

"I wish I need not acknowledge him my brother," Meg complained, "curse him to hell!"

This was not the first such opinion Isobel had heard. She bit her lip and then decided to ask the obvious question. "Why do you hate him so?"

Meg shot her a scathing look. "Are there not a multitude of reasons?"

"Maybe. But I think you are a woman who deals in specifics. Will you tell me?"

Meg swore bitterly. "Is it for me to recount your husband's sins and failures? Let him tell you himself."

"Failures?"

Meg gave Isobel a disparaging look. "What do you know about Dougal's past?"

Isobel shook her head. "Nothing."

Meg turned away, walked to the window and stood looking out.

Snow fell steadily and cold crept over the window sill in an unremitting wave.

"You have courage, Isobel," she said unexpectedly. "I respect that." She looked over her shoulder. "So I warn you again, do not lose your heart to him."

"No?" For the past fortnight, Isobel had been struggling to convince herself that had not already happened. "Why, apart from the obvious?"

"'Tis a fool's task, falling in love, especially for a woman. We open ourselves to all sorts of pain, betrayal, and disappointment."

"Some man has disappointed you?" Isobel hazarded.

"What man has not, from my father on down? But we speak not of me. Guard yourself carefully, Isobel, against Dougal. He has, in the past, betrayed a woman who loved him right well."

"Oh, yes?" Isobel felt her heart sink, and hoped her emotions did not show on her face. "Who was she?"

"My good friend, named Aisla. We all grew up together, and she wanted Dougal for as long as I can remember. My dear brother—strong, handsome, aye, but not so much a devil, then. We thought they would wed. Everyone thought it. And he professed himself in love with her, but he lied. For when it came down to it, he refused to save her from a fate she did not deserve."

The pain in Meg's voice gave Isobel pause, yet she had to know. "What fate was that?"

It seemed Meg would not answer. She faced Isobel, and the bitterness in her eyes was shocking. "Aisla's father—bastard that he was—decided to give her in marriage to a man of wealth and substance."

Realization struck Isobel all at once. "MacNab?"

Meg's expression tightened. "Aisla was Bertram MacNab's first wife—the one he killed with cruelty and abuse."

To Isobel's surprise, she saw tears in Meg's dark eyes—tears of anger, surely, as well as grief.

"Sweet, gentle Aisla," Meg went on, "who would not raise a hand to swat a naughty pup. I saw her three times after she was wed, and the change that came over her horrified me. She begged me for help, for rescue. I vowed I would save her."

Meg's features pinched with pain, and she no longer looked beautiful.

Isobel's stomach clenched in dismay; she did not want to hear the rest of this tale.

But Meg tossed her head. "Like a fool, I went to Dougal, my grand warrior of a brother, who feared nothing and could do anything. He was like a god to me then—at twenty, he had just taken over the estate following our father's death. I thought he loved Aisla— loved her as I did or, more, loved her like a woman. But do you know what he said to me, when I told him of her plight?"

Isobel shook her head.

Fiercely, Meg told her, "He said, 'She is another man's wife.' As if that meant anything. As if it changed her sweetness, her vulnerability, her trust in him, or how much we cared for her. I could not believe my ears. I told him he must save her anyway. That she needed him. That she looked but a shadow of her former, happy self... He turned from me. His face grew hard and his heart also. And after that he drank and haunted the roads, and he let her die in that bastard's hands!"

"How long ago was this?"

Meg, deep in memory, did not answer.

"You said he was but twenty, then. How long ago—"

"Eight years. It took Aisla five years to die. I saw her not again during that time, for MacNab kept her locked away. 'Tis said, by the end she had become a jabbering madwoman."

And this, Isobel thought with a flash of pain, was the fate she had spared Catherine, and that she herself had narrowly escaped, by the grace of the Devil Black MacRae. Her own father must not know how his good friend's son had treated his first wife.

She whispered, "What did Bertram MacNab do to her, do you know?"

Meg stared at Isobel with empty eyes. "Word

trickled out by the servants. What did he not do to her? Confinement, whippings when she did not produce a son. Vile rape, I have no doubt. 'Tis said a man cannot in fact rape his own wife—you and I know better. I will never forgive Dougal for failing her, and I will never respect him again. I left here to marry shortly after Aisla's death. My own marriage did not work out, and I am forced to return here. But I need not like being under the same roof as my accursed brother."

"He does hate MacNab very deeply," Isobel began.

Meg glared at her. "Do you defend him? I hope, for your sake, 'tis not a sign of attachment on your part. For be fairly warned, Isobel, he will forsake and abandon you just as he did poor Aisla. If you believe in God, you had better pray you fall not into MacNab's hands."

A shiver traced its way up Isobel's spine. "But I am Dougal's wife, now. Surely that offers me some protection."

"Do not be a fool! This is an ancient part of Scotland—wives have been snatched, traded, and raped before now. Do not say you have not been warned. Men are vile creatures, not to be trusted, and I have no use for them."

"All men?"

"All of them!"

"Even," Isobel asked tentatively, "your brother's companion, Lachlan MacElwain?"

Meg glowered. "Him, more than most. If you will speak of a fool—"

"He is a good-looking fool."

"Aye, and that is the worst kind. Such charm cannot be trusted. I have known him since we were all children, and he does not improve with acquaintance."

"From what I have observed, he has feelings for you."

Meg laughed cruelly. "Aye, and the name of his feelings are 'lust' and 'desire.' He is capable of nothing else."

"He shall not succeed then, in his suit for your affections?" Isobel asked curiously.

"Is that what you think it? I should have called it seduction."

Isobel lifted an eyebrow, and Meg laughed reluctantly. "If I want him in my bed, I shall have him there, but that is all there will be to it. I am too wise to involve my heart. And you do likewise, mind."

"Yes," said Isobel gravely.

Surprising her, Meg laid a hand on Isobel's arm. "Truly, Sister, you are an intelligent woman, too much so to get caught by any man's lies or suggestions."

Isobel struggled with it. "You are right," she acknowledged. "But does not your brother's declared feud with MacNab, and the very fact that he stole me away from Bertram, argue he did, indeed, care for Aisla and that he wishes some sort of revenge?"

"You have hope for him yet?" Meg shook her head. "Had he cared enough, had he the courage I expected of him, he would have done something at the time." She added passionately, "He would have saved her."

Isobel nodded, but Meg must have been able to see that she remained unconvinced.

"Ask him, if you do not believe me," she challenged. "Ask about his courage—or the lack of it—and see what answer he makes. He swore he loved her, long ago. He lied! So I warn you, believe no such words that fall from his traitorous lips."

"I will be most careful," Isobel said, despairingly. "And I thank you, Meg, for trusting me with the truth."

## Chapter Sixteen

"You are quiet tonight, Wife," Dougal observed casually, resting one booted foot on the curb before the simmering fire. Outside, the snow still fell, an accursed, early show of winter. He and Isobel sat alone in the drafty, high-ceilinged hall.

He had roamed far this day and taken a heavy load of silver off a fat merchant. All the while, he had thought only of returning home to his wife and the sweet reception she would give him in her bed. He had been nearly too hard to ride comfortably.

And now that he was here and the hour passing late, she began with women's games—the withdrawn gaze and prolonged silences. He had not expected Isobel, so fiery and honest, to lower herself to that petty level, and it annoyed him.

"Have I done something to displease you?" he asked ironically.

That persuaded her to look at him, a searing, blue stare. "How could you, my lord, when I have barely seen you this day?"

"Ah, so that is it? You fancy neglect? Well, I cannot be in your bed all day long, more's the pity. But surely we can repair there now." He had an accounting, in his mind, of the things he wanted to do to and with her—a long accounting.

She got to her feet and glared at him. "Is that all I

mean to you? A warmer for your bed?"

Dougal sighed inwardly, letting none of his aggravation show. Women—almost more trouble than they were worth. Perhaps her mood had swung due to her monthly cycle.

Evenly, he said, "You are my wife and as such deserve respect. And aye, your duties do include warming my bed."

"Duties?" She nearly soared off her toes, in anger. He had never seen her truly enraged, though he had tasted her other passions; it might prove interesting.

He let his gaze travel over her slowly. "I thought, Wife, it was a duty you enjoyed right well."

Her cheeks heated. "That is neither here nor there. Why did you wed with me?"

Dougal got to his feet, a deceptively lazy motion. "If you mean to rant at me, let us go upstairs. The servants will be listening."

"There are no servants."

"I speak of my men, who do for me about the place. Have some dignity."

Her eyes opened in surprise, and then she turned and led the way from the hall. She ascended the stone stairs ahead of him, and Dougal found himself admiring her taut backside, the focus of a large part of his fantasies earlier in the day. His palms itched to touch, yet he could wait and hear her out—he possessed at least that much self control.

The chamber they now shared felt warm and cozy; she had made a few changes these last weeks—chairs, and an upholstered bench before the fire, a rug on the cold, stone floor, and a hanging blocking the cold air from the window. Part of him appreciated that, desired the comforts almost as much as he desired her.

She spun to regard him, wild-eyed. "Now we are alone, will you speak to me?"

"Aye." Damn it, he was still hard; being in her presence acted on him like black magic. "But I will tell you ahead of time I do not appreciate a woman's moods, nor being held victim to them."

"Moods?" she echoed, outraged.

He examined her briefly. "I apprehend this unfortunate display is born of your...monthly sensitivities?"

"No! I am not—" In an effort to control her anger, she paused and drew a breath. "I assure you, I am not in the habit of suffering from 'sensitivities,' monthly or otherwise."

"Well, I do no' appreciate this ill temper."

"And, am I supposed to worry about what you appreciate?"

Dougal felt his own anger—a dark and terrible thing—sharpen. "Presumably."

"Think again. Because you care not for my feelings—shut up in this terrible place virtually alone, fated to provide you comfort, and you will not even answer for me one question."

"I will, if you ask it in a sane manner."

"Sanity? He asks for sanity, in this madhouse? Why did you wed with me?"

Dougal turned away from her and poured a cup of whisky from the flask that stood ready. "You know why. The King decreed—"

"That is not the reason! A man like you—a robber, an outlaw, a thief of cattle and women—cares nothing for what the King bids him. You hate MacNab, and you wed me to get back at him, to hurt him, did you not?"

Dougal drank deep. "Why ask me questions, if you already know the answers?"

"So. It is as I said before, I am nothing more than a weapon, like a sword or a dirk. Why sleep with me, then? Why not just keep me prisoner, kick me into a corner? Would it not serve the same purpose?"

Annoyance blossomed in Dougal's head. He sneered, "I sleep with you, woman, because it is my right. Because your body pleases me, and because MacNab will eventually discover you are here. When he does," Dougal let his gaze flick her again, "I would make sure you already carry my son."

She gasped and wrapped her arms about herself in a defensive gesture. "That—that is your aim?"

"He will not want you back, if you carry the black devil's get. Neither will your father, if he turns up looking."

"My father?"

"Had that no' occurred to you? I figure 'tis but a matter of time. Someone in this household will talk, and word will get abroad that my new wife looks remarkably like Catherine Maitland."

"So—" she sounded as if she had been struck, "you sleep with me to…to stake your claim?"

He shrugged with indifference he did not really feel. "Aye, and will you complain of it? You were willing to give yourself to Bertram MacNab for your sister's sake. Him, or me—where, in your view, is the difference?"

Eyes burning, Isobel stared at him and said nothing.

"You know full well MacNab wanted sons. Should

I be any different?"

"So I am naught but a…a breeding sow, am I?"

"A valuable sow, aye." His eyes were on his cup, so he nearly missed it when she flew at him and aimed a blow with one hand. His instincts being what they were, however, he caught her wrist before the blow could connect, and glared into her eyes.

"Ah! I will not take abuse from you," he snarled.

She refused to back down. "Yet I am fated to accept abuse from you?"

"How and when have I abused you, Wife?" He had been right; her anger inflamed him and made him want her more than ever. He now felt so hard he might burst. "By giving you my kisses, which you returned full well? By removing those garments you could not strip off quickly enough?"

"Curse you!" she spat.

He stared into her eyes. "Too late! I was accursed long before ever I met you."

"Take your hands from me!" She strove to pull away from him.

For an instant he thought about holding her, kissing her as he had longed, feeling her melt against him into a pool of desire, as he knew she would. But no. He would not force her. Let her ask him for it.

He released her as if touching her burned—as it did. Turning away, he began stripping off his clothing—leather tunic, soft wool shirt, overly-tight trews and, finally, the kilt. When he'd finished, he turned toward her, flagrantly displaying his manhood, which surged to attention.

She looked her fill and swallowed hard. "What are you doing?"

"Going to bed, Wife. Surely that is permitted?"

"Here?"

"Have I not the right?"

"Yes, but—I thought you only stayed here when we… I warn you, I will not agree to accommodate you this night."

He lifted a brow. "You complain when I stay only to 'use' you, and then you complain when I stay to sleep."

She flushed again, the color staining her beautiful skin.

"Sleep where you will. I care not. I only want you to understand what will and will not happen this night."

"Oh, aye, you have made yourself clear." He climbed into the bed, taking up as much space as possible. He closed his eyes, feigning weariness. In truth, he felt anything but tired.

Isobel stood where she was for several moments, as if rooted, then went and sat in the chair by the fire.

Time slowly drew out, and Dougal's body relaxed. The long miles ridden that day began to catch up with him, and his thoughts drifted toward sleep.

He nearly slept when he half heard, half felt Isobel move about the room. Peering between his lashes, he watched as his wife removed her clothes and donned her night rail, some of his drowsiness leaving him as a consequence. He knew that body of hers now, could declare the soft weight of those breasts, the silk of her long legs wrapped around him. Desire pricked at him like a fever.

She climbed into the bed, her long hair loose around her. Carefully, she strove to make herself small and assure her body avoided his.

He thought of the many mornings this fortnight past when he had waked to find her limbs twined with his, and the delectable feelings thus occasioned. He had only to reach for her now...

Yet he had vowed he would make no such move until she showed her desire—and a woman locked into a tight ball at the edge of the bed showed none such.

He was a grown man, was he not? A man who had endured tremendous pain in his life with stoic resistance. Surely he could endure this.

Yet he swore at himself bitterly before he closed his eyes again, and he had to force himself to form the mild, ironic words, "Good night, Wife—and be sure to sleep well."

Chapter Seventeen

"MacNab is at the door with that accursed son of his in tow. They demand entry."

Meg delivered the announcement with her back pressed against the closed door of the dining hall and her head high. The four of them had been at dinner. The hour being late and the weather continuing foul, the last thing Isobel expected was this kind of interruption.

Yet Meg, who had gone out to direct one of the courses, returned and shut the door as if against an invading army.

Lachlan MacElwain, their sole guest, exchanged glances with Dougal and straightened in his chair. Isobel, her heart leaping, looked to her husband also.

Dougal stirred, a small, ironic smile touching his lips, picked up the dirk with which he cut his meat and slipped it neatly into his sleeve. "Leave it to the impolite MacNabs to disturb my dinner," he drawled. "Well, Sister," he continued to Meg, "and have you left them on the doorstep?"

"In the hall," she replied, only the glitter in her eyes and the high color in her face betraying her emotion, which Isobel could not quite identify—terror, or excitement?

And surely she saw anticipation in her husband's eyes. Lachlan looked thoughtful but not appalled. Was Isobel, herself, the only one frightened by this awful development?

Dougal looked at her, just as if she had spoken the question aloud. Three days had passed since that night they had spent together and yet apart, in her bed, and they had not had relations once. The wild thought now blossomed in her head: perhaps, finding he had no use for her, Dougal would just hand her over to MacNab after all.

Yet, on his feet, he turned to one of his retainers. "Alert the men, if they are not already aware of our...visitors. Make sure everyone is armed, and close the gates."

He looked at Meg. "How large a party has MacNab brought?"

Meg shook her head. "Not large: just himself, the abominable Bertram, and two attendants."

Dougal's smile sharpened. "Very bold—or very foolish."

Lachlan, now also on his feet, said, "You cannot take him prisoner, Dougal, nor murder him. In all conscience—"

"I have no conscience, a fact MacNab knows right well. And I have anticipated this from the first." He turned to Meg. "I will see him there, in the hall."

Meg nodded, and her eyes moved to Isobel. "Shall I stay with your wife, upstairs?"

Dougal feigned great surprise. "Why would you do that?"

"To keep her out of MacNab's sight, of course." Meg asked Isobel directly, "Will he recognize you?"

Isobel nodded, but Dougal gave her no chance to speak.

"You think I mean to hide her? But nay, Sister, I

will not hide my wife. Why should I, indeed?"

Now Meg and Lachlan exchanged incredulous stares.

Lachlan spoke, "Because she is Bertram's affianced wife, whom you stole?"

"Nay, but she is not. I apprehend 'tis one Catherine Maitland for whom they have come looking—my wife's sister, in truth. Well, Wife, will you greet them with me?"

Isobel narrowed her eyes on his face. So, he meant to brazen it out, did he? And yes, he had anticipated this with great relish, but she had not, and she felt terrified, as if she might lose what little dinner she had taken.

"Come." Dougal stepped to her side and offered his arm. "You look beautiful, as always. It might be better, however, could you manage to look a bit less frightened."

"Impossible!" Isobel's lips felt stiff, and her throat had gone tight.

Now they all stared at her.

"She will be ill," Meg predicted.

"She will faint," Lachlan wagered.

"Nay, she has more backbone than that." Dougal's arm, beneath her hand, felt like rock.

She gazed up into his eyes. "Perhaps I would do better to wait in my room."

"Perhaps you would. Yet, Wife, word of your presence has obviously got round the district at last, and now we must play this out. MacNab will not rest until he lays eyes on you. 'Tis best faced now."

"What must I say to him?"

"The truth: that you chose to wed wi' me."

"What if he insists on taking me away with him?"

Isobel's heart violently protested the possibility. Despite her many doubts about her husband, and the seemingly impossible distance between them, she discovered she did not wish to leave him.

Something flickered in the grey depths of Dougal's eyes. "Then he shall have a war on his hands. You are my wife. I will die before I give you up."

The words found their way to Isobel's soul and took up residence, even though she knew the reason he said them had nothing to do with what was in his heart. He already battled MacNab. This was a skirmish he had contemplated. He merely did not want to lose.

Yet she felt her chin lift anyway. What might it be, to be loved by a man such as this?

His gaze quickened as he read the emotions in her eyes. His hand, warm and strong, came up and grasped her hand, which rested on his arm.

"Very well, I am ready," she told him.

Still, when they began to move, her knees wobbled and sickness rose into the back of her throat. She could hear raised voices in the great hall. They fell silent when she and Dougal entered the lofty chamber and the two men there turned to stare at her.

She recognized Randal MacNab at once, somewhat to her surprise. Tall and carrying enough extra weight to argue affluence, he had a strong, fleshy face and receding hair, now gone grey. Lines scored his forehead and cheeks, but his eyes were those of a young—and angry—man. He wore unrelenting black, no kilt for him, and a sword at his side.

She failed to recognize Bertram, the man she should have married. He had been a man of twenty-one when last she saw him and must be all of thirty now. He had his father's height but none of his bulk, and reminded Isobel of a whip, cruel and dangerous. His brown hair had just begun to recede and his face might be deemed handsome by some. Well proportioned, he looked proud and haughty, and Isobel saw rage in his eyes. Like his father, he wore a sword. Unlike him, he sported the MacNab tartan, its colors muted in the dim room.

She heard what sounded like a growl come from Dougal's throat and felt the hate surge through him like summer lightning.

Bertram MacNab stepped forward with a cry. "Catherine! Father, did I not tell you it was so? Catherine, are you well? We searched the district for you. In fact, this blackguard pretended to help us search, all the while keeping you imprisoned here."

Isobel, still clutching Dougal's arm desperately, said the only thing she could. "I am not Catherine."

Confusion reigned for several moments while both MacNab and his son spoke at once, neither giving Isobel fair opportunity to explain. Dougal stood the while, silent as a rock, even when Bertram stepped up to challenge him.

"What have you done to her, MacRae? What foul magic worked upon the poor lass's mind, that she knows not who she is? I shall have you for abduction and imprisonment."

"I am Isobel, older sister to Catherine," Isobel said, determined now to make herself heard. "I was Isobel Maitland and am, now, wife to this man." Her fingers tightened on Dougal's arm.

"Married? You wed wi' her?" Isobel thought Bertram would explode; the point seemed far more valid to him than her actual identity. It was clever-eyed Randal who stepped forward and said, "Why are you here, Isobel? My son's marriage contract was with your sister, Catherine."

"Just so." Dougal spoke up for the first time. "And you have no business here, having no contract of any kind concerning this woman, my wife."

"One moment!" Randal MacNab held up a hand. "She will explain to us before we go anywhere. Where is your sister, lass? And had your father knowledge of this?"

Isobel shook her head. "My sister and I hatched the scheme between us, to change places. No one knew, save our maid who, I believe, died when our coach crashed."

"Everyone died," Randal said grimly. "The coach overturned in a ravine. We were not sure but you—or rather your sister—had perished as well. We had men search the roads for days."

"And all the while," Bertram seethed, "this bastard knew—"

"Aye," Randal denounced in a hard tone. "And yet he pretended to search, by our sides. Explain that, man. And also why you saw fit to wed with this woman if, indeed, the marriage is no sham?"

Dougal lifted his head arrogantly. "I wed as the King himself bade me—in response to your complaint of me, I believe, MacNab. And the marriage, performed by the priest, O'Rourke, is legal, as well as consummated."

MacNab stiffened like a horse feeling the whip. "O'Rourke? That drunken sot! I believe any ceremony performed by him could well be called into question."

"And the consummation?" Dougal sneered. "Will you question that, as well?"

Bertram turned what appeared to be half crazed eyes on Isobel. "If, Lady, he raped you—well, my father has the King's ear. He shall hang for it!"

For the first time, Isobel felt Dougal tense beneath her touch. The words she spoke now, she knew, could mean his demise—and her freedom.

If she wanted freedom from him, that was.

She drew a breath that seemed to vibrate through her, then leaned toward Bertram and met his eyes, her own narrowed.

"No rape, I assure you, sir. I wanted him. I do, yet. Had I been forced to lie with you in my poor sister's place—now, that would have necessitated rape."

\*\*\*\*

Dougal was still laughing long after the MacNabs gathered the shreds of their dignity and stalked off, their rage tangible. His mirth seemed genuine, and it annoyed Isobel in a way she could not easily define.

At last she turned on him and exploded, "I do not know what you find so amusing. You have not heard the last of this. You heard him say he will send word to my father, and what he may do I cannot say."

"I did, indeed, hear him," agreed Dougal, his eyes still displaying unholy mirth. "Yet, Wife, I can only applaud the spirit you showed. As for your father, surely he will be deep in confusion by now, with your sister having disappeared. Or will he be thinking 'tis yourself ran off, and Catherine here? At least he will be relieved to know you are alive."

Would he? What would Father feel when he learned his daughter had wed with an infamous outlaw?

Would he care? Perhaps all his concern centered on Catherine and he was glad to be rid of his elder, troublesome daughter...

"I do not think 'relief' can describe his possible emotions," she said tersely. "And whether he will actually travel here I cannot say. He has ever professed himself far too busy with the estate to trouble much with us." Her lips tightened. "He is most diligent toward the estate."

"Aye?" Dougal gave her a cool look. "And yet this case may be different, surely? He might well bestir himself."

"He might."

"So I shall be prepared, give my men instructions to expect company at the gates. Eh?" He slanted a brow at her.

Isobel, thinking hard about it, said slowly, "MacNab will send Father word that I am here, not Catherine. So whatever he thinks now, he will soon know the truth." She shook her head decisively. "He will not come."

"We shall see."

She told him, "Whatever my father decides, I doubt MacNab is done with this. Will he complain to the King?"

"How can he, when you have assured him you chose to wed wi' me?" Dougal crossed to her side and lifted a finger to trace her lips. "Thank you for that, Wife."

Helplessly, she gazed up into his eyes, deep grey and as mysterious as a stormy sea.

"But perhaps," he whispered, "words make an insufficient expression of my gratitude. Can you think of aught else?"

Isobel knew she should not melt into a pliable bundle against him; nothing between them had been resolved. He thought of her still as a weapon, something to be used—his heart remained aloof from her, no matter how intimate their bodies became.

Could she live with that? Could she live without his touch? He declared himself grateful, yet he, like his sister, manipulated people with ease.

Isobel should walk away from him now and preserve what little pride remained to her amid this awful mess. She did not need more hurt or more pain. And yet he held, for her, all the temptation of the devil himself.

"I will think of a proper way for you to thank me," she told him. "Only give me time."

## Chapter Eighteen

"I do not need you. I do not want you! Be a sensible man and keep out of my life." The whisper vibrated through the cold silence of the great hall and stopped Dougal in the doorway, unseen. The dawn, just past, had come muffled in deep snow; the couple in the hall, who spoke with their heads close together, stood nearly lost in deep gloom.

Yet, Dougal knew them: his sister, Meg, and his friend, Lachlan—who obviously did not know what was good for him.

As if to prove it, Lachy whispered, "I cannot! You have bewitched me. Do you have any idea how I want you?"

Dougal, unwilling eavesdropper, almost groaned. He—fresh from his wife's bed and another endless night spent struggling not to touch her—understood the meaning of frustration. But he knew his sister also, and Lachy would get nowhere by begging.

As if to prove him right, Meg laughed. "All men want me, most to their sorrow. Do yourself a favor, Lachy, and give it up."

Lachlan's voice trembled when he replied, "I do not think that's possible."

Dougal saw his sister reach up and touch Lachlan on the cheek, a gesture of unaccustomed tenderness. "Lachlan, I have known you since we were both children. You are like a brother to me, almost."

"Do not say that!"

"I stipulated 'almost.' We teased and tormented each other as bairns. I know your mind and your considerable failings, as you know mine."

"Surely that is to the good?"

"I think not. You are fickle as the wind and want always what you have not, simply because 'tis withheld from you. You have never formed a serious attachment in your life, save that to my accursed brother. And what does that say of you?"

"Never, perhaps, until now." The throb of passion in Lachlan's voice opened Dougal's eyes wide. "I would sell my soul for you, Meg."

"A fine declaration. But I have no interest in your soul."

Dougal knew he should withdraw; this scene was not meant for his eyes, or ears. Yet wonder kept him rooted to the spot.

Lachlan shook his head. "I am helpless in your hands. Prudence and wisdom—what little ever I possessed—fly away from me in your presence."

"Do not play the fool!"

"And if I cannot help myself?"

"We can always help ourselves, Lachy, if we try. Do you know what I am? What they say of me?"

"That you are a witch," Lachlan said, so low Dougal, still listening shamelessly, barely heard him.

"A witch, aye. And a murderess. Both are true of me, Lachy. So keep clear and save yourself—for the sake of our old friendship."

"You surely have enchanted me."

Poor sod, Dougal thought, shaking his head. Lachy

never learned. Yet he saw his sister, cruel as fate and twice as fierce, fall into his friend's arms and then, while they were wholly distracted, Dougal did withdraw, for decency's sake.

The incident remained much on his mind and later that day, when he and Lachlan, who seemed, now, virtually to live at the keep, were busy inspecting the fortifications one more time, he tried to broach the subject.

Knowing Lachy had stolen at least a kiss from the object of his desire, Dougal expected him to be enthused and energized. Yet as they stood together on the walk that ran along the keep's top battlements, Lachy seemed quiet and morose.

"What is troubling you, then?" Dougal asked impatiently. "Are you sickening for something?"

Lachy rolled his eyes like a wayward pony. "Sick, aye, 'tis a terrible sickness."

"What is?"

"Love."

Despite what he knew, Dougal almost choked on his tongue. "Please say you do not fancy yourself in love wi' my sister. It is a sickness indeed, one that will destroy you if you let it."

"Oh, aye? And I apprehend you do not in fact feel the same toward your new wife?"

"I do not," Dougal declared bitterly. "I am, aye, attracted to her, and she serves to warm my bed." *Though not lately.* "But you know very well I believe not in 'love.' "

Lachlan looked stubborn, one of his worst moods. "You did, once." He spoke the name Dougal wanted never to hear again. "Aisla—"

Pain rushed through Dougal in a staggering wave, and he reacted in the only way he could—with anger. His hand flew to his sword and he rounded on his companion.

"I was a lad then," he growled, "a deluded fool."

Lachy's blue eyes met his, unflinching. "And you loved her. I daresay you do yet. We all loved her—who could fail to? Will you betray her by denying the truth, the value of what you felt? Must you, Dougal?"

Dougal's rage nearly strangled him. His voice sounded rough as gravel when he spoke again. "I do not deny I thought I loved her. But I assert such love is an illusion, a false emotion. How did any love I thought I felt for her benefit her, Lachy? You speak of betrayal— aye, I carry that sin every day of my life."

Lachlan's expression turned to one of regret. "I did not mean that. God knows, you did what you could." His voice lowered, even though they stood isolated in the cold wind at the top of the keep. "I know—"

"You know nothing! And you will forget what you think happened. I warned you before, if ever you speak of it, I will slit your throat, friend or no."

Lachy glared. "Have I ever spoken a word, all these years? I am not sure what happened, by any road—only that you made a bid—"

"And failed," Dougal said, like a man stabbed to the heart. "My own conviction in the power of love availed me nothing then, Lachy. If you want to buy into the delusion for the sake of your loins or your conscience, though by the devil's horns, I do not know why, then find yourself some meek miss who can decide herself equally besotted with you and give you a crop of sons. Do not entangle yourself with my sister."

"So you have advised me, over and over again. And I say to you, Dougal, love is more than the side effect of a stiff crotch. 'Tis a kind of magic, that strikes where it may. You canno' choose it, or refuse it."

"You truly are a fool."

"So you have also advised me, repeatedly."

"Tell me then, Lachlan. If you languish in the pleasurable pool of love, why do you also mope here, showing the aspect of a man who has been kicked in the teeth?"

"You know why. Meg leads me a merry chase. She spends most her time warning me off and then, just occasionally, tosses me a scrap of hope, barely enough to keep me panting after her."

"So, be a man. Command her, or leave her."

"As you do your wife?" Lachlan slanted a curious look at Dougal. "I suppose you command all of your emotions, where she is concerned?"

"Of course," Dougal lied.

"I have to admit," said Lachlan, who seemed to have a penchant for putting his foot in his mouth this day, "I never expected to see you wed—after Aisla, I mean. And Isobel is naught like Aisla, is she? 'Tis like comparing chalk and cheese."

"And why should she be like—" Dougal found that even after all this time he could not speak her name.

"Full of spirit," Lachy went on, oblivious to Dougal's state of mind. "And I cannot imagine her weeping in that soft way, as Aisla used to."

"Shut up, Lachlan."

"Eh?"

"Stop talking now, or I swear I will silence you!"

Lachlan shot him an injured look.

Silence fell on the high walk, save the soughing of the endless wind that seemed to bring the chill of the distant hills.

"All I am saying," began Lachlan, who never knew when to keep still, then, "is I hope your new wife proves worth it. You do know you have war on your hands? Her father may or may not bring you trouble. With MacNab, 'tis assured."

"I welcome war with MacNab, Lachy. I have long desired it."

"You want revenge, and to pay him back."

"We have established that."

"And if it costs your lands? Your bonny new wife?"

Dougal shrugged. "The cost be damned. Just so I bring him down—with me or without."

"Aye, so!" Lachlan tossed his head. "I suppose that proves you have no real love for Isobel."

"I have told you over and over again, Lachlan, I am incapable of love."

\*\*\*\*

Lachlan's words returned to Dougal later that evening when he and Isobel sat by the fire in her chamber, prior to retiring. He felt restless and irritable, and Isobel's presence acted on him like strong drink, turning his mind. He wanted her, aye, but he would be damned if he would jump through hoops for the privilege of enjoying her body. Why did he put himself through this particular hell? He would be better off taking a turn among the guard he had posted on the battlements, or sitting up alone in the great hall.

Or, if he chose, he could just take her—as her husband, it was his right. But self-prohibition that went beyond conscience kept him from that. And, curse her, she had not reached for him.

She spoke suddenly into the stillness of the room. "Do you think MacNab truly will bring trouble over our union? I have been thinking about it for days, ever since his visit, and contemplating my rash action in taking my sister's place. Perhaps I should write to my father and explain, take all the blame onto myself. He cares little enough about me anyway. Perhaps he could diffuse the situation with MacNab, since they are such close friends."

Dougal turned his head and looked at her in surprise. She stared into the fire, so he saw her in profile. She looked like a girl turned into a woman by sorrow, and he experienced a twinge of nameless emotion. It had been days since he had considered her state of mind or, in truth, anything save his hatred for MacNab and the ache in his crotch. Now the parallels between her situation and what Aisla had endured long ago leaped at him. Isobel had fire and courage, and little of Aisla's gentle spirit, yet she must feel afraid and very much alone, her only companions himself—Satan help her—and his witch of a sister.

He drew a breath and thought, actually contemplating his words before he spoke them. "I appreciate your concern, but I cannot imagine any letter of appeal to your father that might change things now. We are wed, and naught can undo that."

"No?" She looked at him, her eyes wide and filled with reflected firelight.

By the devil's horns, she was beautiful, from the hair that tumbled down her back to her bare feet.

"Yet," she spoke on, "Meg says you could lose

everything if this, this war goes badly—this place that means everything to you, your ancestral lands, your life."

He smiled. "Nothing means everything to me, save revenge. You might as well know that of me now. You had best believe it."

She lifted her chin. "You could renounce me. Send me home to my father."

"The marriage has been consummated."

"So it has. Yet I would be no more shamed than I already was, in my father's eyes. Make some excuse, say the priest was drunk when he joined us, or—"

"O'Rourke was, indeed, drunk. But that does not render the joining invalid." He frowned at her. "Do you want to escape me so badly that you would rather choose shame beneath your father's roof?"

She shrugged. " 'The devil you know,' as the saying goes. At least, if I return home to a life of obscurity, it will not cost you all you value."

"Allow me to worry about my costs, Wife. I am no bairn, unable to make my own choices."

"Nor am I."

Just as well, with the way he felt right now: enflamed, ready to push her to the hearth rug and take her there. Could she see the desire in his eyes? He had done his best to hide it these past days and nights, but it grew more difficult. Sleeping beside her proved tortuous, yet he could not keep away. And even when he did remove himself, pacing the battlements or riding the fields, she obsessed his mind.

He did not know what he saw in his eyes, but she reached out, her fingers barely brushing his sleeve, withdrawing and then grabbing hold, hard.

"You carry old wounds, deep ones," she whispered. "I would not have you acquire more because of me."

Astonishment touched him. "You are a merciful woman, I think," he told her. "Just how much pity, Isobel, do you have in your heart? Naught can heal those old wounds of which you speak. Yet there is a fairly constant ache you might ease."

He had never come closer to asking, but his blood fair burned inside him, and he found himself awaiting her reply with held breath.

Her eyes fell and then came up to meet his again, spilling over with wicked light. She tumbled forward into his arms and lifted her lips. "I feared, Husband, you would never ask."

Chapter Nineteen

"Husband, are you awake?" The words came from Isobel in a whisper as she turned to the man beside her in the bed. Early dawn light crept over the windowsill and past the curtain she had hung to block the cold, barely lifting the gloom that filled the chamber. But she could see Dougal, and the sight caused a pain in her heart.

He slept on his side, turned toward her, his black hair tangled on the pillow with her own. In repose, his face looked almost beautiful, like something carved of ivory, all the wary cruelty gone. His eyelashes, sinfully long, made twin fans against his skin, and only the deep scar beneath his left eye marred his perfection.

Isobel's fingers tingled with the desire to touch him, smooth his hair, which she knew felt like silk, caress the supple muscles beneath every inch of skin even as she had most the night long. No wonder he still slept, after their excesses—she doubted either of them had more than an hour or two's rest, and she could still feel his touch everywhere.

Only a madwoman, such as she surely must be, would awaken early following such a night just to look at her husband. Yet that temptation, following all the others of the night, would not leave Isobel alone.

She had made a number of mistakes in her life, some of them disastrous: falling victim to the charms of a wastrel, trading places with Catherine and, quite possibly, marrying this man. Yet no mistake would be so disastrous as falling in love with him.

She lay gazing at him and prodding the tender regions of her heart as one might a fresh wound, testing its depth and risk. She had never been in love and did not understand the emotion. And what she felt toward Dougal did not resemble in any way what she had imagined love to be. This felt raw and wild, desperate and unbidden, yet it differed from the desire she also felt when in his hands. She had thought love a soft, comforting thing.

Yes, surely this was but some form of mad desire, never before experienced. After all, she had encountered many forms of desire at his hands— wicked, immensely pleasurable, and heretofore unimagined. She had never dreamed a man and woman could use their lips, their mouths on one another's bodies the way she and her husband did, nor that the responses could be so shattering and miraculous. Just thinking on it now set her body throbbing again.

Surely, in light of all that, what she felt for him must be mere attraction. Yet the thought of her father journeying north with a household guard or, worse, help from his friend MacNab to reclaim her, caused deep pain. For whatever reason, she did not want to leave this man.

Could it happen? Could her father declare her marriage contract invalid, take her by force or persuasion and give her to Bertram, for his wife? The very idea made it hard to breathe. She would not survive a week, a day, an hour.

Was this love, or need? Need to see Dougal

MacRae walk through a door in that arrogant, confident way he had, need to watch the intelligence flicker in his eyes when he spoke, to catch the rare, wry smile he tossed at her when the two of them found something humorous. Need to feel the warmth of his big body in her bed, and even when he slept drink in the feeling of safety brought by his presence, as if no harm could find her when she remained with him.

A lie, that. They were surrounded by harm, risk, and danger. The trouble was, she cared for none of that while he was within her reach.

And what would this day bring? She dreaded to think. She dreaded the possibility of anything coming between them.

The thought made her reach out and touch his hand, which lay upon her pillow. It, like much of the rest of him, was scarred, and once again she wondered about the origin of those wounds.

His fingers clasped hers strongly in his sleep. But no—he slept not; his eyes came open and stared deeply into her own.

"Wife," he said groggily, and drew her closer. Though, she acknowledged, she could hardly get much closer. As he pulled her against him, her traitorous heart began to pound out a dangerous rhythm.

She wondered what would happen if she confessed to him all of what she felt—the confusion, the wonder—if she employed honesty and risked her sanity and made herself completely vulnerable. Perhaps he knew how to identify love.

But if he did, if he knew, it was because he loved Aisla still. Aisla, never Isobel.

She should get up out of the bed, walk away from

him, try to save herself. She should welcome the possibility of rescue by her father. Instead, she found herself pressing her naked body against his and feeling the liquid fire begin to pour through her veins again.

At least they had this.

And she knew he desired her, believed that without doubt. She saw the flames in his eyes, felt his body quicken, and wondered what form the delight would take this time.

His long-fingered, clever hand, with the rough palm, skimmed over her body and slid downward until it reached the juncture of her thighs and parted them.

"Ah, Wife, will you have me again?"

"I will," Isobel breathed raggedly.

"I am surprised you did not have enough of me last night."

"I seem to be insatiable," Isobel admitted, supposing it fruitless to try to hide the obvious. At this moment, could she hide anything?

"I can feel that," he said, those long fingers doing things that made Isobel's mouth go dry. He kissed her lips softly and ran the tip of his tongue across them. "How will it be? How will you have me, bonny Isobel?"

She wanted it all: the heat and strength of him bearing down upon her, the wild abandon when she rode him like some half-broken stallion, the raw taste of him on her tongue. She whispered helplessly, "I cannot choose. Dougal, I—"

Fortunately, he kissed her again, stopping the traitorous words that might have slipped out, her confession of love. For he did not want to hear it, did he? And she, who had already exposed every part of herself to him, need not expose, also, the innermost regions of her soul.

Because he loves Aisla still, she reminded herself yet again, even as he came to her. Never, never me.

Tears blurred her vision then, despite the tenderness with which Dougal treated her. They burned and stung and trickled from the corners of her eyes even as she held him to her. She did not expect him, in the throes of passion, to notice, but she should have known this man noticed everything.

His hand came up. He used his thumb to wipe the outer corner of her eye. "Isobel? Did I hurt you, lass?"

"No."

"Then, why do you weep?"

Isobel, unwilling to answer, was spared when a thunderous pounding erupted at the chamber door. Dougal swore and, moving like a panther, leaped from the bed almost before she could draw a breath.

He stalked, naked, to the door and hauled it open. She heard muffled conversation and sat up in the bed, clutching the blanket to cover herself.

"What is it?" she asked when Dougal turned back from the door, his face gone hard as stone.

"Soldiers at the gate."

"Soldiers?"

He dressed hurriedly and without looking at her, throwing himself into his clothing and, lastly, strapping on his sword. "'Tis a party of the King's men accompanied by MacNab and a band of his warriors."

"The King!" Horror touched Isobel and she slid from the bed, dragging the blanket with her. "Have they come to take me? Can they take me from you?"

He shot her a look across the chamber, hard and

level, that had the impact of a touch. "They may well try."

"Dougal! I will come with you, tell the King's men I am here voluntarily. That—that I wish to remain your wife!"

"You will stay here."

"Dougal, no! I—"

"You will stay here with a guard at the door." He shouted it at her and went out.

"Damned if I will." Isobel muttered, and began dressing as hastily as he. She must act quickly before he had time to post a guard who would keep her in. Because, if her fate rested on what happened downstairs, she meant to take part in it.

Her fingers tripped over themselves as she struggled to fasten herself into last night's gown. She gulped air as she tried to bundle her hair into some kind of order—she did not want to go below looking the wanton but a respectable matron content with her lot.

When she opened the door mere moments later, she could hear voices from below, hear shouting and MacNab the Junior's unmistakable, raging whine countered by Dougal's biting lilt. Her heart began to pound double time, and she headed for the stairs, only to find her arm caught in a fierce grip.

"Do not go down!" It was Meg, herself fully clad but with her black hair down. In the dim light at the top of the stairs, she looked every inch the witch, eyes narrowed and filled with cunning.

"I must. They mean to decide my fate. Let go of me!"

"They cannot take you. Surely this is just harassment on MacNab's part. Let Dougal handle it."

"But I must show I am willing to remain here."

Meg examined Isobel slowly. "Are you, then? Has the Devil Black woven a spell that has ensnared you?"

"I love him," Isobel said, speaking the words she had sworn she would not. She tore herself from Meg's grip and flew down the stairs.

The scene in the great hall screamed of danger. Men stood everywhere, all of them armed. Most were Dougal's warriors, his household guards, one among them no doubt the fellow assigned to guard her door, unable to tear himself from this tableau.

Among this rough crew, the King's guard stood out like silver from dross, in bright red jackets and with glittering swords. With dread, Isobel counted them: only five, one obviously an officer, yet Randal and Bertram MacNab stood at their back, with at least six of their own warriors in tow.

Madly, Isobel wondered who had let them all in. What had been the meaning of keeping a watch and staking men at the gates if the enemy were permitted to walk right in?

She paused in the doorway and her eyes sought her husband. There—in his shirtsleeves and with his sword strapped on, the black hair streaming across his shoulders. He faced Randal MacNab and did not yet see Isobel, but others of the men did, including MacNab himself.

"You see her!" he declared, his voice throbbing with indignation. "That is the woman in question. Abducted against her will, her attendants murdered! Imprisoned here, forced into marriage by this man. He deserves, I tell you, to be tried, sentenced, and hanged!"

Chapter Twenty

"That is a lie!" The words burst from Isobel, sounding clear and certain despite the fact that her legs had no strength beneath her and for one terrible moment she feared she would fall down. Every face in the hall turned toward her, expressions ranging from curiosity to outrage. Isobel could not identify what she saw in her husband's eyes, but his head came up when he saw her, like a horse with the whip laid on.

The captain of the King's guard, identifiable by the amount of silver on his jacket, stepped forward. "You say, Lord MacNab, this is the woman in question?"

"It is! Daughter of a dear friend of mine who sent her north from Yorkshire, in all good faith and trust. I have already notified him of his daughter's abduction, and he repairs here with all haste."

Her father? On his way? The knowledge hit Isobel hard. She'd believed her father would never stir himself for any reason but estate business.

"But I," MacNab went on, his voice rich with indignation, "will not rest until she is out of this blackguard's hands and somewhere safe."

"She is somewhere safe," Dougal snarled, snapping his gaze back to Randal MacNab's face. "In her own home. The woman is my wife."

"Forced into marriage, as I say!" MacNab bellowed. "The good God knows what torments he employed, to bring her to it."

"Enough!" The King's captain, a handsome man of perhaps thirty-five, held up a hand, looking pained. "Since the lady in question is here, I shall inquire of her and determine just what has occurred."

MacNab tossed his head. "Unacceptable, sir! You know the nature of this man." A bit wildly, he indicated Dougal. "We have appealed before to the King concerning him. Many in the district have complained. He is a devil, his sister is a witch, and he may well have employed dark arts to turn this woman's mind. I say you cannot trust anything she tells you."

"I shall speak with her, and all involved parties, nonetheless."

Bertram MacNab, stationed at his father's side, spoke up. "Better to take MacRae into custody. Question him in the King's dungeons!"

The captain gave him a sharp look. "I shall make that determination. Mistress MacRae, is it?" He gestured to Isobel. "Please, come in."

Dougal's own men stood nearest the door, their hands hovering above the hilts of their swords. They parted to make way for Isobel, whose feet still felt disconnected from the rest of her, and who could feel her heart pounding so hard it made her ill. The MacRae warriors glared at her as she passed, but she saw only the expression in her husband's eyes, hard and unwelcoming as a wall of stone. He did not want her here—he feared she would speak words that would hang him.

But she would sooner die herself.

Lifting her head and drawing on every bit of comportment she had ever been taught, she looked up into the captain's face. "Am I to be given the courtesy of your name, sir?" she asked.

He bowed smartly. "Your pardon, Mistress. Captain George MacBain, of the King's Edinburgh regiment, at your service."

"Captain MacBain," Isobel repeated graciously. "Must we conduct such private business before an audience?" She indicated MacNab and his warriors. "Surely you and I might speak alone?"

"I will be damned," Dougal muttered beneath his breath, but MacBain heard; his eyes swiveled to Dougal's face and back again to Isobel's.

"I protest!" Randal MacNab cried. "I am here on behalf of this woman's father. I stand her guardian in proxy."

The very idea turned Isobel pale. "The captain and I shall speak privately," she declared, "or not at all."

She could feel the intensity of Dougal's stare bent upon her. Did he think she would betray him? Did he truly trust her so little?

She sent him a look in return, trying to convey assurance. He looked unconvinced. She knew how hard it was for him to trust.

Captain MacBain made his decision. "Very well, Mistress MacRae. You and I shall speak privately."

Now it was Dougal who protested. "As her husband, I have a right to be present when you question her."

MacBain rounded on him. "A number of parties here claim rights, sir. It is my task to either validate or dismiss them. I can speak with your wife privately, or you may accompany us under guard to Edinburgh."

Dougal raised his head. "Then, sir, I choose to

accompany you."

"Do not be a fool," Isobel told him. She stepped forward and laid her hand on his arm, willing him once again to trust her. He glared his answer, a wealth of pain and doubt in his eyes.

"Enough of this!" Randal MacNab shouted. "I must insist custody of this woman be given to me. Otherwise, Captain MacBain, the King himself shall hear of it!"

That caused MacBain's guards to shift uneasily. The captain shot an unfriendly look at MacNab.

"Do as you will, sir, but I have been sent here as the King's agent. I will gather the facts and report my findings."

"Facts? You expect to get those from this chit of a lass?"

"I do. Mistress?" MacBain gestured to Isobel. Head high, her legs wobbly, she led him from the great hall and across the way into the solar.

No fire burned here at this early hour, and only darkness showed through the windows, yet the familiar place eased her a bit. She turned and faced him. She must speak carefully now. She knew she would have but one chance to defend herself—to defend Dougal and remain with him.

The only light in the solar came from a single torch near the door. It left MacBain's face in obscurity, though Isobel imagined he could see hers well enough.

"You are Catherine Maitland?" he began.

"No. Catherine is my sister, whom my father wished sent north to wed with Bertram MacNab. My father, Gerald Maitland, and Randal MacNab are close friends. My sister, Catherine, did not wish for the marriage, as her heart was otherwise engaged. So I took her place."

"Without your father's knowledge?" MacBain's wits moved quickly.

"Yes. My sister and I hatched the deception between us."

"Ah, that explains the confusion. The story that came to Stirling was muddled, talk of two women— Catherine and Isobel."

"I am Isobel."

"Where is your sister now? The message sent by your father expressed deep concern about the whereabouts of at least one of his daughters."

Isobel's heart leaped. Catherine must have made good her elopement.

"Sir, I do not know. When I left, her intention was to elope with the son of our father's bailiff. Please, do not tell my father."

MacBain drew a breath. "Do you fear him? Does he use you harshly?"

"I do not like to think what he would do, if he learned the truth."

"Mistress, I do not see that you can do aught but tell him. He will undoubtedly press for the truth concerning your sister, and my understanding is, he is already on his way here."

Isobel's stomach clenched hard, and her knees wobbled. MacBain reached out and steadied her.

"Is it true that Dougal MacRae snatched you on your way to Randal MacNab's keep and coerced you into marriage?"

Isobel shook her head. "It was not like that at all. Our coach wrecked on the road. I wandered from the wreckage, not knowing where—or to be truthful, who—I was, for a time. Dougal MacRae lent me his assistance."

"So he is a hero, eh?" MacBain's voice was rife with skepticism.

"You might say so."

"And why did not this hero convey at once a message to MacNab, who expected your—or, rather, your sister's—arrival?"

"I—I did not at once remember whence I was bound."

"So MacRae merely took you in, without inquiry, and married you? Are you aware that he and MacNab are old enemies and that Randal MacNab has complained of him to the King many times?"

"All you need know, sir, is that Dougal MacRae is my husband and I wed with him by my own free will. I am content with my present situation."

"Why did you wed with him?" MacBain asked frankly. "A stranger to you, a suspected outlaw?"

"He offered me shelter and protection."

"From what?"

"Among other things, from Bertram MacNab. Sir, you have met him and his father. Were you a woman, would you choose to marry into that brood? I came to Scotland prepared to sacrifice much for my sister's sake, but when it came to it... A woman has very few choices in life, sir," she concluded truthfully. "I chose MacRae."

The captain remained silent for a moment, apparently thinking hard. "This wedding, then. Tell me about it. You were not forced or constrained in any way?"

"I was not. I had time and opportunity to refuse as I would. MacRae's sister Meg, who lives here, counseled me. An itinerant priest called O'Rourke performed the rite."

"I have heard much of O'Rourke from MacNab. It is possible he has been defrocked."

"I am assured he has not." Isobel held herself proudly. "I wished to make quite certain before going to my marriage bed that the joining was legal and binding."

"Ah." For the first time, MacBain seemed uncomfortable. "And, Mistress, can you assure me the union has, indeed, been, er, consummated?"

"It has. Repeatedly," Isobel told him crisply, "and with great enjoyment. I am content with my marriage to my husband, Captain MacBain."

"Forgive me asking, but Lord Randal MacNab asserts you were, indeed, forced—"

"He was not here, and he is wrong. Just because he and his son treat their own women badly does not mean my husband does so."

MacBain bowed. "Aye, Mistress."

Isobel extended her hand to him. "Captain, I have every wish to remain married to Dougal MacRae. Will you do your part to assure it?"

"You have my word, Mistress. But in truth I can do little besides report back to higher authorities in Edinburgh. This I shall do faithfully."

"Thank you."

"Indeed, Mistress, you would do well to speak with your husband, if you wish to stay married to him. If he does not curb his activities, I can assure you he will be hauled away, and you may well end a widow."

Isobel raised her hands to her lips. "I understand."

"And now, Mistress, I must go speak with your husband. It has been a pleasure meeting wi' you."

He turned smartly and marched back to the great hall, Isobel following, where MacNab and MacRae were, predictably, more angry. Things had grown heated indeed, and more than one man's hand gripped the hilt of his sword.

They broke off and stared as MacBain and Isobel entered the chamber. Isobel saw Dougal narrow his eyes and set himself, a man expecting a fight.

But it was to Randal MacNab the captain spoke first. "Sire, I find myself satisfied this woman has not been constrained into marriage. I shall report my findings—"

"What!" MacNab's bellow tore through the hall. "How can this be? The blackguard snatched her off the road, held her here in secret, procured a drunken priest—"

"Mistress MacRae assures me she married by her own volition, sir, and is satisfied with the union."

Randal MacNab's face grew dusky with rage. "Well, aye, she may say that. The bastard will have enchanted her in some way."

"Enchanted her?" Dougal lifted a brow and smiled nastily. "Am I now supposed to be a purveyor of the dark arts?"

"Aye, like your sister. Everyone knows what she is, and the fate that befell her husband. And they do no' call you *Diabhal Dubh* for naught."

Captain MacBain stiffened. "I am no' here to deal with superstition. MacRae, your wife has spoken and attested to the validity of your marriage."

"Aye." Dougal shot a quick look at Isobel, which she failed to interpret. "You will see, only, that I obeyed the decree of my King, who bade me wed, settle, and get my house in order."

MacBain smiled tightly. "Aye, sir, and I need only confirm one thing concerning how Mistress Isobel MacRae came to be in your household. She has given me an account—yet I need verify it with your own."

No fool, the good captain, Isobel thought, her stomach muscles clenching again. He suspected Isobel might have spun him a tale and thought still to catch Dougal out, here before everyone.

And Randal MacNab, like a wolf scenting blood, went silent, gestured to Bertram, and the room went suddenly still.

Isobel knew she could not speak, not even to hint to her husband what path her story had taken. Fools that they were, they should have established a likely tale before it came to this. Now, Dougal might well be caught and, if MacBain had reason to suspect, hauled off to answer for his crimes.

Dougal, eyes still narrowed and head thrown back, had never appeared more dangerous. He looked once at Isobel, a searching glance during which she tried to convey—wordlessly, by magic if need be—the tale she had told MacBain. Because she now knew, to the depth of her soul, were this man to be hanged she might as well end her own life, for she could not exist without him.

Dark grey and mystical as smoke, his eyes met hers before returning to the captain's.

"Ah," he said, "you will be referring to the rescue, when her coach overturned. I happened to be out riding that evening and found her unconscious on the side of the road. I had no idea her companions had ended in the ravine, nor did I know at first who she was. I believe her own wits were addled for a time. When I did learn the truth—"

Randal MacNab, no longer able to control himself, interrupted, "When you learned the truth, you did not, as might any reasonable man, inquire round the district about a lost lady of quality, nor let it be known she had been found. Instead, you decided to ruin and then marry her, no doubt thinking her father's lands must be worth something to you?"

"It did not happen that way." Isobel spoke in a clear voice that failed to disguise her anger, and glared at MacNab as she stepped to Dougal's side. "How dare you so insult me?" Ignoring the irony inherent in speaking the words, she went on, "How dare you imply I would submit to any man before marriage?"

"He is a devil," Bertram MacNab responded, "who has ruined good women before you, Mistress Maitland."

"Mistress MacRae," Isobel corrected him haughtily. "And I quite think this has gone on long enough. Sir," she turned to Captain MacBain, "we have answered your questions fairly."

He executed a bow and signaled to his men. "Thank you, Mistress, for your patience."

"Do not be deceived!" Randal MacNab howled. He turned his glare from MacBain to Isobel. "And you, lass, just wait until your father arrives. I thought to get you away out of here and spare him this distress, but you will answer to him, and he will not be so easily deceived."

Isobel's heart sank in dismay, but she kept her head high. "I shall, of course, be pleased to welcome my father into my new home." Shocking, how well she now lied. Her life had, in fact, become unimaginable, the one consistency her feelings for the man who stood, like a rock, at her side.

And it was to Dougal that MacNab directed his parting words, in a sneer.

"This is no' over, MacRae. Do not think you have escaped judgment. I will not rest until you hang!"

Chapter Twenty-One

"Tell me MacNab can't really carry out that threat he made—tell me he cannot assure that you are hanged."

The whispered plea came suddenly out of the darkness, issuing from the woman who lay, obviously sleepless, beside Dougal. He twitched in response. Since the departure of their unwanted guests, Isobel had barely spoken to him. He had spent a large part of the intervening time riding and tramping his borders and battlements, making sure the guard stood strong. Only in the wee hours had he retreated, ducking the icy wind outside to crawl into her warm bed.

"You should be asleep," he said softly. He wanted only to lie here and absorb the wondrous heat of her without thought or question. The devil knew he felt unready to contemplate what had happened earlier.

"I know, but my thoughts will not be still." She stirred restlessly, and the scent of her came to him, subtle and seductive. Despite his bone-deep weariness and his set intentions, his body responded to her nearness involuntarily.

"Husband, where have you been? I had begun to suppose you meant to forsake my bed this night."

Dougal shook his head. That he would not—could not—do. He had spent every night since his marriage with her, even those when, out of stubbornness, he did not touch her. He could not explain why he should so torture himself, save he felt caught, and never more deeply than now.

"I was busy seeing to our defenses," he told her. "I do not ken what is coming, but I can sense something. I know MacNab. He will no' back down. Once your father arrives, he may launch an all-out attack. Tell me, is your father a warlike man?"

"Warlike?" She seemed to muse upon it. "Not at all. He is stern, upright, demanding, and commanding. He believes there is a clear division between right and wrong—"

"Does he believe it strongly enough to accept MacNab's offer of arms? For you know, he will offer."

"I am not sure. Nor can I imagine what must be in my father's mind right now, learning it was I and not Catherine who came north. He will be furious with both of us. He does not take well to deception."

"Few men do." Dougal fought the desire to stroke her arm. He knew how she would feel: soft and supple, enough to distract him even from the problems at hand.

"If they do come to your gates seeking battle, my father and MacNab together, what shall you do?"

Dougal answered without hesitation, "Give it to them."

"Would it not be better and easier for you just to hand me over?"

That did make him turn toward her in the bed. "I have never yet done things the easy way, and you are my wife. You told MacBain you want to stay with me."

"I did."

"Is that the truth?"

He heard her breath catch in the darkness. "It is."

"You are certain? Before this comes to bloodshed—for I declare it to you now, Isobel, if you wish to be with me, I will fight to the death to keep you here."

"Must we speak of death?" All at once, she was in his arms, burrowing into him strongly and then wrapping her arms around him, tight. "By heaven, you are chilled to the bone."

"The wind outside is keen as a knife." Without his permission, his fingers buried themselves in her hair. "And, aye, I fear we must speak of death. For I warn you, it will come if this trouble I sense rushes in upon us."

"Just so long as you, Husband, remain safe," she breathed, her lips but a whisper from his.

Did she truly care? Could she care? Or were these just woman's words, meant to cajole and manipulate? She did not want to return to her father, that was clear, nor did she wish to go to MacNab. Perhaps she just found him, the Devil Black, a less horrific alternative—which, in itself, held a ludicrous irony. She hoped he would defend her, when he had failed to protect the only woman he had ever loved.

He understood what he was—and was not—even if his bonny wife had not yet discovered it. Yet she was here, so close and warm, and his body thrummed in a way he found hard to deny.

"Tell me, Husband—Dougal," she appealed, "how did you know what story to give MacBain, what tale to spin him—the very same I had chosen: that you rescued me from the road after the coach had wrecked?"

Dougal shook his head in the darkness. He could not quite explain how he had known what to say. He had looked at her and the words just came to him. The fey Scot in him made him ask, "Did you will me to know?"

He expected her to deny it, perhaps scoff at the idea, half Englishwoman that she was. But she whispered, "Yes. Yet, I will many things where you are concerned. Why should that particular wish prove effective?"

"I do no' ken." Dougal thought hard about it. A practical man, he nevertheless believed in Second Sight, messages from beyond the grave, and even visits from departed spirits. Was the transference of thought really so much more absurd? Yet the ability to pass a message from her mind to his argued some deep and fast shared connection, and that he was reluctant to warrant. After all, he had shared no such connection with Aisla, whom he had loved better than his own life.

"'Twill be a fluke," he whispered, "a chance or coincidence."

"You think so? Perhaps, Husband, we should test it. Can you tell what I am thinking now?"

He need not read her mind for that. Her warm body said it all, wriggling against his and conveying her desire far better than words. He slid his hands from her hair down her back, then further to cup her buttocks, drawing her closer. She opened herself to him like a flower. He longed so to plunge himself into her, it fairly unhinged his mind. Yet certain things must be said.

"Thank you for championing me this day, Wife. I confess, such defense half surprised me, given your past anger with me for—as you have repeatedly accused—making a weapon of you."

She sighed deep in her throat and twined her arms

around his neck, curling her fingers into his hair. "I no longer feel angry. Hurt, perhaps, and wishing things could be different between us, that you were not still in love with someone else—Aisla."

At the sound of the name, pain clenched at Dougal's heart, nearly crippling him. "I will never— never love anyone else," he admitted, the confession torn from him.

"I know. And no woman wishes to learn she will always come second, even in her husband's bed."

"I desire you," he told her—impossible to deny it in the present circumstance. "Is that not enough?"

"At some moments it is." She brushed her lips across his lightly. "At some moments, I find it is not."

"Which moment is this?"

"Let me warm you, Husband. Let me warm you to your heart."

She warmed him three times before dawn. Even then, when he rose to leave her, his desire remained unspent. He eyed her where she lay in the bed, lit by the dull morning light, stark naked and drowsy, her rounded breasts and slightly parted legs a rampant temptation. What was this madness he felt for her, that refused to calm? Aye, so, he found her beautiful. But no matter how many times he accommodated her physically, he could never satisfy the longings he now suspected of occupying her heart.

"I am sorry," he whispered, and she widened her sleepy eyes at him.

"For what?"

He shook his head. He did not want her to care for him, for his heart was a wounded and blackened thing. The devil knew, he did not deserve a woman like this.

"For continuing to use you, I suppose," he told her wryly, "despite your forgiving heart."

"Do you hear me complaining?" she asked. "Come back to bed, Husband, and use me sorely again."

He smiled despite himself. "Wicked!"

"Am I not? As befits, perhaps, the wife of an infamous devil."

"Aye." Despite himself, his fingers tarried in the act of fastening his clothing. The tightness beneath his kilt told him he would be well able to take her again.

She sat up in the bed and her red hair swung across her breasts. "Where do you go?"

"Out to check the fortifications, one more time."

"Would you not rather stay here? It sounds to be sleeting again."

"I would rather stay here—temptress!" Yet he turned away, wondering whether she could possibly come to terms with what he was, and was not, able to give her.

She flopped back into the bed. "I suppose I shall just have to wait until later, then."

\*\*\*\*

Curse her, it proved all Dougal could think about that whole day long: the warmth of her in the bed, the promise in her eyes, and what he meant to do about it. Even as he rode his boundaries with a party of his men, enduring the stinging sleet, even as he conferred with Lachlan concerning likelihoods and possibilities, and when he weighed the odds for battle, Isobel occupied his mind.

Not even the view from his battlements, one that usually filled him with a feeling of deep possessiveness, served to distract him. Late in the afternoon, when he and Lachlan stood on the walkway of the highest tower braving the wind, his eyes caressed each fold of land, outlined in light and shadow, but his mind dreamed of caressing his wife.

"I mean to ask your sister to marry me," Lachlan said.

"Eh?" Dougal turned and directed a stare at his friend. "Have you lost your mind entirely?"

"You know," Lachlan looked thoughtful, "I believe I have. 'Tis the only explanation for what has come over me these last weeks, since she returned home—unless, of course, you allow for the possibility of love."

"I do not believe in love," Dougal said harshly.

"And I say to you again—you did, once."

"That was a long time gone."

"So," Lachlan tossed his head, "you mean to tell me you will never love again?"

"Never!"

"Never is a great span of time. I should think you might find yourself tempted by that bonny wife of yours, spirited as well as beautiful."

"Oh, aye, I am tempted by her, all right." Dougal laughed harshly. "But not into the trap of love. I know my own mind, Lachy, and 'tis made up."

"Ah. I hope your sister is not equally stubborn. I have been trying to get her in my bed, but," he added frankly, "though she will kiss and cuddle and tease, she will no' commit to the act."

"My sister, cuddle?" Dougal echoed incredulously. "Impossible!"

Lachlan grinned. "Grope and fondle, then. She has had her hands up my kilt more than once."

"Spare my ears!" Dougal cried in agony.

"I thought if I offered her marriage—a better marriage than she last endured—with a man sincere in his affections—"

"You?" Dougal howled. "Sincere? The world must be ending."

"I am desperate here, man. She has fair enchanted me. I would say or do anything!"

"The cry of man since the beginning of time. But, Lachy, that does no' make you sincere."

"I ken that, fine. Do you suppose Meg can tell?"

"I think it likely, since my sister is no fool."

"Perhaps you are right," Lachy admitted ruefully, "and wise to keep yourself free of all ties and so save yourself. 'Tis no fun, this, finding yourself at the mercy of—"

"Wait." Dougal laid a hand on his friend's arm, silencing him, and narrowed his eyes in an attempt to peer through the gathered gloom. "What is that?"

"Where?"

"There, in amongst the trees, and in the folds of the land. They are out there, Lachlan."

"Who—?"

"But why did my guards fail to come and warn me?" Dougal felt a chill race up his spine, closely followed by a surge of anger. "Come on!"

"By the devil's horns, Dougal, I do not—"

"MacNab has us surrounded," Dougal shouted. "'Tis war now, and certain!"

Chapter Twenty-Two

"How many of your men are dead?" Isobel asked her husband, trying to sound calmer than she felt. Dougal and Lachlan had come in just at dark and she had gleaned the details of their situation in pieces: MacNab haunting their borders, lurking not quite beyond sight, attacking when he could and withdrawing again when Dougal himself rode out. The guard Dougal had assigned to patrol the perimeter had been slaughtered, the message clear.

She had never seen anyone wear the look now on her husband's face, grim, stark, and blank with anger, enough to justify his name. He had not expected an attack so swift or stealthy. Unable to sit still, he paced before the fire in the great hall while Lachlan sat silent with his head in his hands, and Isobel, with Meg at her side, stood by.

"Four," he answered in a voice rough with emotion. "Every man I sent out on this last patrol— their horses, as well."

Meg swore bitterly, and her brother glanced at her. "Aye," Dougal said, "he needs to pay. He *will* pay."

Lachlan raised his head. "Aye," he agreed in turn. "But MacNab has made his position evident, has he no'? Not a man comes or goes until your wife's father arrives and this matter is settled. You do not ride out, I do not go home. You cannot even send a message to the

King."

"As if I would appeal to that trumped-up bastard!" Dougal fairly shouted the words, his rage overflowing. "I take care of my own troubles and fight my own battles."

"And how are you doing at that, Brother?" Meg asked nastily. "MacNab has you in a slip knot. If you ride out with a band of men to meet him fairly, at arms, he will melt away and you will find no enemy."

"At least that may keep the villain clear of my borders." Dougal looked at Lachlan. "We will ride out at dawn—until then, let him freeze his balls off in the cold. I have fallen men to honor, and clansfolk to comfort."

Isobel whispered, "What comfort can you give them?"

Dougal's profile grew hard as iron. "All a laird has to offer—his vow to provide for them so long as I am able."

A chill of apprehension snaked its way up Isobel's spine. "Might you lose your lands over this? Could you lose everything?"

All three of them stared at her. Dougal pivoted on his heel to face her. "No one takes my lands!" he declared. "I may lose my honor, my standing, my head, but MacRae lands, where MacRae blood has been spilled, will remain. 'Tis a sacred trust."

Isobel nodded. She had thought her father obsessed with the lands he oversaw in Yorkshire, lands that had come to him as her Scottish mother's dowry, no doubt a throw-away entitlement on her maternal grandfather's part. For, as she had come to see upon acquaintance with her husband, Scotsmen did not part with Scottish lands. The Yorkshire holding, profitable as it might be, had never belonged to her grandfather's ancestors and was not tied to him by blood.

Looking at her husband now, Isobel saw MacNab might as well steal his limbs as deprive him of his lands—or emasculate him. Isobel needed to understand his feelings, and how deep they ran.

She lifted her chin and looked him in the eyes. "There is another solution."

Impatient and enraged, Dougal barely acknowledged her. "Aye? How is that?"

"I could give MacNab what he wants, what he says he wants, that is, and stop this horror where it stands, before any more blood is shed."

"You?" Dougal's smoke-grey eyes narrowed in an unfriendly way. "Again, how?"

"By handing myself over to him." The words sounded bolder and far braver than Isobel felt. In truth, the very idea sickened her and made her heart beat high up in her throat. Yet she found she would be willing to do even this, for his sake.

Meg gasped, and Lachlan's head swiveled toward Isobel violently. But Isobel barely spared a glance for them. She continued to gaze into her husband's eyes, looking for something she failed to see. Acknowledgement? Gratitude? Affection? Isobel's heart clenched in disappointment.

What she did see was a flare of rage so bright it seared her. "You wish to leave me?" he roared. "Despite all you said? Now that he looks to prove victorious, would you rather throw in your lot with my fiercest enemy?"

"No!"

He reached out with one arm and cleared the table beside which they stood, sweeping it of cups, bottles, papers, and a candle that flared before going out.

"You decide your chances look better with MacNab, is that it? You look to abandon the ship I sail? You believe I shall be bested—again?"

"No, I—" Isobel's heart fluttered, and she struggled for words in the face of what she now saw flare in his eyes.

He lowered his voice to an edge of danger, cutting as a blade. "Or is it you would simply prefer his bed to mine?"

Isobel reacted without thought and lashed out, intending to strike him. He caught her wrist before she could land the blow, and held her tight.

"So it is to be that way, is it? By how many means will you punish me?"

"You misunderstand me," Isobel cried, not even attempting to struggle against his bruising grasp. "But you will not listen, stubborn savage that you are."

He sneered into her face, "I am not in the mood to listen."

"I can see that." From the corner of her eye, Isobel saw Meg grab Lachlan's sleeve, pull him to his feet and tow him from the room. Save for the guard who doubtless waited outside the door, she and her husband were alone.

"Can we not speak reasonably?" she appealed. "Can we not try?"

He swore and released her, turning away to the fire, giving her his back. "If you wish to leave me, do it," he growled.

"I do not wish to leave you." How could she tell

him she wanted anything before that, and given the choice would sooner die than go to MacNab?

"If you wish to leave me go," he repeated, "but I will never see you released to MacNab. Go to your father if you must—or to hell—but I will fight to the death before I see you in that animal's hands."

"Why will you not listen?" She walked round him and stared up into his face. "Much as you would deny MacNab the victory of gaining possession of me, I deny the possibility of you losing your lands and all you hold dear, just to keep me. These lands are your life's blood, while you have not known me a month. Rather would I act to put an end to this conflict."

"You cannot. The devil himself could not resolve what lies between MacNab and me. Is that what you truly think, that I would steal victory from MacNab by keeping you?"

"Yes."

He searched her face. "Nay, Wife, but I would spare you the agony, torture, and abuse that befalls any female who comes to his—or his cur of a son's—hands."

"Aisla," she said.

Pain flickered in his eyes. "Aye, Aisla."

"What did he do to her? She was Bertram's wi—"

"I do not wish to speak of it."

"No." The echoes of his pain gripped Isobel's heart. "Yet the love you once felt for her finds its reflection in the hate you feel now for MacNab. Judging by the depth of your hatred, your love must have been deep indeed."

Dougal fairly howled, "I have said I do not wish to speak of it!"

"And I say we must, since what you felt then affects us now. I am caught in this. Do you not think I have a right to know exactly what MacNab did to Aisla—and thence to you—that killed your ability to love?"

Dougal became very still, like the surface of the ocean before a storm. Like the ocean, Isobel could feel currents stirring, violent and terrifying. When he glared at her, she saw vicious rejection in his eyes.

"Love is a lie," he told her, "a fool's cruel delusion. It is weakness rather than strength, a myth that begets vulnerability. A claim of love changes nothing. It saves nothing! And I do not want to hear the word spoken between these walls again."

"Then perhaps I *should* leave you. Maybe when my father arrives I should pack up the nothing with which I came and just leave with him. Because I will not live with a man who supposes he can tell me how to speak, think, and feel."

Dougal's voice dropped to a harsh whisper. "Surely you did not expect me to love you."

Isobel took the blow without flinching, at least outwardly. "Of course not. It is a ridiculous premise. What, after all, is there about me to love? And why should my life take such a turn, in a direction it never before headed? Obviously I am not worthy of any such fine emotion. I might as well slink home behind my father and live out my days in disgraced obscurity."

He took a step nearer her, lifted one hand toward her face but stopped short of touching her. "You deserve better than a lie, Isobel. I value you—the devil knows, I desire you! I admire your courage and would be glad to see you bear my sons. But I cannot offer you more than that. Should there not at least be honesty between us?"

Isobel's heart, struggling beneath her breast, admitted she did not want him to lie. She wished the words to tumble from his lips, soft declarations and promises. Yet this man would never give her that, and she began to see his harsh demeanor revealed a stark honor.

If she told him how she felt, confessed the wild, tumultuous feeling possessing her, he would scoff, call her deluded, declare her feelings unfounded. And she could not bear the pain of that—not now, and possibly not ever.

For the first time, her eyes dropped from his. "Honesty." She repeated the word as if she fathomed not its meaning.

"Aye." His hand at last touched her cheek, cupped it almost tenderly, sending through her a shiver of involuntary response. Traitorous flesh, that wanted him so! "'Tis all I can offer you, Isobel—that and my promise, as your husband, to hold to you and no other."

"So, you offer your disbelief in love to me, alone. It is a grand compliment!" She drew a ragged breath. "You speak over and over again of honesty, yet you refuse to say, honestly, what happened between you and MacNab."

"Do not ask that of me. Anything else."

"Yet it is what I need to know."

"It is not." His thumb brushed across her lips, causing her to part them and draw a breath—causing desire to flare low down in her belly. What would she not do for this man? Yet what he demanded of her—to live with him without love—must prove hardest.

"All you need to know, Wife, is I will fight with the last of my strength to keep you." He laughed harshly. "Poor reassurance as that may be."

Somehow, Isobel found the strength to pull free of his grasp. "And if I ask Meg for the truth?"

"Do not do that," he said. "I warn you—do not, if you wish to retain any semblance of harmony between us."

Chapter Twenty-Three

"A party of riders approaches, Laird! A large party, and flying MacNab's banners."

The bellow from the battlements froze Dougal's heart in his chest. A fortnight had passed, awaiting the arrival of his new wife's father, and the situation in the keep had steadily deteriorated. His warriors were edgy, Meg irascible, Lachlan gloomy. And Dougal's relationship with his wife veered between cautious hostility and passion so bright it seared him to the bone.

Now on this cold, bright, snow-dusted morning it seemed something would happen—at last.

Dougal had been up since dawn, unable to sleep and unwilling to disturb his wife's slumber. In the chilly dining hall, he nursed a mug of ale for his breakfast and half listened to Lachlan whine about his continued ill-treatment at the hands of Meg. When the summons came, he and Lachlan stared at one another, and then Dougal swore viciously. His sword was in his hand even before he rushed to the outer door with Lachlan in his wake.

Aye, and there they were, Gerald Maitland no doubt among them. They made an impressive showing in the clear light, a group at least a score strong with their pennants snapping in the cold wind.

Dougal's warriors, no doubt as eager for action as he, formed a group around him, and he knew the men on the walls would be ready to fight as well. If it happened here, on his doorstep, so be it. 'Twould not be the first time blood had stained this ground.

As the party approached, Dougal's quick eyes dissected it. He saw no agents of the King, just a strong battalion of MacNab clansmen at Randal and Bertram's backs. And there at Randal MacNab's side a stranger, well-muffled against the cold, who must be Gerald Maitland.

Dougal sneered. He supposed he could not offer his wife's father a naked blade in greeting, much as he longed to. The blood pounded in his veins, and he felt rabid for a fight. Yet talk must come first.

The party came to a neat halt perhaps thirty feet from Dougal's doorstep, the horses blowing steam into the cold air. Dougal, with his entire birthright at his back, felt the weight of the moment. The choices he made in the next few minutes could cost everything. And he had never been a man to play it safe.

Yet he had a wife now to defend, as well as an inheritance—and, perhaps, a child on the way? He had wondered about that this morning before dawn, when he ran his hand over her naked belly. She showed no sign, yet, of increasing. But how could he pump so much seed into her without founding a bairn?

His narrowed eyes moved to the man at Randal MacNab's side, searching for some resemblance to Isobel and finding none. The man's high forehead and prominent nose made him look pained, his grey hair gave no hint as to its original color. But the expression he wore defined, quite well, his mood.

"MacRae!" Randal MacNab hollered. "Do you mean to give us battle? Or let us in?"

"A braw question," Dougal returned. "Which does your arrival warrant? And what of the fact you ha' been haunting my lands for weeks, trespassing and tempting my warriors' swords?"

"Looking after my interests," MacNab maintained.

"You have no interest in what is mine." For a thousand pounds sterling, Dougal could not have kept the disparagement from his voice.

"But this man does." Randal gestured to the rider beside him. "This is Gerald Maitland, father to the woman you abducted and raped."

"Oh, aye?" Dougal snarled. "And can Gerald Maitland not speak for himself?"

"I can." Maitland edged his mount forward. "Are you holding my daughter? Did you seize and force her against her will?"

Dougal struggled to remind himself this man knew only what MacNab had fed him—a poisoned fare. He considered giving Maitland the benefit of the doubt, and failed to persuade himself.

"And which daughter might that be?" he shouted, knowing his very tone was an insult.

Even at that distance he saw the angry flush rise to Maitland's cheek. "Isobel, as you know right well."

"Truly? Yet I perceive, sir, 'tis your daughter Catherine you sent north as a bride for Bertram MacNab."

Maitland exchanged an incredulous look with Randal MacNab before saying, "I thought to send my daughter Catherine but was deceived in that. Isobel took her place."

"And you did not miss the one for the other? Tut, tut, sir. What sort of father must you be?"

"Cur! Answer my question, else you will do so at the demand of my sword! Do you hold my daughter Isobel?"

"She abides here with me, aye."

"Do you hold her against her will?"

"I do not."

"You imply she chooses to be here with you and is not, in fact, captive?"

Dougal had already parted his lips to answer when something struck him in the small of the back with the force of a hurled boulder. He jolted forward and then pivoted as his wife pushed past him, half fastened clothing and hair flying, to face the party on the doorstep.

"Father? So, you came."

"Isobel! Daughter, are you safe?" Very little emotion, besides anxiety, colored Maitland's voice. Dougal heard no hint of affection, and he scanned his wife's face for her reaction. She looked stricken, guarded, and angry. Aye, by now he knew what passed for anger in her eyes.

"Has he harmed you?" Maitland shouted, giving her no chance to reply.

"No." Isobel shook her head violently, her hair tumbling. "But why are you here?"

"I am mounting a rescue, of course. I have come to take you out of this prison—by force if need be."

"Well!" Isobel glanced into Dougal's face and back at her father. "Then I suppose you had better come in so we can discuss it."

\*\*\*\*

"There is absolutely nothing to discuss," Gerald Maitland said in a voice whose educated accents barely covered the basic Yorkshire. A tall man who, at close hand, displayed the bones and blue eyes of Viking forebears, he paced the hall before the fire, the sword he wore rattling.

Dougal thought Maitland did not look entirely accustomed to that sword, yet the glint in his eyes, not unlike Isobel's, argued he would use it.

Dougal hoped not. He would hate to fell Isobel's father at her feet, even though on the face of it there seemed to be very little affection between them.

Only a small group occupied the hall—Maitland with both Randal and Bertram MacNab, Isobel, Dougal, and Lachlan. Dougal felt some surprise about Lachy's presence—until now, he had kept the full extent of his relationship with Dougal under cover. And being here was a virtual declaration of war. But Dougal could spare little attention for that now; he was far too fascinated with watching his wife.

She glowed and shimmered with emotion, like a candle that would not blow out in a gale. Dougal could not, however, quite read the emotions, especially when she looked at her father, for she guarded them then. Rage? Distrust? Determination? All he knew was, she looked rampant as a warrior queen.

"This farce is over," Maitland went on. "You are coming home with me. And if this blackguard who calls himself your husband objects, I shall take you back by force—just as you came into his hands."

Isobel shot Dougal a cautionary glance. This one he interpreted quite clearly: it said, *Let me handle this.* And, aye, he was willing, for the moment. But if things went badly, he would step in. No one would take her from him.

"He is my husband," Isobel said in a voice that struggled for steadiness. "We were wed—"

"Under duress, no doubt. He pulled you from the wreck of your carriage and brought you here only half conscious, had the priest mumble a few words, and thought, so, to steal an interest in my lands."

"Ah!" The tone of Isobel's voice altered. "It is about the lands. I thought it must be."

"Do not be foolish!" Maitland barked. "I care about your welfare also, far more than you seem to. You have yet to explain to me why you came to Scotland, and where your sister has gone."

"You mean, you do not know?"

"I have been half mad with worry! I thought it was you who disappeared the same morning she came north. I sent men out searching—there was no trace. At length, my bailiff came to me, confessing that his son, Thomas, had also disappeared. I thought you had run off with him, willful, ungrateful daughter that you are!"

Isobel seethed. "I warrant you were relieved then, to have me, disobedient and damaged, off your hands?"

"It made some sense. You had transgressed, so, before. When my good friend MacNab's messenger came advising me Catherine had never arrived and that it was you, and not she, being held captive, I did not know what to think. But relief never came into it."

"If you do care about my welfare, as you claim, then you should thank that man, my husband. He rescued me on the road, brought me here, and kept me safe."

"Rescued you! I have it on the best authority it is more likely he held up the carriage, abducted you, and forced the marriage."

Head high, Isobel demanded, "Do I look like a woman who has been forced to do anything?"

Dougal, remaining silent with difficulty, had to admit she did not. She looked proud and magnificent, but Maitland's nostrils flared in anger.

"You have never known what is good for you, Daughter. Would you even recognize coercion in the form of kindness?"

"I would, despite the fact that I have seen so little warmth or kindness my life long."

Maitland's stern face convulsed with rage, and he lashed out for Isobel's cheek, but fast as he moved the blow never landed—Dougal caught his wrist in a grip of iron.

"Nay, sir, you will not," he growled. "That is my wife."

"She is my daughter, and I will discipline her as required."

Dougal stared into the man's eyes. "And you wonder why she fled you?"

"Do not speak to me that way, you snake," Maitland began.

Isobel pushed her way between them, breaking Dougal's hold upon her father. "I know not what lies your friend MacNab has told you, but I am clearly not in need of rescue. Father, it is Randal MacNab who would use me, who uses you now in an effort to further the quarrel between him and my husband."

"Now, just a moment!" Randal MacNab started up. "I have acted, in this, only for the good. This man—" he gestured at Dougal, "has a reputation in the district as a rogue and a lawbreaker. Abduction is surely not beneath him. Your daughter, Gerald, was contracted to my house. I had a right to step in—more, a duty to do so."

"Aye, well, your duty ends here," Dougal grated. "You have brought the man, and he sees his daughter is content. And when it comes to it, MacNab, your spawn was never contracted to this woman but to her sister."

MacNab glanced at Maitland. "He took your daughter in marriage only to get back at me, and to stake an interest in her inheritance."

"Aye?" Dougal heard himself say. "And why should I wish to get back at you? Why do you not tell the man how your fine son used his first wife, and then he will see what a narrow escape his daughter has had."

Now it was Bertram MacNab who pushed forward. "If you, bastard cur, believe that old score remains unsettled, perhaps you will fight me on it—single combat, one on one?"

Rage rose to Dougal's head, so intense that for a moment Bertram's sneering visage flickered before his eyes and the room dimmed.

"You will pay," he promised, low and agonized, "for every indignity you forced her to suffer, for every bruise on her body, each tear she shed."

"Aye?" Bertram MacNab's face became a leering, taunting mask. "It is an old matter, that. I acted with a husband's right to discipline a wife who needed it."

"She? The sweetest soul ever born to this world?"

"If you wish me to pay," Bertram goaded, "then draw your sword and face me here and now—coward!"

Dougal felt the rage explode in his head and leapt at his tormentor, welcoming a rush of relief when his hands closed on Bertram's throat. He had lived nearly eight years for this, and every fiber of him wanted to mangle and harm. He heard Isobel's cry of alarm, and any number of hands seized him and pulled him away.

His vision cleared slowly. The first thing he saw was Bertram MacNab's face, blood on his jaw and triumph in his eyes, letting Dougal know he had played right into his enemy's hands.

"You see?" Randal MacNab bellowed. "The man is dangerous—violent! Gerald, you cannot leave your daughter in his keeping."

Before Gerald Maitland could speak, Isobel pushed forward once more to face her father.

"If you cannot see, Father, what has just happened here—"

"Oh, I see, Isobel. Pack your things. You are coming with me."

"I have no 'things.' All was lost with the coach. And I am going nowhere."

"Obey me, daughter—for once in your life!"

"I obey now only my husband. Father, the marriage is valid. It has been consummated—"

Maitland flushed with anger. "No matter. I am willing to take you back anyway."

"Is that not decent of you?" Dougal stepped up to his wife's side. "She stays with me." He looked Bertram in the eye. "And, I will fight—and best—any man who says differently."

Bertram sneered, "I have heard that claim before."

"Aye, and this time 'twill be fairly done."

Randal MacNab bridled. "Do you accuse us of falsity? You, who summoned that malodorous excuse for a priest to perform your scurrilous joining?" To Maitland he said, "The priest is morally fallen and well known in the district as a drunken fool. We shall prove the marriage invalid and take your daughter back, under weight of law."

Maitland nodded and looked at Isobel. "I shall yet rescue you, Daughter, and that is a promise."

## Chapter Twenty-Four

"My father does not make promises lightly," Isobel said unhappily, dread forming a corrosive ball in the pit of her stomach. She lay curled in a tight crescent on the bed in her chamber and spoke over her shoulder to Meg who, rather surprisingly, had brought a tray in an effort to persuade her to eat.

Three days had passed since her father's visit. During that time Dougal had kept away from her, had spent his daylight hours—and nights, for all Isobel knew—riding his boundaries and pacing his battlements. When Isobel saw him from her windows, he wore a grim face and an ugly air of gloom that befitted the name they called him in the district, Devil Black.

Isobel craved the reassurance of his presence. Even a single visit from him in the night would give her something to hold on to in the midst of all her uncertainty. She knew he did not love her, but an indication he wished to keep her for some reason beyond his desire to spite MacNab would go far to bolster her spirit.

"In fact," she mused to Meg's silent presence, "I can count but three times my father made any promise to me." The first had been when they stood watching Isobel's mother being put into the ground, Isobel holding Catherine's hand, and he promised he would look after them. She supposed he thought he had done that, to the best of his ability, and he thought he was looking after her now. If he believed the lies MacNab poured into his ear, then he believed she needed rescue and of course he would listen not to what he considered Isobel's misguided words.

He had made his second promise when he told both Isobel and Catherine he would see them well married and cared for. That was before Isobel's seduction and downfall, when she had completely disgraced herself in her father's eyes. Then, he had promised her she would live to regret her deflowering.

And she had—oh, she had!

"You need to eat." Meg slid the tray onto the bedside table. "You have taken nothing in three days."

"I do not care," Isobel admitted, still surprised Meg apparently did.

"You should." Meg seated herself on the foot of the bed so Isobel could not escape looking at her. "What if you carry my brother's child? Have you not thought of that?"

Isobel sat up abruptly. "But I have no reason to assume I am with child. Have I?"

Meg shrugged diffidently. "You expect me to know?" She inspected Isobel slowly. "Surely it is possible, given the joining has been consummated as vigorously as you continue to claim."

"I feel no different."

"Still, would you gamble on it, if 'tis possible you carry the heir my brother so deeply desires?"

"Does he, truly?"

"Aye. These lands may not seem much to you, coming from the sweet south, but they are Dougal's life's blood."

"Yorkshire is scarcely the sweet south."

"Well, we live simply and starkly, here. You had better take something to eat, for the sake of us all."

"All right." The food on the tray looked unappealing, but Isobel took up a crust of bread. "Will you stay and talk with me while I eat?"

"I am no fit nurse or companion."

"Tell me what's been happening. What is going on downstairs?"

Meg scowled. "Naught to the good. My brother wears himself thin minding his borders, and that fool, Lachlan, minds me. I wish he would take himself off! I will never give him what he wants."

Distracted momentarily from her own troubles, Isobel asked, "Why not? You admitted he is a fine-looking man."

"A pretty boy!" Meg's lip curled in derision. "Oh, I am not saying he lacks a fine body—long limbs and a good set of shoulders. But I am through with men."

"Forever?" Isobel asked incredulously.

"Aye, well, I will allow I have been tempted to use him for the one purpose…but then how would I get him out of my bed again? I doubt a good kick to the rump would be enough to remove him."

"Perhaps you could make a deal before hand," Isobel suggested, barely noticing now the food she ate. "Take him to your bed once, on the condition he leaves you alone, after."

Meg smiled slowly. "I like the way you think. The trouble is, as I say, I have known Lachlan most of my life, and I know he would agree to the bargain only to follow me like a hound pup, after." She sighed. "I doubt 'tis worth it; I would be better going without."

Isobel, tearing her crust into chunks, did not comment.

More briskly, Meg said, "Why do you not get out of this room and take the air? The kitchen garden is sheltered and pleasant enough. I would go mad, shut up in here so long."

"What is the weather, outside?"

"Snowing, though the wind keeps it from lighting on the ground."

"I fear my husband's health will suffer, and him out in this cold."

"He is healthy as a horse." Meg tipped her head, her quick, clever eyes looking deep into Isobel's. "You really do love him, by God! Incredible as it seems."

Isobel flushed. "Much good may it do me. He cares so little for me, he has not come near me in three days."

"That is one way to look at it. Another is that he cares so much he rides in the snow and the wind, to keep you safe."

"No, even that can be laid down to his desire to spite MacNab. He still loves Aisla. You cannot deny it."

Meg remained silent.

"How am I to fight that?" Isobel appealed. "She is ever perfect, in his mind."

"In all our minds," Meg said softly. "My dearest friend. I will never forget her, nor will I ever forgive my brother for failing to rescue her from that fiend who held her and tortured her. So how can I fault your father, Isobel, for wishing to rescue you, now, from what he believes to be a similar situation?"

"Yet I have told my father and MacNab I am not in

need of rescue, that I wish to remain here. No one listens to me."

Anger flashed in Meg's dark eyes. "A woman will say anything, under duress. Aisla made a similar claim, even with the welts Bertram had inflicted bright upon her flesh, for fear of what he would do to her, did she speak the truth."

"Your brother has not treated me that way."

"No, but how can your father be certain?"

Isobel hesitated. "What did Bertram MacNab do to Aisla? And how do you know—?"

Meg looked away, toward the window. "A servant smuggled out a letter Aisla had written to me. I could scarcely believe how it read! I wept over those pages for hours, and then I took the burden to my brother, sure he would act immediately to save her, the woman he loved. Because I knew how he loved her—how he claimed to love her.

"He read that letter with a face like stone. He said if he took our warriors to attack MacNab's stronghold and lost, 'twould be the end of us here in Scotland. MacNab would appeal to the King and sue for our lands. He had done it before to other, weaker neighbors. And we were not so strong then as we are now. My father was not long in his grave and Dougal yet finding his way. He has built our strength since then. I am sure he vowed never to be caught so again.

"Yet it was Aisla! Her grief and suffering cried out from those pages. One of her tears was worth risking all we owned. How could he leave her there to die?"

"I cannot imagine he made the choice lightly," Isobel pointed out. "He still holds MacNab responsible—"

"Curse Bertram MacNab and his bastard of a father! I wish them naught but ill, and I will never forgive them. But neither can I forgive my brother. He might have ridden out to defeat, aye, but he should have made the attempt. Can you imagine her there, alone, and no one coming for her? No one at all?"

"Dougal has spent the intervening years—?"

"Aye, strengthening his holdings, his clan, and antagonizing MacNab any way he might. Though you will never hear him admit it, he garnered most of our current wealth through risk and thievery. It is a fine and dangerous line to walk. As you have learned, now the King's eye rests upon him."

"You say you despise him for his cowardice."

"So I do."

"Yet you admit he has not stopped fighting, and opposes MacNab yet." Isobel felt uncomfortably aware of her own status as one among her husband's weapons.

"Too late. 'Tis too late for Aisla, is it not? She lies in the ground, even her wounds turned to dust. But the wounds inflicted on the rest of us are still raw."

Meg lowered her voice. "They say round here my brother is a devil and I am a witch. I will tell you, I have studied the black arts. A woman has few enough weapons to her hand, and I do not like feeling helpless. My husband betrayed me, and he paid the price. MacNab, too, shall pay, but 'twill take strong magic, indeed, to bring him down."

Isobel, not sure how to reply, fought a shiver. At that moment, with her dark eyes gleaming and her black hair flowing round her, Meg looked every inch the weaver of spells.

"Would it not be better," she suggested tentatively,

"to use your...talents and work together with your brother against MacNab?"

Meg sprang up from the bed, suddenly restless. "For that, I would need to forgive him."

"Would you?"

"And that is something I can never do. So long as my friend remains in my heart, my heart will remain turned against him."

Isobel thought of Catherine, for whom she had been willing to sacrifice so much, and understood. She wondered where her sister was right now. Was she wife to her Thomas, settled in happiness and security? Her heart ached over the long years stretching ahead before she might hope to see her sister again. Yet she had that hope, however faint, that Meg had not.

"I am sorry," she whispered. "But I wish you would consider forgiving your brother. It is no way to live, in bitterness and grief."

Meg made no answer other than to stiffen her spine and take herself from the room, leaving a deep chill in her wake.

Later that night, when the keep lay eerily quiet, Isobel got up and crept from her chamber, down the stairs to the great hall. Cold scuttled across the stone floors, and the silence seemed a living entity that accompanied her.

Even the wind had died.

The great hall lay steeped in gloom. The fire burned low and the shadows were so thick at first she saw no inhabitants. Yet there were two; with a leap of the heart she saw her husband sitting with one booted foot propped on the hob, and Lachlan beside him, both unmoving.

The silence seemed to ripple as she stole in on careful feet. Quiet as she was, Dougal heard her and turned his head, his narrowed eyes gleaming at her.

What did he see when he looked at her? A wraith with wild, tumbled hair? A woman driven to desperation? His expression, hard and set, did not change nor did he move but sat like a master hunter luring prey.

Isobel would not let herself hesitate over what he might think. Never had she felt this kind of hunger, this consuming need.

And by heaven, he made a beautiful devil with his long limbs poised and graceful, the black hair streaming over his shoulders, the shirt beneath his vest torn open, revealing flesh turned to amber by the firelight. She now knew every inch of that flesh—the feel and taste of it—and seeing him so made her mouth go dry.

And Lachlan—with relief she saw that Lachlan slept, his head canted to one side, his chest rising and falling slowly.

"Husband!" She did not intend the word, spoken softly, to make a claim upon him, yet it did. She reached out and caught his hand where it rested on his knee, drew it to her breast. "Husband, please—will you not come with me?"

He rose without a word, his long fingers twining with hers. They climbed the stairs like shadows and entered her chamber, where Isobel shut the door and leaned against it, heart pounding and breath quick.

"Isobel..." he began then.

"No." She shook her head. "Please. I need you with me."

His face inscrutable, he stood insubstantial as a

shadow. He wetted his lips before he said, "I cannot give you what you want."

"You can." She untied the laces at the front of her sleeping rail and let the garment drop to form a pool around her feet.

What cared she now for modesty? What was politeness, to a starving woman?

His gaze caressed her, lingered long on her breasts before it dropped lower. Yet he shook his head. "I cannot. My heart is mangled, a dark and useless thing. It comes to me, you deserve far better."

Slowly, Isobel approached him. "I do not care, tonight, for what I deserve. In the morning, I may again. But not now."

He drew an unsteady breath that expanded his chest. "You reproach me, Wife, for using you as a weapon in my private war. These past days, riding my borders, being brutally honest with myself, it comes to me you are right. I have, aye, taken my pleasure in your bed, but my motives had little enough to do with you."

Isobel stepped closer. He need only reach out, now, to touch her naked flesh.

She whispered, "If you have, indeed, taken your pleasure in my bed, then I beg you please, do so again this night."

He closed his eyes and groaned. "Isobel, I am trying to deal fairly with you—"

"I know, and I am grateful. Yet, is life fair? If you cannot give me your heart, mangled as you say it is, can you not at least give me that for which my body aches?" One step more and she stood virtually within his arms.

He opened his eyes and she fell into them,

consumed by grey mist, the contact so strong she barely noticed after all when his hand cupped her breast.

"Come to me," she begged, "and we shall worry about the world come the morrow."

Chapter Twenty-Five

"The world is a mad place," Lachlan said judiciously, and tipped a mug of ale to his lips: liquid breakfast. Dim light crept round the stones of the keep, and a chill pervaded the air. After enjoying the warmth of Isobel's bed last night, Dougal felt the cold intensely, like a blight of frost in his bones. And aye, her bed had been warm, her kisses sweet, and her passion strong enough to heat him through, repeatedly.

The memory of his wife's soft flesh clinging to him distracted him so completely he barely heard Lachlan blather on.

"I mean, to make sense of aught that happens— well, it cannot be done. Women, for instance. Has ever a man made true sense of a woman? I speak in particular of your sister. Shall I tell you, Dougal, what passed between us last night?"

"Please spare me!" Dougal drank from his own mug. The ale tasted sour on his tongue, but then anything would, following the honey he had so recently tasted.

"I met her—by chance, so I thought—in the solar before she went up to bed. We exchanged a few kisses, as I told you we have been doing. This time, she did not seem inclined to stop. I thought—well, I need not say what I thought. Indeed, I doubt my mind kept working at all. I begged her to put a spell on me—life is short and uncertain, I told her—and she… I can barely stand to speak of it!"

"Pray, do not." Savage emotion rose in Dougal's breast. He must spend this cold, wretched day riding his borders when he wanted, himself, only to return to Isobel's chamber.

She would be lying abed still, no doubt warm and willing. Just the thought of her gave him a rod of iron beneath his kilt, despite the fact that she had drained him dry mere hours ago—thrice.

"And then," Lachlan continued to confide, oblivious or indifferent to Dougal's mood, "while still my flesh tingled from the caress of her lips and mouth, on at least a particular part of my flesh, she arose, looked me in the eyes, and told me not to suppose 'twould ever happen again. Said she cared not a whit for me, and would I cease following her like a hound pup deserving a kick."

"Then stop following her," Dougal advised, thinking about Isobel's mouth and tongue, with which she did such remarkable things—and aching with need.

What would she say if he came to her later, when this day was done? Would she deem it an unjust use of her? Would she once more claim him, as she had last night? He thought he might be able to survive whatever the day ahead brought him, if he might promise himself Isobel at the end of it.

And aye, Lachlan might be right in that the world was a mad place. His feelings for his wife—which, he told himself, consisted mostly of lust—might be mad as well, but, by the devil's horns, she was a lovely thing with that wild, red hair and those eyes that sparkled with humor, desire, or intelligence. She might not be soft and gentle like Aisla, fragile as porcelain. But then, there could never be another Aisla in this world.

Or, perhaps, another Isobel...

That thought startled him so much he barely noticed when Lachlan asked him, "So, man, do you think I should?"

"Eh?" Dougal responded vaguely.

"Ask her."

"Isobel?"

"Nay, you gormless fool, have you not been listening? I speak of your sister, still. I thought of bearding her tonight, asking where I stand with her."

"You stand nowhere." Dougal looked Lachy in the eye. "No man stands anywhere, with Meg. Have you no' learned that yet? If she pleasured you last evening, it is because she sought to pleasure herself."

"Aye, well." Lachy did not look so crushed as Dougal felt he should. "I am willing to let her take her pleasure wi' me again."

Dougal experienced a flash of annoyance with his friend, and then wondered whether he, himself, did not represent his sister, Meg, in his own relationship, and Isobel represent Lachlan... Yet he did not think less of Isobel for her willingness to accept him into her bed. The words he might have spoken to Lachlan died on his lips and he said, instead, "Talk to her, Lachy. Speak honestly and earnestly. Deal with her as you mean to go on."

Lachlan looked surprised, but Dougal gave him no chance to comment. "Now, come. We have borders to ride, and MacNab clansmen to put to the chase."

The day proved as lengthy and wretched as ever Dougal anticipated. A keen wind blew from the northwest, sweeping over hill and moor like a drawn sword, cutting him to the bone. The sun barely struggled over the horizon, lending no warmth. Shortly after midday, he and his band encountered a group of MacNab warriors on his western boundary and gave hard pursuit. They seemed to disappear of a sudden, just as an icy rain began to fall, and Dougal turned his party for home, with a sense of having accomplished nothing.

He reached his own land to see a single rider approaching from the direction of the keep, coming hard. When she drew near enough, he saw she was Meg, stretched out along the back of her pony with her hair flying like a black banner, and urging her mount desperately.

He and Lachlan rode to meet her, the rest of the band trailing them more slowly.

Meg's hair glittered with icy rain, and her face looked white and drawn. Her eyes met Dougal's without prevarication.

"I came at once to tell you—she is gone. Taken! She must have been walking in the kitchen garden. Days ago, I suggested she take the air there, where 'tis sheltered, and she has been doing so from time to time. If you want, you can blame me. But who thought she would be in any danger, with the guard all about? Rab has found a trail leading out from the woods behind the keep, and has gone in pursuit—"

"Who?" Dougal asked, even though his plummeting heart proved he already knew. "Who is taken?"

"Isobel! Rab found the guard assigned to patrol the rear wall dead, with an arrow through his back, and there can be no question whoever killed him seized Isobel."

"Nay!" Dougal protested fruitlessly. "It cannot be! She should have been safe anywhere inside our walls. Have we not been out all this while defending the borders?" *Aye, just to keep her safe.*

Meg glared at him impatiently. "Do you really want to argue about it now? Be grateful she is well and warmly dressed in the cloak and fur boots she had when she arrived. Rab and three others have gone after her, as I say, but whoever took her was mounted—"

Dougal's blood, inside him, turned as icy as the rain. "MacNab—I will kill him!"

"You will need to catch him first. Come!"

Meg turned her mount and started away, quick enough to outrun the wind. Dougal urged his own mount to follow. He had no need to hear more. Heart nearly bursting, he passed and then outdistanced Meg, Lachlan and the rest of the group. He reined up in the forecourt of the keep just as a number of his warriors appeared, Rab among them.

"MacNab has your lady wife," Rab greeted him. "We followed the tracks that curved round into the woods and then joined up wi' the long trail that leads across the moor, westward. No sight of them, ahead, but that way leads to MacNab's keep and no mistake. We ha' one man dead."

Lachlan, arriving in time to hear, said, "That skirmish in which we were caught, on the far border—that was just a distraction. This was planned."

"Of course 'twas planned." Viciously, Dougal rounded on him. "But how could they know she would be outside?"

"They must ha' been watching," Rab said, "from some point high in the hills, waiting for a chance to strike." He hesitated. "And she did go out ever' so often. We thought you knew."

"I did not!" Dougal felt sick. Isobel, snatched against her will, frightened and alone...the last place he could bear her to be.

He glared at his men. "I cannot believe no one saw anything, heard anything."

"Only Ian," Rab said laconically, "and he is dead."

"Is it possible they could have coaxed her away?" Meg suggested.

"Nay," Dougal denied it, remembering her in his arms last night, clinging to him as if she would never let go.

Meg said emotionlessly, "If they had her father with them and he persuaded her, convinced her she could save you from persecution, and possible death? She might so sacrifice herself."

Everyone stared at Dougal accusingly. He met Meg's gaze and saw she knew. Meg knew that Isobel loved him. His wife had never spoken the words, but the truth was reflected from her eyes, it told in her touch. He knew he deserved no such devotion. He was a ruined man with a savage heart, capable of loyalty and nothing more. Poor lass. Would she truly sacrifice herself for such a worthless specimen as he?

"We are wasting time sitting here blathering," he said viciously. "Come on, show me this trail."

The falling rain, icy as it was, had nearly obliterated the sea of tracks when they reached it. Dougal's own men milled about, restless for action, and the light already waned in the west. Dougal set men to search the immediate area again, but knew it to be an exercise in futility.

"What to do?" Lachlan asked uneasily.

"If MacNab wants war, he shall have it." Dougal felt desperate at the thought of Isobel spending even one night in MacNab's hands, yet demanding her back, as every impulse bade him, was not the best strategy. That would come, aye, but not yet.

Lachlan offered, "Surely, if her father is with her, she will be protected from the worst of MacNab's perversions?" Lachy, knowing what had befallen Aisla, knew the demons that haunted Dougal.

Aye, there was that, the faintest glimmer of hope. And if it came to it, Isobel was no timid Aisla, to let herself be used cruelly. She would fight like a wildcat.

Yet even a strong woman could only fight so hard.

"Lachy, I want you to ride and fetch O'Rourke. He will prove valuable to us now—the only proof my marriage is valid. Should he be found and murdered, 'twill be easy for MacNab to wed Isobel to that damned whelp of his, and 'tis a thing to which Isobel's father might well agree. Can I trust you in this?"

Lachlan nodded. "I promise my best efforts. But, the rest of you?"

"We are going cattle raiding," Dougal said grimly. An ancient activity from the Highlands to the borders, cattle raiding represented far more than mere thievery. It was a goad, a dare, a taunt, and an act of one-upmanship no clansman could refuse to answer. It had, in the past, started many a feud or war, for cattle represented wealth.

Lachlan departed into the gloom, and Dougal quickly organized his men. They were gathered in the forecourt, ready to leave, when Meg rushed out.

"Are you mounting a rescue?" she demanded, pulling a shawl up over her hair.

"Not yet."

Meg ignited like dry wood. "You cannot intend to leave her there—"

"I do not!"

Meg ignored him and completed her thought, "the way you left Aisla!"

The forecourt went suddenly silent, all Dougal's men shooting crosswise looks at him before gazing elsewhere.

Dougal leaned down from his horse to speak directly into his sister's face. The pain rising inside him made his voice harsh. "Do not ever make such a suggestion again. Do you trust me so little?"

"I did trust you, once," replied Meg, unintimidated, "and look what came of it."

"This will no' end so."

"'Tis not just the ending that concerns me, but what happens to Isobel before then. I wish to come with you."

"No."

"Why—"

"We will be riding hard."

"You think me incapable of keeping up?"

"I do not wish to have to worry about you, Sister. Get you inside and do what you are best at."

Meg stiffened. "What is that?"

"Employ that devious mind of yours, bend it to your dark arts. We may yet have need of them."

He led his troop away before she could protest further. The night, still vicious with wind and rain, at least held gloom enough to lend cover to the activities undertaken in the next hours. In his youth, Dougal might have enjoyed the odd spot of cattle-thieving. Now, distracted by worry and doubt, it became a nightmarish thing of stinging sleet, mud, and naked blades. MacNab, like any careful land manager, kept his cattle spread out. Dougal knew this first raid would go easiest; once Randal knew Dougal's intentions, he would post a heavy guard. As it was, the fast-moving raiding party encountered only two MacNab clansmen, who were dealt with summarily.

Fine and good, Dougal thought at the end of it, so long as he did not lose any of the stolen cattle, his men, or mounts to a bog, burn, or darkness on the way home. They were frozen through, all, before MacNab's cattle were stowed safely in his own far pasture, and dawn stained the sky in the east.

Dougal still felt sick with worry about Isobel. Nearly a whole night gone. How did she fare? He could scarcely bear to think of her frightened and alone, yet thinking of her being not alone was worse.

He brought all his raiding party into the great hall to warm by the fire and drink a dram. There he found Lachlan returned with O'Rourke, which lifted his spirits slightly.

The priest, quite obviously drunk, had claimed for himself a place before the fire and held a tankard in his hand. He raised it when he saw Dougal.

"To the Devil!" he cried, and drank.

Dougal looked at Lachlan, who rolled his eyes. Lachy appeared as wet and cold as the rest of them.

"Good work," said Dougal, crossing to Lachlan's side. "Where did you find him?"

"In the stinking, dank hidey-hole he calls home," Lachlan replied distastefully, "and already with a skin full. He had earned himself a jug, earlier, by performing a christening."

O'Rourke got to his feet and stumbled over. "I thank you, Laird MacRae, for your kind offer of hospitality. 'Tis a vile, wet night to be abroad."

Dougal eyed Lachlan in question, and Lachlan explained, "I told him he had a bed here for the time, out of the weather."

"'Tis good of you," O'Rourke decried and attempted to bow. "And I am sure the things said of you in the district are greatly exaggerated."

"Aye," Dougal told him ironically, "and I may need you to return the favor by speaking up for me when the time comes. That marriage you performed for me—you recall?"

For an instant it appeared O'Rourke did not. Then his bleary, pale blue eyes cleared. "The bonny lass with the red hair?"

"My wife, Isobel, aye. She has been stolen away from me."

"An ab-abomination!"

"It is. And I may need you to swear to the validity of our joining. Accept my hospitality, so, until this business is done."

O'Rourke thought about it with apparent difficulty. "But—I am needed in the district, to perform various services. What if a babe is born too soon? What if someone should die?"

"Oh, aye," Dougal murmured. He had determined someone would die, for this. But amidst his ale fumes, the priest truly looked troubled. "If you are needed,

Master MacElwain, here, will escort you wherever you need to go. Will you not, Lachlan?"

Lachy looked disgruntled. "Me? I am no priest-minder."

"More like a bodyguard," Dougal said. "I need someone I can trust to keep him alive at all costs."

"Aye, well," O'Rouke spoke before Lachlan could, "I am all in favor, me lads, of keeping alive."

## Chapter Twenty-Six

"At least I am still alive," Isobel told herself, in an effort to battle the panic that had overtaken her mind: alive, imprisoned, and far more terrified than she had ever been.

Terror, she knew, made a poor companion, especially in her present circumstances. A weakening emotion, it might render her helpless when the moment to act arrived. She would do better to feel anger, indignation, determination—anything that might empower her.

And yes, she felt all those things: anger at her father, that he had allowed his friend MacNab to snatch her like a bundle of goods, that he did not intervene now to set her free; indignation that Randal MacNab should arrogantly decide he could get away with such a deed; determination to free herself, if no one else would help her.

And longing for her husband... She could scarcely let herself think about Dougal, the pain was so bright. He would be furious over this, she knew—his wife in the hands of his enemies—but why? She feared he would feel anger that MacNab had got one over on him, not distress for her own sake.

Her new prison, and she did not mistake it for anything else, was a well-appointed bedroom twice the size of her chamber at MacRae's keep. It had a fine curtained bed, a chest for the clothing she did not possess, and an upholstered bench in front of the fireplace. She wondered if Aisla had inhabited this room before her and how much suffering it had seen. It had been Aisla's former husband, Bertram MacNab, who escorted Isobel here: she had not liked the barely veiled eagerness in his eyes.

Whatever he and his vile father planned for her, she knew to her toes it would be unpleasant. She meant to fight them to her last breath. If she could not escape any other way, she would jump from the window, and if she could find no other weapon she would set fire to the bed. But first she supposed she should attempt to employ reason.

Marshaling her wits and determination, she marched to the door and tried to yank it open. To her surprise it was not locked; the man standing guard—a huge fellow armed with not one but two swords and wearing MacNab tartan—turned to look at her in a reproving manner.

"I wish to see my father," she told him. She had managed only a glimpse of her sire when Bertram MacNab dragged her in, kicking and struggling. He had been standing beside Randal in the doorway of a chamber off the great hall, and though she called to him he had not responded.

"You are to stay here," her guard pronounced. "My orders," he grinned, "until young master comes."

Isobel liked neither the grin nor the implications. Her stomach clenched, and she struggled to look imperious. "I wish to see my father. I have that right! You can either take me to him or bring him here to speak with me—I do not care which."

"Get ye back inside and wait," the man advised. "I take no orders from you."

Isobel looked him in the eye, stiffened her back and screamed. She had a good set of lungs when she chose to use them, and this was a shriek worthy of an eldritch delivering a curse. It bounced off the stone walls of the corridor and reverberated painfully.

The guard flinched and drew one of his swords. "Stop that! Foolish wench!"

Isobel sucked in a breath and screamed again, louder.

People came running—first two more guards and an ancient servant, a woman who looked like she worked in the kitchen. Isobel wanted to see but one face, her father's, so she screamed on.

The guard with the sword raised his free hand to strike her. She ducked, wove between two of the other men, and ran for the stairs.

"Catch her!" someone cried, and swore.

Isobel did not hesitate. She reached the top of the stone stairs, knocked the serving woman aside, caught her foot in her skirt, and nearly tumbled all the way down.

She caught herself with the help of the balustrade and charged down with at least five people following her.

"What in hell is this commotion?" Randal MacNab stood once more in the doorway of the chamber off the hallway. Like a small battering ram, Isobel bashed her way past him, her eyes wild.

The room, a chamber similar to the solar at MacRae's, looked pleasant and comfortable. Two benches flanked the fire, and on one of them her father rested. Bertram MacNab she saw nowhere.

"Father!" Isobel started forward, but Randal MacNab reached out and nabbed her shoulder, his grasp anything but kind.

"What do you think you are about, miss?"

"I want to speak to my father." Isobel glared into MacNab's eyes. "You cannot prevent me. I have a right, a daughter's right to see him."

MacNab grinned unpleasantly. "Then see him."

He released her, and she stumbled to the bench before the fire. "Father," she began.

Gerald Maitland did not so much as glance at her. He sat canted to one side, his neckcloth loosened and his eyes half closed. Isobel's heart, already beating triple time, sped further. Was he ill? Dead?

"Father, speak to me. Answer me! You must get me away out of here—we both must leave! These men are not your friends, as you think. Take me home to Yorkshire if you will, punish me as you may. But let us be gone—"

She paused, stricken by her father's continued failure to respond. The empty cup sitting on the bench beside him gave her the answer: drunk. Her father, who never touched what he called the demon whisky and frequently lectured on its ills, had now taken so much he did not know where he was or who she was.

He could not understand the danger she faced nor lift a finger to help her.

All the breath rushed from Isobel's body. She turned her head slowly and looked at Randal MacNab.

Once more, he smiled that unpleasant smile, the one that left his eyes cold. "Stupid girl, you have been far too much indulged. That is the error my good friend, here, has committed. But as you can see, he has now entrusted you to my hands."

"He has not!"

"Can he say differently? Bertram!" He bellowed the name, which was the last Isobel wanted to hear, and when his son came trotting in, the cold and sleet upon him as if he had just returned from checking his borders, Randal gestured at Isobel.

"Our charge needs to learn obedience."

Isobel looked at Bertram. His eyes, unlike his father's, did not look devoid of emotion. Emptiness would have been much better than what Isobel saw: eagerness, anticipation, cruelty. He seized her arm and twisted. "Come."

No fear Isobel had ever felt rivaled what assailed her as Bertram dragged her back up those stairs, past the old woman from the kitchen, past the guards and other servants, all staring. She struggled, kicked, and lashed out, injured herself on the stones, but did not break free. She did not care how badly she hurt herself. She suspected if she once more entered that bedchamber she would never again come out, but she would suffer—this man would assure it.

At the top of the stairs, when one of her wild blows connected with his face, he shouted, "Stop it!" He then released his hold on her arm and seized her hair instead. Isobel howled as the excruciating pain brought immediate tears to her eyes.

The door of the dreaded chamber still stood open. Bertram threw her inside like a bundle of sticks, and she landed hard on the stone floor and skidded. He followed her in and slammed the door behind him.

For an instant, winded, Isobel lay where she had

fallen. Her scalp roared with pain and her shoulder, which had absorbed most the impact of her landing, screamed at her.

Bertram stood over her, legs spread, like wrath impersonated.

"You are wanting discipline," he pronounced, "and I can give it." He fumbled with the front of his kilt. "On your knees."

"No."

"That is a word which will never cross your lips again! When I tell you to act, wench, you will obey." He reached down and seized her hair again. Isobel gasped as he hauled her to her knees, but she had not yet lost her fight.

"If you put any part of your vile body near me, I shall bite it," she promised.

He struck her across the face so hard it sent her sprawling backward. She fell onto her injured shoulder, hit her head, and saw stars.

Bertram loomed over her, pointing a condemning finger. "Do not ever threaten me! You will obey, understand?"

Isobel raised a shaking hand and wiped blood from the corner of her mouth.

"You will accept me the next time I walk through that door," he continued, "and you will prove willing. Else we will see how well you learn obedience, tied spread on that bed whilst each member of my warrior guard takes you, one after the other."

Somehow Isobel scrambled to her feet. "You would not!"

He grinned cruelly. "Try me, lady. Try me, just as each of them will try you."

A wave of nausea surged through Isobel, so strong it nearly knocked her down again. For the first time she realized she stood where Aisla once had—poor soul!—and Aisla had not survived.

*Evil*, she thought, as Bertram took himself out through the door and slammed it shut. This time she heard a bar being lowered across it. The man personified evil, walking. And Dougal—

She quivered with longing at the thought of him. Would he tumble to where she was? Would he attempt to rescue her? Did he care enough? Oh, yes, though it might not be love but hate that brought him. Yet he would come; he would never allow MacNab to keep the woman he called his wife.

The question remained: would Dougal come in time?

Slowly she walked to the bed, a fourposter, the frame carved of dark wood which, when she inspected it closely, chilled the blood within her. For each of the four posts bore chafe marks as if rope had been threaded around them and had bitten deep.

Isobel believed it then: Bertram would follow through on his threat, carry out his vile plan as he had done to Aisla in this very chamber. She had suffered here unspeakable hurt and humiliation. Had she died in this room? Had her last breath tainted the air?

Isobel's heart went out to her, poor lass, alone and frightened beyond the bounds of sanity. But her backbone stiffened. She had no intention of repeating Aisla's fate. She would, first, die fighting.

Yet what options did she have? She went to the door and tried it, even though she had heard the bar drop. It held fast against her. She needed either a weapon or a plan. How much time did she have before Bertram MacNab marched back in and reasserted his demand for obedience?

She went to the window, pulled aside the drapery, and looked out. Early dark cloaked the countryside and obscured the ground below, but she could see enough to tell it would be a vicious descent. Fifty feet of sheer wall fell unbroken to the cold, rocky turf. Yet the wall itself, built of stones rough cut, had gaps between them for toes and fingers, and the ground below was just that—grass with a stone wall beyond, not a paved courtyard. The breath caught in her throat. Dangerous, oh, yes, but possible, if she had the courage. And she would take her chances any day in the wild countryside before testing the cruelty in Bertram MacNab's eyes.

"I will escape him," she told the deepening darkness, "or die trying."

Chapter Twenty-Seven

"You do realize your wife may well be dead," Lachlan said gloomily. "MacNab might have been forced to silence her, or she may have fought a bit too hard."

Dougal shook his head. He had no doubt his wife would fight against her abductors, but he thought Randal MacNab must be canny enough to keep her alive for a time. Isobel had become a pawn in a dangerous game, the best weapon MacNab now had to his hand. "You forget her father is there. Surely his presence will serve to protect her?"

Even as he spoke the words, Dougal took little comfort in them. There were ways and ways of making a woman suffer. The prospect of Isobel enduring any of them turned him sick inside. But he thought he would know if Isobel no longer lived: had he not felt it the moment Aisla died, like a sword plunged into his soul?

But...he had loved Aisla; at best, he desired Isobel. It was different, was it not?

Lachlan remained unconvinced. "You may launch an all-out attack on MacNab's keep only to recover a corpse. 'Twill be war, Dougal, and costly. You do know that?"

"My men are prepared to fight."

"By throwing themselves against MacNab's walls?"

"It is not the only way." Dougal, brooding, stared into the fire. He and Lachlan stood beside the hearth in the great hall while, outside, his warriors organized for the trek to MacNab's stronghold. "I may, instead, offer him what he wants."

"And what is that?" Lachlan slanted a look at him.

"Single combat," Dougal replied.

Lachlan drew a breath, and his gaze sharpened. A number of emotions chased their way, one by one, across his face. "Would you dare, after what happened the last time?" He broke off abruptly.

Dougal returned his look, unflinching. "You know nothing of what happened before, Lachlan. Nothing." Slowly he raised his hand and touched the scar on his cheek. Deeply puckered, it made a crater of memory, regret, and shame.

He saw Lachlan's eyes narrow and wondered again how much Lachy guessed about what had happened eight years ago. But no, even Lachy considered him a coward, rather than what he was in truth—a failure.

"You must care for Isobel a very great deal," Lachlan ventured. "Dare I say, even, you must love her? I know how you felt for Aisla."

From somewhere, Dougal summoned a harsh laugh. "How many times must I tell you I do not believe in love? 'Tis a fool's pursuit! Yet would I allow that bastard to keep from me aught that is mine?" The last four words rang with conviction.

"Aye, well." Lachlan backed off. "When do we act?"

"Tonight. By a miracle, the clouds have cleared, and the moon is out. We will bait the badger in his own den."

Meg found him a short time later, while he donned his weapons and downed a mug of whisky. His men awaited him in the forecourt, their mounts restless beneath the moonlight.

"So," she said as she broached him, like a ship in full sail, "you have found the courage to go after her?"

"Hold your tongue, Sister. I need none of your mettlesome opinions."

"You shall have them anyway. I hold my tongue at the bidding of no man."

"A sad truth! Yet I warn you, I am in no mood for your haranguing. Have you finished speaking your spells? Are the gods—or the devils—on our side?"

"Curiously, they are." She tipped her head, and the firelight slid off the length of her unbound, black hair. "The Spirits are strong with us, this night."

"Good. I go to discover how badly MacNab wants the return of his cattle, and whether he is willing to trade for them something I hold even more valuable. I will return with Isobel or, as our forefathers used to say, on my shield."

"Lachlan says you mean to challenge Bertram MacNab to single combat."

"Lachlan has a terrible great mouth."

Meg's lips curved in a wry smile. "He is under my enchantment, so tells me everything."

"Poor sod!"

Meg's dark eyes met Dougal's grey ones. "Brother, do you have any idea how I have hated you—hated you deep and strong—for failing to go to Aisla's rescue when she needed you? She was my dearest friend and, I dare say, the last person I have ever loved."

"Aye?" They had that in common, then.

"She was my opposite, to her bones—sweet and gentle, deserving of any sacrifice, the kind of woman for whom a man might well lay down his life. So why did you fail her then, yet propose to sacrifice yourself now for that red-haired Southern hoyden?"

Dougal lifted a brow. "You do not like my wife?"

"That is the second curious thing of the night—I do. I find I like Isobel enormously, if not as I did Aisla. Isobel has fire and courage, she possesses a sense of humor. Yet she is not Aisla, and it makes me wonder why you would bestir yourself for her."

"Aisla died many years ago. Do you not think I have learned something since her death? Do you not think I am changed by her death? Besides, Isobel is my wife, as Aisla never was. I have a right to protect her."

"Then go and get her, and this time, Brother, do not measure the cost. And should Bertram MacNab fall during the ensuing encounters, 'twill make of the world a finer place."

Dougal nodded—'twas another point on which he and his sister agreed—and went out.

**\*\*\*\***

The wind that surged across the dark countryside and round the stones of MacNab's keep had chased the clouds far to the east. Isobel would have preferred rain, sleet, and darkness, even if they made the descent she contemplated more dangerous. She had rifled her bed and tied the linens into long ropes of fabric she then grounded to the foot of the wooden chest beneath the window. She donned her cloak—which Bertram MacNab had torn from her and hurled into the corner when first he brought her in—with fingers that shook. She refused to hesitate long enough to contemplate her terror.

She hoped, and doubted, the hastily-constructed rope would prove long enough. Her mind, which seemed to have cleared like the sky beyond the window, told her it would likely fall short. Her true difficulty, she knew, lay in her injured shoulder, which burned with fiery pain every time she moved it. Would it fail her? Could she ignore the pain long enough to scramble down the wall to that beckoning green turf below?

And if she fell but did not die, if Bertram MacNab found her, what would he do then? Would he drag her inside, bent and broken as she might be, haul her back to this hated room to tie her to the bed and carry out his dreaded scheme of discipline?

The very idea got Isobel over the window sill and scrabbling with her toes for gaps between the outer stones. The wind seized her like cold fingers seeking to pluck her from the wall. She clutched the linen rope, and her shoulder shrieked in protest. She gasped, set her teeth, and endured.

A glance over her shoulder told her the ground looked much farther off from her new perspective. The stones, still wet from the previous bout of sleet, proved slippery, and rough enough to tear her fingers. The thought came into her head she might well slip and die.

Then anger flared again. Better to perish while attempting to escape than to suffer what Bertram MacNab threatened. She began to edge her way down the rope, pinned against the wall by the moonlight, and prayers crowded her brain. She had not attempted to pray since shortly after her mother died, when she became convinced that God, if he indeed existed, failed to listen. But now she asked fervently that no member of MacNab's guard should come round the corner and look up, for then she was surely done.

Haste and the weakness in her right shoulder nearly caused her to fall not once but thrice. She stretched her ears, listening beyond the roar of the wind for a shout from above or below. If Bertram entered the bedchamber he would be quick to haul her back up. She heard nothing but the wind that enfolded her, and her own desperate breathing.

And then she came to the end of her rope. A terrified look told her the distance below her feet remained greater than she had hoped—a drop of perhaps twenty feet yawned beneath her. She hung for several, endless moments, whimpering at the pain in her shoulder, toes reaching desperately for secure holds, and then she fell.

She hit hard, struck her head, and once more saw stars, as she had in the room above. But she had landed flat on her back, and the turf made a cushion. For an instant she stared up at the high window—incredibly high—that made a tiny, lit square in the wall with the linen rope dangling pale against the stones. She struggled to breathe and assess herself and then, spurred by the sharp fear of discovery, scrambled up and ran.

Before the descent, while still inside, she had tried to determine direction. She knew Dougal's lands lay east and thought she could guess a likely path. Now panic licked at her and she merely fled, directionless, wanting to lose herself as swiftly as possible in the nearest inky darkness.

She ran hunched over, wracked with pain and afraid to pause. The moon spotted her shadow before

her and she knew how visible she must be. Surely
MacNab had men on patrol and the odds of failing to
meet one now were poor indeed.

She never paused until she reached a stand of dark
pines, where she fell to her hands and knees, her lungs
pumping like leaky bellows. Her heart, beating double
time, cried for mercy, and her shoulder roared at her so
fiercely she almost missed another pain stabbing deep
inside her belly, low and relentless.

*What now?* she wondered, as she fought her way to
her feet, once she had breath enough to stand. Did
MacNab's warriors ride these woods? Would she hear
approaching horses, with the wind soughing in the
trees? She blinked as phantom rays of moonlight
flickered between the branches. If she chose the wrong
direction now, the mistake could prove fatal. She might
wander miles into unknown country, or back into
MacNab's hands. Yet staying here might prove just as
deadly.

The next minutes and hours proved a confusing
nightmare as she dodged trees, boulders and fallen
limbs, following nothing more than blind instinct. In
her mind she carried a picture of her husband's face—
guarded, shadowed, the magical grey eyes half-veiled—
and it was that which drew her. When at last she
reached a narrow track, cutting like a sword blade
across the dark turf, she followed that also, too close to
exhaustion to fight her way any further beneath the
trees.

In the end, the wind betrayed her; she did not hear
the party of mounted men coming up behind until it was
too late. At the last moment she whirled and saw the
cluster of riders looming over her, nothing more than

black shapes silhouetted against the moon.

A number of images flashed across her mind: being dragged back to MacNab's keep, the dreadful chamber where Aisla had suffered before her, the fourposter bed, scarred by pain.

She turned about and ran, knowing she had no real chance and that a mounted man could bring her down the way a fox ran down a hare. The track made a narrow gleam of moonlight; she lifted her skirts and pounded along it.

A cry came from behind her, almost lost in a gust of wind. She heard the fierce rhythm of hoofbeats, stumbled and almost fell, picked herself up somehow, and thought she heard her name on the cold air.

"Isobel!"

Something other than pain, fear, or exhaustion made her hesitate then. She half spun just as the rider reached her. His arm came down, snatched her from the ground, and swung her onto the horse before him. The arm felt like iron. An instant's terror convulsed her before she went suddenly still. She knew that touch, hard as it might be. More, she knew the scent of him and the profile just visible beneath the plaid he wore.

"Isobel," he repeated her name and pushed the plaid back from his hair, onto his shoulders. Wild, black locks streamed loose in the wind and grey eyes, glittering like the moonlight, stared into hers.

"By all that is holy," he exclaimed, which seemed an amazing thing for a devil to say, "how came you here?"

Isobel began to tremble, which did not prevent her from pressing closer, burrowing into the warmth and strength of him. She clutched his plaid as a drowning woman might a thin curl of rope.

His arms drew her in closer. They hurt, but she reveled in this ache.

"I escaped," she said brokenly. "I was trying to come to you."

His hands, gentle now, caressed her, stroked her back, her hair. "And MacNab?" he began.

"Hunting me." She shivered. "He will be hunting me by now."

"He will not have you," Dougal vowed. "That I swear, on my life."

## Chapter Twenty-Eight

"Your wife is in a bad way," Meg said flatly, but with sympathy in her eyes. "She may be dying, I cannot tell."

Dougal, who once more sat with Lachlan in the great hall, choked on the mouthful of whisky he had just taken and looked at his sister, stricken. He leaped to his feet without intention.

"Eh? But her injuries did not seem so great. Her shoulder—" Isobel had cried out when he lifted her down from his horse, in the courtyard.

"'Tis not her shoulder," Meg interrupted him. "There is somewhat amiss inside. She bleeds profusely."

Dougal felt the color drain from his face. "What did that bastard do to her? She swore to me he did not rape her."

Meg shrugged. "Were I to venture a guess, I would say she is miscarrying—at a very early stage. I just thought you should know."

"My child?" Dougal swayed on his feet. "She carried my child? She never said."

"Likely she did not know," Meg told him tersely. "She seems baffled, now, as to what is amiss, but cries out with the pain."

Dougal stood like a man struck and stared at his sister. His child, the heir he so desperately needed to secure his lands. And Isobel...

"I thought you might wish to see her," Meg said dryly, "before it is too late."

Lachlan surged to his feet and clasped Dougal's shoulder. "Go, man!"

All the way up the worn, stone stairs, Dougal's thoughts hollered. Men lost their wives in childbed, he knew—it was a fact of life. Yet this could be laid directly at MacNab's door, another thing the bastard had taken from him, and bitterness burned in his chest.

"Women lose bairns," he said, "and do not die of it."

Meg glanced back at him. "She bleeds too heavily. If she dies, 'tis that will take her."

Dougal's throat closed. "There must be somewhat you can do—women's medicine?"

"I am no physician."

"Send for one! I will send Lachy."

"Is there a physician in the district? I cannot bring one to mind."

"In Stirling—"

"Aye, send Lachy if you will, but I doubt 'twill be quick enough."

They reached the top of the stairs. Dougal seized his sister's elbow and gazed into her eyes. "Somewhat else, then. Magic. There must be spells, you will know them. Save her, Meg, and you will never want for anything so long as I live."

One of her brows quirked. "A bargain? Now, brother, you speak my language—'tis how I live, that. But I do not know if I have the ability."

"They call you 'witch,' do they not?"

Meg tossed her head in scorn. "Ignorant folk use

meaningless words. There is a power, Brother, but I do not possess it. It must be sued from one far more elevated than I."

Dougal studied her hard. "The devil?"

Meg laughed. "And what sympathy might he have for the plight of women? He is but a construct of the priests, a boogie man meant to frighten. I deal with a far older power, the one that makes the doe to run before the hunter, and puts the trees in leaf."

"Can it save Isobel?"

"It can."

"Will it?"

"Well, now, that would depend very much on your reasons."

"She is too young to die so." Too full of life, and passion.

"You have to need her to live," Meg told him mercilessly. "And, for the right cause—not because you want a child out of her, or because you do not want MacNab to win in this. You must care for her, herself."

Dougal nodded. Leave it to Meg to demand the one thing he could not give—his heart, that blackened, damaged stone incapable of what Isobel required.

He pushed past Meg and through the door of his wife's chamber. The smell of blood assailed his nostrils, raw and intense. He knew then a battle took place in this chamber, as grave as on any killing ground.

A woman from the kitchens sat beside the bed. She rose when she saw him and stepped away, but Dougal barely noticed her. His eyes were all for Isobel.

She lay sprawled like a man in death, her face devoid of color and her eyes narrowed in pain. Dougal had seen warriors who wore that same look as they gazed beyond this world to the next, whence they traveled. Fear—real fear—seized him, and he knew Meg had not brought him a whit too soon.

"Isobel." He went forward and perched on the edge of the bed, reaching for her hand. She turned those distant eyes on him, and he wondered what she saw in his face—rage? Grief? Terror?

"Husband." Her lips moved feverishly, and the words came in gasps, "I do not know what ails me. I climbed down from MacNab's prison—I fell part of the way."

"Did you fall hard?" He wanted desperately to touch her but feared causing more hurt. He reached out and brushed the tangled hair from her brow. Could such a fall bring about a miscarriage?

"Very hard." Pain gripped her, and she writhed in agony. When the wave passed, her eyes sought his again. "The chamber in which I was held—my prison—was that of another before me—your love."

"My love?"

"Aisla, she whom you love. The only woman ever you will." The words hung between them, indisputable. Dougal wanted desperately to refute them but could not. He looked round, but both Meg and the serving woman had gone; he and Isobel were alone.

Gently, for him, he said, "Do not try to talk if it causes you pain."

"I must speak now, or perhaps not at all. Do you know what is the matter with me?"

"Has Meg not said?"

Wildly, Isobel shook her head.

"She thinks you miscarry." His voice sounded

harsher than he would have liked. But her eyes flew to his, and clung.

"A child? But I was not carrying—"

"Are you sure? Meg says 'twas very early." Seeing the look that came to her face—one of stunned grief— he gripped her fingers hard. Another wave of pain seized her, and she rode it out in obvious agony.

Then she asked, "Am I dying? Tell me the truth."

"The truth? I do not know." Before seeing her, he would have said she could survive. Women did. But now his heart stuttered with fear.

"I must tell you—not much time." Her fingers twisted in his, bit into his hand with painful intensity and her eyes—wide, now, and eerily blue in her white face—captured him. "If I do not tell you this now, I may never have the chance."

Dread blossomed in Dougal's chest, spread upward, and closed his throat. He knew what she would say as if the words were already spoken.

She drew a ragged breath. "I love you, Dougal MacRae—devil or not, I do not care—and I am helpless to deny! I did not ask to love you, do not understand the feeling, but my heart, poor gift that it may be, is yours."

"'Tis not a poor gift." Dougal barely recognized his own voice. He reached out to smooth the skin of her brow, thinking of the many ways he had touched her these weeks past. But a declaration of passion was not what she wanted, and lust was not love. He would give much to return the words to her, but even now he could not lie.

"I am honored," he told her, feeling humble. "I do not warrant such feeling, nor deserve—"

She smiled ruefully. "You do not welcome such

feeling," she corrected. "Yet I cannot help but tell you. I hope you understand."

"Isobel, my heart is a damaged, blackened thing. 'Twould make no worthy return for you."

She whispered, her strength failing, "You love only her, will always love only her. Will that truly never change? Can you give me no hope?"

Terror gripped Dougal's heart: she was dying right here beneath his hands, in a welter of blood.

"Isobel—Wife—you must hang on. You must fight! There will be other bairns—"

"Can you want my child, even though you do not want me?"

That he could answer, and truthfully. "With all my heart! There is naught I can imagine better than an heir with your courage, strength and fire. And, Wife, I never said I did not want you. Of that you may be certain!"

Another spasm gripped her. They endured it together. He found himself wishing he could pray, and seeking words that, to her, would make a difference.

"Listen to me, Isobel," he told her when the pain eased again. "I know fine 'tis a poor offer, since I cannot give you my heart, but I vow to you, everything else I am is yours. Hang on for me—fight—and we will build a life, a future together. A good life."

He had never before made such a promise, not to anyone, and it frightened him that he should do so now, but he gave it completely. His crippled heart aside, he was willing to live with her—and for her—all his days.

"Will you fight, Isobel, for me?"

She nodded.

Behind him he heard the door open as Meg reentered the room. He bent and kissed his wife's brow, then rose and released her fingers. Her eyes drifted closed.

When he joined Meg at the door, she gave him a searching look.

"What can you do for her?" he demanded. "Her strength fades! You said I must need her to live—" He gazed into his sister's black eyes. "Well, I do. I will give whatever you ask, if you save her. Is it enough?"

Meg nodded, and Dougal went limp with relief. Did he believe in his sister's purported powers more than he believed in God? Yet Meg insisted the powers upon which she called were not her own, nor of the devil. He did not know, yet he clung to a slim shard of faith.

"Leave us," Meg said. "Wait below and think on the debt you incur—not to me but to the woman who lies there. If she lives, it will need be paid in care, loyalty, and fidelity."

He left the room and stumbled blindly back down the stairs, where he found Lachlan waiting for him. One glance and Lachlan looked away.

"As grave as that, is it?" he asked awkwardly.

Dougal reached for his cup, which proved empty. He splashed whisky into it and drank deep.

"I would send to Stirling for a physician, but Meg insists there is no time. I have left Isobel in her hands."

"I will ride to Stirling, if you like," Lachlan offered.

Dougal considered it. "At the rate she loses blood, I do not doubt Meg is right. But, aye, go! I would appreciate it."

Lachlan got at once to his feet. "I will go as swiftly as I may."

Dougal reached out and grasped Lachy's arm. "Thank you."

"She will survive it, man."

"If she lasts the next few hours, 'twill be due to Meg's magic. I will then be in debt to my sister—a frightening enough thought."

"It is, that." Lachlan could not but agree.

He went out, leaving Dougal to brood at the fire alone, the victim of his thoughts, dark and fierce. He thought of what Isobel had said about Aisla, and the room from which she had escaped. The blood pounded in his ears. He had already lost the child Isobel carried. If he lost his wife as well, MacNab would have a heavy price to pay.

"And you will pay it," he said aloud to the shadowed room. "That I do vow!"

## Chapter Twenty-Nine

"The Lady uplift thee, the Lord defend thee; strength flow to you from the winds that cleave the world, the fire that purifies us, the water that speaks to us, and the earth itself, clothed in beauty. Vigor return to thee, and may those I sue banish all harm. Awake!"

The words drummed in Isobel's ears, interrupting a dream of pain, and called her from the far darkness. The summons possessed power she could not deny, and she came back to her body the way one returns to a dwelling after a long absence. It felt changed, not quite as she remembered. Her limbs felt light, her flesh insubstantial. All the agony she had known was gone.

She drew a breath that felt like the first she had taken in a long while, and opened her eyes. A face hung above her, one she remembered seeing often between the flickers of nightmare—with deep, black eyes tilted slightly at the outer corners, pale skin, and a wealth of black hair, now tumbled and untidy. Isobel knew those eyes, intent and unsparing, as well as the touch of the hands, hard and competent.

"Meg," she said, only it did not come out sounding so much like a word as a hoarse croak.

Meg smiled, reached out and touched Isobel's brow, and Isobel saw unexpected kindness in the dark eyes.

"So," Meg said, "we have our answer. How do you

feel?"

"Awful. Weak, and strange. Where am I?"

"Your own chamber, safe."

"What happened to me?"

"Do you not remember? No matter. You are back with us now."

Meg turned away, and Isobel heard her whisper, apparently to someone else in the room. Her sense of hearing seemed more acute than her other senses. The rest came in pieces that did not seem to belong to her. The bed beneath her—her own bed, yes—felt like an illusion. Pale daylight stole over the windowsill that she could just see. She felt too weak to turn her head.

"Dougal?"

At the name, Meg turned back to her. "He is waiting below. I will bring him, but first, have you any pain?" Meg touched Isobel's stomach gently. "Here?"

"Not now. Why?"

Meg's expression tightened. "You had a fall and have been unwell." She turned once more to the other person in the room. "Nell, let us change these linens again. We will not have her greet her husband decked in gore."

When the other woman leaned over her, Isobel recognized Meg's tirewoman. Her confusion increased along with her sense of unreality. She barely felt the movement as they shifted her in the bed, stripped off her night rail, and washed her body, tussled with the linens, and dressed her again.

"Drink this," Meg told her then.

Suddenly, Isobel thirsted unbearably. The contents of the cup—not water—tasted sharp and bitter but refreshed her.

"There, now." Meg smoothed her hair on the pillow.

"What day is it? How long have I been ill?"

"A while. You journeyed far. Do not think on it now. I will bring your husband."

Isobel heard her hurry away, heard Nell move about the chamber, then voices and more footsteps, including some that made her heart leap in her breast.

Dougal's face swam into view. Oddly, he too looked changed. She vaguely remembered clinging to the idea of him, the desire for him, the intense need. Yet she had never seen him like this, subdued and tentative, even the wild, black hair tamed at the nape of his neck.

He seated himself on the edge of the bed, and she realized he had been there before this, had gripped her fingers and cradled her hand. She gazed into his eyes—the color of the sky after storm—and gasped at what she saw.

"Wife," he said. Only that, but it held claiming and gladness that buoyed Isobel's heart.

She reached out, and he twined his fingers with hers. She realized Dougal, seldom at a loss for either words or confidence, did not know what to say.

So she spoke. "Meg will not say what befell me."

"Do you not remember?"

Isobel frowned. "I have pieces of it: being here in this bed, ill, floating in darkness and pain. But I do not understand."

Dougal glanced over his shoulder at his sister and the servant, who moved about gathering the used bedding and other paraphernalia.

Meg shook her head and shooed the servant before following her. "Since she does not remember, you will have to tell her, Brother. I did my work, now you do yours."

He whispered a curse softly and turned back to Isobel, his expression grim.

"What must you tell me?" Isobel asked. "What has befallen me?"

"You suffered a fall when escaping from MacNab's keep. Meg has been busy healing you."

Amazement touched Isobel, and then perplexity. "Escaped!"

"He held you captive after snatching you from within these walls." Dougal looked fierce. 'I must apologize to you, Wife. You should have been safe in your own home. I failed you."

The look in his eyes told her he did not speak the words lightly or with ease: admitting failure of any kind nearly choked him.

Isobel's sluggish mind began to waken, aligning some of the pieces. "What is it you are keeping from me?"

"Meg employed magic to heal you. It may have stolen some of your memory."

"But you can tell me all. What is it you refuse to say?" Isobel struggled with it. "MacNab snatched me? Why?"

"In an effort to hurt me, of course. Do you not recall? Your father is with him."

"Yes." The memories came slowly, but they came. "I was in MacNab's stronghold... I went to my father to sue for rescue. I found him drunk. But my father never drinks to excess."

"Your father is securely in MacNab's pocket." He squeezed her fingers. "But, Wife, the courage you showed in the face of danger was remarkable. One of my warriors could not have been more valiant."

"I fell! I fell climbing down the wall from the window, in the dark. I ran—"

"Aye. My men and I came upon you, exhausted and half raving, in pain."

Isobel recalled flames and darkness, pain that came in waves and cleaved her like a sword. "I feel so weak now."

"You bled much. We thought we should lose you. Lachlan rode to Stirling for a physician, who has promised to come later this morning. No sooner did Lachy return than Meg told me she thought you would survive."

Again, Isobel searched her husband's eyes. "There is more? Tell me!"

He drew a ragged breath. "When we got you here, safe, Meg realized you were miscarrying. You have lost our child."

"What?" Isobel felt amazement widen her eyes; her fingers spasmed in his, but he did not release them. "I did not even know I was carrying."

"No, it was very early. But you bled so much, we thought we must lose you also."

His expression—calm, almost wooden—was belied by the agony in his eyes. Isobel, beholding it, knew it must be for the child she had carried so briefly, his heir. For had he not told her, fairly, he would never love her?

Grief rose in a towering wave, and she did not know if it was for the lost child—his child—or the fact that he valued her only for what she could, or had failed to, give him.

"Do not look so," he bade her, and touched her

cheek gently. "'Tis hard to bear, I know, but there will be other bairns."

"Will there? Yet I have failed you now—"

"Isobel, Wife—" He seemed to search hard for words. "There is no blame to you in this, no fault. All the blame lies at the feet of Randal and Bertram MacNab. They will pay for hurting you. That I do avow."

Isobel pulled her hand from his and covered her face. "I have failed you in the only way that matters." she grieved. "Leave me, please!"

He did not move. "Isobel, listen to me. We are engaged in a war, and in such, there are casualties. 'Tis a bitter thing to swallow, true. Yet, had one of my warriors fallen in a skirmish or, indeed, in attempting escape, I would not fault him but those whom I fight."

Isobel did not speak. Other memories now streamed in upon her, the way water gushes from a broken ewer: the dreadful room at MacNab's keep; the cruelty and anticipation in Bertram MacNab's eyes; the marks left by the deep bite of rope on the posts of the bed. She knew, now, exactly what had befallen the woman her husband loved. She would have to tell him. But not now. She could not bear it yet.

"Leave me," she begged again, unwilling to look into his eyes.

"Not until I know you are all right."

Isobel, convinced she would never again claim that state, turned her face away.

Just then she heard a rap at the door, followed by the voice of one of Dougal's warriors. "My Laird! The bastard MacNab waits below with your Lady Wife's father, asking to speak wi' you."

Isobel felt Dougal stiffen. Just as when they lay together in passion, it seemed she could sense the emotions moving through him—rage and now, strangely, regret.

"Do no' fear," he told her. "I will deal with him, and speak with your father as he deserves. Be well, Wife. I will return."

He removed himself from the room like a thundercloud rolling before a strong wind. Isobel felt relief, overwhelming sadness, and bone-deep exhaustion.

Meg came in, so quietly Isobel barely knew she was there, and interrupted the tears that had claimed her patient.

"There now," she said, never one for softness. "Did it go badly with my brother, then? He never blamed you for this?"

"He did not." Isobel wished only to go on weeping. "But I will need to tell him... He loves her still."

"Her?" Meg frowned.

"Aisla. I remember... I know, now, what she suffered while in MacNab's hands. He threatened to treat me the same. If I tell him, Dougal will never let go of his feelings for her."

"Do not think on it now. There will be time for talking when you have regained your strength. You need to sleep, and so heal."

"I am afraid to sleep, and dream."

Meg touched her brow. "You will not dream. I shall stay here with you, if you like."

"Thank you. You are good to me."

"Sleep, Isobel. The physician is on his way. When he comes, will you see him?"

"Can he tell me if I will conceive again?"

"No one can tell that."

"Then I do not want him. I want only you, Meg— no one but you."

"So be it," Meg said, and it sounded, to Isobel's ears, like a promise. "I will keep you safe."

Chapter Thirty

"What goes on between my wife and sister?" Dougal asked Lachlan, even though he doubted Lachy had a fit answer. "They formed some mysterious bond while Isobel was ill, and now they seem nearly as close as Meg and Aisla were. Meg fights for Isobel like a she-wolf defending her cubs. I cannot get near my own wife."

To Dougal, it seemed all he had done these many days past was fight. Aye, so, and he had no quarrel with that—the anger inside him desired expression with the sword or any other weapon that might come to hand.

Three weeks had passed since Isobel's miscarriage, since what Dougal thought of as his final declaration of war with MacNab. By any account, his wife should be regaining her strength and her health. Dougal had spent most of the intervening time out riding his borders in the blustery cold, stealing MacNab's cattle and setting fire to his outbuildings. He had also, in no uncertain terms, repulsed not one but three visits from Isobel's father, the first in Randal MacNab's company on the day after she miscarried.

"You allowed this to happen to her," he accused, staring Gerald Maitland in the eye. "As far as I am concerned, you are no longer Isobel's father, and I will die before I see her in your hands. As for you," to MacNab, himself, "the next time you darken my door—

you or that misshapen demon you call a son—I will see you dead!"

After that, Gerald Maitland came alone, to be turned away with alacrity. A period of filthy weather ensued, and Maitland did not show his face again. Dougal did not know, and little cared, if he remained at MacNab's keep or had returned home to Yorkshire.

What did worry him was his wife's state, both mental and physical. She languished in her room, took little to eat, and worst of all refused to see him.

"What has Meg told you?" he asked an uncharacteristically quiet Lachlan now. "I know you are sleeping with her—'tis the talk of the household."

"Is it?" Lachlan raised a brow, along with his cup of whisky. The hour being late, the two men shared spirits and a fire in an attempt to defrost their toes.

"Aye. In the kitchens, the maids whisper of little else. They all fancy you, it seems."

Lachlan smiled briefly. "The maids will have to languish in vain. I waited fifteen years to get into your sister's bed. If you think I mean to stray from her now, you are very much mistaken."

"Oh, aye?" Dougal's attention, very nearly snagged from his own grief, focused on his friend. "So, 'tis love, is it?"

"I thought you did not believe in love—or so you swear, over and over again. Call it enchantment, and have done."

"I am pleased for you." Dougal added in mock disgust, "But you may wish to keep a muzzle on your cries of joy—the two of you can be heard all over the keep."

"What can I say? Your sister is a magnificent

lover."

"Stop, else you will turn my stomach and ruin my sleep."

"You have not been sleeping anyway, from the look of you." Lachlan eyed him wisely. "You're spent."

"Aye." Dougal could not tell when he had felt so tired, weary to the bones. His worry for Isobel haunted him. She had sent away the physician, declined to leave her chamber, begged off seeing him. He felt as if he had lost her, though he could not express that even to Lachlan.

"My wife should be recovered by now."

"Meg says the loss of a child takes women in strange and various ways," Lachlan offered diffidently. "It follows no map, no set time."

"Aye, so. But why must she shut me out?" Broodingly, Dougal stared at the fire. "'Tis almost as if she dreads seeing me."

Lachlan shrugged. "Go to her while she sleeps, be there when she awakens."

"With my sister guarding her like a mastiff?"

Lachlan slanted a look at him. "I happen to know that in approximately one hour your sister will be well occupied elsewhere. She gives Isobel a sleeping draught—which, I understand, rarely works but does serve to calm her fears—and then retires to her own chamber to wait for me."

"Aye?" Isobel should have no fears needing calming, Dougal thought, not under his roof and his protection. Yet he had failed to protect her, had he not?

"Aye," said Lachlan decisively, and put aside his cup.

Some time later, Dougal climbed the stairs to his

236

wife's chamber, where he had not slept in many nights. The keep was very nearly silent, as if even the night held its breath. Outside, for once, the wind had stilled, and his warriors quietly stood their watch.

Reluctant to frighten Isobel, he eased the door open and slipped in. The room, lit only by a low fire, also lay in stillness. He heard Isobel sigh and shift in the bed even as he closed the door softly behind him.

What dreams possessed her rest, if rest she found? And why would she not turn to him for comfort?

Softly he moved across the room and called her name. "Isobel, 'tis I. Are you awake?"

She murmured something, and the bedclothes rustled. Disrobing as he went, he approached the bed, slipped in, and took her into his arms.

Instant warmth swamped him, and comfort such as he had not known in days. By the devil's horns, he had missed this—had not realized how much. Still not certain if she slept, he cradled her carefully, as one might a treasured child.

For a moment she stiffened, then eased against him, accepting what he offered. She wore only a thin night rail, and he could feel all of her, fragile and thin— she had wasted to almost nothing. He cared not for the changes—she was Isobel, with the same scent and spirit, all he desired.

"Sleep." He put his lips against her cheek, and her hair. "Let me hold you."

She murmured desperately, and he wondered what moved in her mind. He could virtually feel the shadows that enfolded her, yet she did not push him away. A miracle!

She lifted one hand and touched his face. "I cannot

sleep," she confessed. "Not since... I have but snatches of rest before I come awake again, and no peace."

"Perhaps I may bring you a measure of peace, Wife. Sleep."

To his surprise and relief, she cuddled in still closer against him but did not relax completely.

"I have something to tell you," she began, sounding tormented. "But I do not know how."

"Hush," he bade, with tenderness foreign to him, and stroked her hair. He knew only that he needed to be here with her, under any circumstances.

She ignored his directive. "I have been remembering things—they return to me whether I want them or not. It has all trickled back in bits and pieces. I now remember escaping from MacNab's keep. And I recall where, and how, I was held."

"Do not dwell upon it, Isobel. It is over now."

That made her stir in his arms, seeking to gaze into his face. "It will never be over, so long as you love her."

"Her?"

"Aisla."

Dougal felt himself tense at the sound of the name, as does a man receiving a grievous wound. "What has she to do with it?"

"I know what befell her, in MacNab's hands." Isobel barely breathed the words. "I was held, you see, in the same room as she. And Bertram MacNab threatened to do to me what he had done to her."

Dougal's throat closed abruptly. Part of him wished to hear what more Isobel had to say, wanted to gather every detail; most of him did not want to know. He managed to say, "Whatever befell her happened long ago."

"But," Isobel reasserted, "you love her still."

Dougal considered the words, as best he could. The tangle of emotions he felt for Aisla certainly could not be expressed in a single word, and he was no longer sure love was uppermost in the mix of guilt, anger, regret, and shame.

"She relied on me," he said with difficulty. "I failed her."

"How?" Isobel moved restlessly in the bed, escaping his arms.

"I did not give her the one thing she so desperately needed," Dougal admitted wretchedly.

"As I have failed to give you a child?"

"It is no' the same, no' at all!" Dougal sat up so quickly he knocked her back onto the pillow. "You could not help what befell you. I failed! Sometimes of a night I lie thinking how it must have been for her, waiting and waiting for me to come, believing I would—for I had pledged myself to her. That is the thing you do no' understand."

"I do," Isobel whispered. "We all make promises."

"And now you say you saw the very room where she endured her nightmare? Tell me!"

"Perhaps it is best if I do not. Nothing can now be gained—"

"Nothing but that I may flagellate myself as I deserve. Tell me, Wife—what tortures befell the woman I had vowed to protect?"

He heard Isobel draw a breath, like a woman backing away from a cliff edge. She glimpsed, now, the hell in which he lived day after day, night after night.

At last she said, "Upon consideration, I think such

things should not be spoken, even here. Bertram MacNab is a depraved monster who needs to be destroyed, for the good of the world. For all I have suffered, I am yet glad I was able to keep my sister from his hands. And I am grateful, Husband, you snatched me on the road that night."

Still upright in the bed, gazing down at her, Dougal said bitterly, "Would you rather be tied to a man who cannot keep his promises? Who does not deserve love?"

"Far rather." To his surprise, she reached for him, pulled him into her arms to lie against her. "You know, Husband, there is such a thing as forgiveness—even forgiveness of self."

"I will never forgive myself," Dougal said, and knew the words for truth. "And I know better, now, than to make pledges I cannot keep. I could not even hold you safe in your own garden. There is naught I would like more than to vow MacNab's destruction for your sake—and hers. But I know better, now. I know myself, and him. MacNab does no' play fair."

"No."

Dougal laughed harshly. "Aye, well, during the intervening years I, too, have learned the value of cheating. I can now lie, steal, and deceive wi' the best of them. For honor gets a man nowhere, and the devil laughs at good intentions."

"Is that what you have striven to do these many years—make yourself more despicable than MacNab? Is that why they call you Devil Black MacRae?"

"I ha' learned to fight on my enemy's terms, and MacNab knows naught of mercy—why should he?" He thought hard on it and added, "The difference between us is, MacNab hides his black heart behind a smiling and compliant face. I, being an honest man, flaunt mine."

At least, he thought, even in the face of cowardice he could claim honesty. And that honesty kept him silent about what he felt for Isobel now—possessiveness, caring, and a surprising amount of tenderness—because the word she wanted from him he could not, in conscience, give.

"Why can you not forgive yourself?" Isobel asked. "You have forgiven me. Would you forgive Lachlan, if he failed you in some way?"

"Ah, Lachlan!" Dougal laughed more naturally. "He is another thing altogether. By the way, did you know you were right? He is sleeping in my sister's bed."

"Yes, and she is quite content with it. I think she will take from him what she needs, and give what she can." Isobel hesitated. "Not an ideal situation, perhaps, but one that serves them both."

Dougal grimaced in the darkness. "Meg, you are thinking, is as damaged as I. And are you, too, willing to accept broken and unsatisfactory offerings?"

"Broken, maybe," she whispered, "but never, never unsatisfactory."

Chapter Thirty-One

"It is unsatisfactory!" Dougal declared viciously. "I will not rest until I have brought that bastard to his knees. I do not care what it takes."

Meg looked at her brother impatiently and then, once more, at the letter in her hands. It had arrived by courier from a woman she knew in Stirling, named Elizabeth Carstairs, whose husband held a place close to the King. Elizabeth had written not out of any sense of finer feeling but from spite, to inform Meg the King had Dougal MacRae in his sights.

"Do you not hear what I say?" she asked. "MacNab has once more complained to the King about you, and it seems this time the King means to act. He is due to arrive in Stirling within the fortnight and means to summon you thence."

Dougal remained unmoved by the news. "MacNab needs settling," he reiterated. "I will declare as much to the King or anyone else."

A week had passed since the night Isobel took him back into her bed, which seemed to prove a turning point of sorts. Isobel's health at last improved; Meg told him she now took her meals without protest and last night—miracle of miracles—his wife had allowed him to make love to her. It had been gentle, careful, nothing like their old couplings, yet it had shaken him to the core. His foolish heart had begun to hope they might build a future together after all, and now came this accursed missive, once more promising MacNab the upper hand. It enraged him.

Still perusing the letter, Meg went on, "MacNab tells the King you steal his cattle, torch his outbuildings and withhold from him his son's betrothed."

"She is my wife! Did not the King, himself, command me to marry?"

Meg grimaced. "What shall you do?"

Dougal considered it, scowling. "I shall tell the King, and fairly, there is no proof I have stolen MacNab's cattle—"

"They roam your hills."

"Strayed there. Is it my fault MacNab proves a careless landsman? Nor can he prove who burnt down his outbuildings and slaughtered the guards he posted. It might have been anyone. I assure you, Sister, we have been careful with our back trail."

Meg did not look content.

"As for Isobel's abduction... I would like the King to learn what goes on in MacNab's keep. Perhaps 'tis time justice was sued."

"You will not ask Isobel to go to Stirling! I doubt she would stand it."

"Surely I can speak on my wife's behalf."

"And if her father also appears before the King and tells a different story?"

That, Dougal had to admit, would not be to his advantage. Yet he would die before he allowed Isobel to be harmed again. "We must determine whether Maitland has returned to Yorkshire."

The door to the great hall where they stood flew open, and one of Dougal's guards thrust his head inside.

"Riders, Laird. Two of them—escorted by our own outriders."

Dougal's heart clenched. What now? "Can you tell who they are?"

"Laird, 'tis snowing too hard to tell."

Dougal followed the man to the forecourt just in time to see that, indeed, two riders—well-wrapped against the cold—approached along with a band of his own men, through snow blowing almost horizontally. One of his warriors broke away and came forward at a trot.

"Laird MacRae, the lady there says she is sister to your lady wife—one Catherine Hewett by name—and she requests shelter."

Dougal blinked in astonishment. "By all means, Rab, show them in."

****

Isobel sat combing out her hair beside the fire when the message came. She still felt weak most days and unwilling to venture out of her chamber, but when a breathless Meg delivered the news, she abandoned her comb and ran, quite fleetly indeed.

"Catherine? Here?" she asked Meg in disbelief. "Are you certain?"

"Aye, so she says. And she looks enough like you to be your twin."

Thus prepared, Isobel burst into the hall to find an impossible sight: Catherine, as out of place as a delicate flower in a byre, looking tired and worn, and beside her the tall figure of Thomas, with whom she had eloped nearly two months ago.

Catherine turned toward her, and Isobel saw she was no longer so slim as before. Her pregnancy now

244

showed clearly, and lines of strain marked her pretty face.

They flew into one another's arms. At the feel of her sister against her heart, Isobel's tears rose in a storm. She clutched Catherine tightly and said in a choked voice, "Oh, God, I thought I would never see you again! But, how come you here? How did you find me?"

"The worst of ways!" Catherine released Isobel and looked into her face. "We have had a terrible time of it, Thomas and I, since we left home—naught but struggle, hard travel, and disappointment. In desperation, I thought to come to you at MacNab's—"

Isobel gasped. "You never went there?"

"No." Catherine shook her head, looked helplessly at her husband who stood silent, and then, in wonder, at Dougal. "These men stopped us on the road—they seemed to recognize me. They questioned us and said you lived here. I did not know what to think, but they proved insistent, so we came with them."

"Thank heaven," Isobel breathed. She turned to the guards, with Rab at their head. "I am grateful to you all."

"We are after stopping everyone, Lady," Rab told her, "since your father's arrival."

Catherine looked confused. "Father? But he is not here—he is at home. We went there first. He flew into a rage at the sight of us, and sent us off again." Her face crumpled. "And we have nowhere in the world to go."

Isobel looked a question at Dougal, beseeching. "This man, Dougal MacRae, is my husband. He will stand you shelter, Sister."

And Dougal replied without hesitation, "To be

sure. Consider this your home for so long as you need."

Some time later the four of them—Meg and Lachlan having tactfully excused themselves—sat by the fire in the solar, the two sisters with linked hands, words flying between them. Dougal had said little beyond telling Rab and his men they had done well, and so far Thomas had barely spoken. But he held his hands out to the warmth of the fire like a man frozen to the bone, and his face appeared so drawn and grim, he barely looked like the handsome lad with whom Catherine had fallen in love.

"Explain how you came here," Catherine begged her sister, with a doubtful look at Dougal. "When we parted, the plan was for you to take my place in wedding with Bertram MacNab."

"Yes, well," Isobel cast her eyes down, "that plan changed. MacNab, as it proved, is not the man Father thought him. Rather, he is a villain and a brute, virtually at war with my husband. Dougal...intercepted me on the road to MacNab's keep and most fortuitously redirected me here."

Catherine cast a doubtful look at Dougal, who sat watchful, his grey eyes hooded. "Intercepted?"

"You need not put too fine a point on it, Wife," Dougal said. "Lady Catherine, I abducted her on the road—took her by force."

Thomas came to his feet. "That is an abomination! A crime!"

Dougal barely stirred in response. "To be sure, it is. But this is not Yorkshire. Do not be a fool, man. Sit down."

Thomas's fair skin flushed. For a moment it appeared he might quarrel further. Then the fight went out of him. "The world," he stated, "is a mad place. I cannot account for it."

"Well said." Dougal reached to pour more whisky into Thomas's cup. "Never mind. This will warm you."

Isobel, watching the emotions travel across her sister's face, asked, "What of you? You were set for Bristol, and Thomas's new employment. How come you here?"

"The place I was promised fell through," Thomas admitted gloomily. "When he heard our tale, my father's cousin, who originally offered the situation, decided he would not risk offending your father by taking me on, since my own father yet hoped to win back his old place as Bailiff. And other places proved deuced hard to find."

"We have been roaming and traveling," Catherine confessed, "sometimes sleeping rough, once in a ditch. When we were robbed of what little money we had, we knew we must turn for home and face Father's anger. I never dreamed he should turn us away after coming so far through that vile weather."

Isobel looked at Thomas. "Could you not apply to your father?"

"I could, but your father has dismissed him for my role in stealing Catherine away. Father has not yet managed to win back his place on your father's estate, and will not if he is found helping me."

"So unfair!" Tears flooded Catherine's eyes. "What did we do that was so wrong, except love?"

"I am sorry," Isobel murmured, heartfelt. She could scarcely believe the plans she and Catherine had hatched together so innocently had caused such devastation.

"Your father is a bailiff?" Dougal asked Thomas. "And, what work can you do?"

Thomas shrugged. "I was promised a place in Bristol as a clerk. I and my two older brothers were taught to read and write, but Father also brought us up learning to run the estate."

"Fine, that, and I can use you. It is as my wife says, however. We are at war with a neighbor. MacNab is a treacherous bastard who has captured the ear of the King and speaks poison of me. I should like naught better than to see both Randal and Bertram MacNab dead. I mean to achieve it if I can. I am known in the district as the Devil Black MacRae." He paused to drink from his cup. "If any of that daunts you, then, aye, you had better take a day's rest and be on your way. For things here are ugly now, and bound to grow still uglier."

Thomas's face, usually so open and sunny, looked guarded. The bailiff's lad, Isobel thought, had changed; a man appeared to have emerged in his stead. He said, "I shall be glad of the place. And I shall fight whomever necessary to keep my wife safe."

Dougal did not smile, but he did extend a hand. "Then, man, we are of exactly one mind."

Later, in the privacy of Isobel's bedchamber, the two sisters exchanged whispers and further confidences. Isobel knew Dougal was out riding his borders. She had no idea where Thomas might be—perhaps finding remedy for his exhaustion in sleep. She knew her own healing, as so often in the past, lay in confessing her thoughts to her sister and trading accounts of hardships. Sleepless, they spoke long into the night, and Isobel was hard put to tell which of them had the harsher tale. Catherine clung to Isobel and wept over the account of her sister's miscarriage, and shuddered at her depictions of Bertram MacNab.

"To think what I so narrowly escaped! And, you, also! But, your husband—is he in grave trouble over this business with the King?"

"I hope not. Losing his lands would kill him. And should I lose him," Isobel added simply, "it will kill me."

"You love him!" Catherine spoke in wonder. "Yet he is nothing like the lads of whom we dreamed as girls."

"What did I know then?"

"There seems a darkness in him," Catherine proposed, "a ruthlessness."

Isobel conceded, "They do not call him Devil Black for naught. Yet he has claimed my heart." The next words came harder. "My sorrow lies in the fact that he can never love me. His heart will always belong to another." She told Catherine briefly, in a whisper, of the woman who had died in MacNab's hands, and the grief that yet rode Dougal MacRae.

"It is a grief that time has not put right," she concluded. "I cannot put it right, either. I fear nothing can."

"Except your love for him," said Catherine, almost with her old innocence. "I know love can overcome anything. You must believe!"

"I wish I could," Isobel said sadly. "My heart is not the hopeful thing it was, when we were girls. But oh, Catherine, I never dreamed it could love so strong. If I follow it, I will follow him anywhere—through any difficulty, storm or fire—if only he will let me."

Chapter Thirty-Two

"You must allow me to accompany you," Isobel beseeched her husband, not for the first time. "As your wife, it is my right to be there and speak on your behalf. It may make a difference. I have much to say to the King, and you shall not face him alone."

And, Isobel thought to herself, she refused to watch Dougal ride from her, not knowing if she would ever see him again. The summons from the King had come three days ago, and since then she had been sick over it, and desperate to persuade Dougal round to her thinking.

She could beg the King for her husband's life if necessary, and promise anything in return for mercy. But Dougal shook his head, a closed look coming to his face—just like every other time she asked him.

"Stay here," he bade, "where you are safe."

"What good is my safety, if I lose you?" They stood in the bedchamber they now once more shared. "If you do not return to me?" Isobel felt perilously close to tears—they threatened to blind and choke her. "I could not bear it!"

Dougal caught her shoulders between his hands and stared into her eyes, and she found herself unable to hide anything from him. All her love and longing must be visible, for he lowered his voice and his tone became unusually gentle.

"Do not worry, Wife, I will return. Do I not take

your brother-in-law, the erstwhile Thomas, with me to speak as to the situation, and MacNab's part in it? The King shall hear how events transpired, and that MacNab is not blameless."

"Oh, Thomas!" Isobel exclaimed with some disparagement. She found herself unimpressed with Catherine's husband, who now seemed almost staid and lacking in fire. "Why should the King listen to him?"

"He can give the truth of it, how Bertram MacNab's betrothed was actually the woman who became his wife, not mine, and how the switch came about."

"And I can tell the King the truth about MacNab— how he abducted me from my own garden—"

"As I abducted you on the road?"

"—and what he meant to do to me, had I not escaped."

"Wife, I ken fine you are afraid—"

"You know nothing of it. Can you imagine how it will be for me waiting, not knowing how you fare? Surely I will be safer, even traveling, in your company."

Some emotion moved in the stormy grey eyes: caution, perhaps. "Nay, but I would not have you possibly return from Stirling alone—"

"Alone?"

"Should I be taken into custody."

Isobel's heart dropped sickeningly. "You say that will not happen."

His lips tightened in an ironic smile. "It should not. Still, if happen it did, you would be vulnerable."

"I would be with the erstwhile Thomas, would I not?"

That made Dougal grimace. "Stay here under guard, please, with your sister and Meg. Do this for me."

Since he asked it so, Isobel could not refuse—she would deny him nothing. But her head came up and she met his eyes in challenge. "I will, Husband, but only if you will do something for me in return, before you go." At the question in his eyes, she began to unfasten his tunic, and tug free the shirt beneath. "Lie with me now. If I am to be left without you, I would at least have your child."

The mist in his eyes ignited and transformed into fire. He would not deny her this, Isobel thought, and she would savor every kiss, every touch. For this memory might have to last her a lifetime.

****

"For the love of all that is holy, will you not sit down?" Meg begged impatiently. "You have been pacing for hours; you will drive me round the twist."

The three women shared the solar, on a day turned vicious and cold. Outside, the wind once more tore at the stones of the keep, shrieking like a woman in mourning.

The fire in the hearth barely succeeded in fighting back the pervasive chill, which seemed to have penetrated clear to Isobel's heart.

"I cannot help it," she said. "I am unable to settle. They will be in Stirling by now, yes? Do you think he has seen the King?"

Meg shrugged. "The King is capricious and lives by his own rules. He may not have arrived as expected. The weather may have kept him."

"I will go mad with not knowing!"

252

"And you will drag us with you." Meg sounded truly exasperated. She shot a look at Catherine. "Can you not reason with your sister?"

Somewhat to Isobel's surprise, her sister and sister-in-law got on amazingly well. At the moment, they definitely stood united.

"Sit down, pray, Isobel," Catherine bade. "Give us all some rest." In an aside to Meg, she went on, "Isobel has always been headstrong which, indeed, began all this trouble."

"Me? And I suppose you have naught to do with it? No matter," Isobel exclaimed bitterly, "recount my past sins if you will. I care for but one thing."

"You should care for your own well-being," Meg said. "Lachlan tells me MacNab has sent out raiding parties these two nights past—when Lachy and our warriors rode out, they saw the tracks in the snow."

"I am concerned with my own safety." Isobel knew full well MacNab wished to get his hands on her again, his sole purpose, now, revenge. MacNab could have no way of knowing Catherine—Bertram's true intended—was now here at MacRae's keep, nor that she had also become another man's wife. He wanted to cause pain, distress, and fear.

"Then behave accordingly," Catherine said. "Sit down and sew."

"I cannot possibly!" But Isobel did pause in her pacing to eye Catherine's needlework. She labored at embroidering a tiny white gown for her baby, a lovely thing that evoked pleasant images. Fleetingly, Isobel wondered if her seduction of her husband, the morning he left for Stirling, had good effect. He had certainly been thorough in his pursuit of the task...

"Since when do you sew?" she demanded of Catherine.

"Motherhood requires patience," Catherine told her implacably, placing one hand on her expanded belly. "As you may one day learn."

Isobel, spared from answering that ridiculous statement, swung round as the chamber door opened and Lachlan came in. She did not miss the way Meg's face lit at the sight of him.

Lachlan, clad for the outdoors and wearing his sword, looked unusually grim. He beckoned to Meg, who rose and went to him. They held a whispered conversation.

"It is rude, that," Isobel protested, "keeping secrets in front of others."

The couple parted and looked at her. Lachlan spoke, "I am saying only that I will be out riding with a troop of men. I have doubled the guard—"

"Why?" Isobel demanded. "Because you saw tracks in the snow?"

Lachlan exchanged looks with Meg, who shrugged.

"Aye," Lachlan spoke directly to Isobel. "I swore to Dougal I would keep you safe while he was away. I would sooner perish than fail in that."

"You believe we are in danger?"

Lachlan scowled. "I do. The weather is vile, and I am thinking raiders from MacNab's keep could use that as cover for creeping in close. I mean to ride the borders, even if I freeze myself through."

"Dougal has a good friend in you," Isobel told him.

Lachlan's eyes once more flew to Meg. "Aye, so, but do not forget I have a treasure of my own here to guard."

He went out and a brief silence ensued. Then Isobel observed, "He is in love with you, Meg."

"Foolish man!" Once more Meg sounded exasperated.

"How do you feel for him?" Both Isobel and Catherine stared at their companion, awaiting her answer.

"I swore off love long ago," Meg replied acerbically, "if that is what you ask."

"Just like your brother," Catherine observed comfortably. "But the head cannot always command the heart, and yon Lachlan is a charming bugger. How do you truly feel?"

For an instant it seemed Meg would not answer, then a spark of mischief entered her dark eyes, and her lips curved in a smile. "I have to admit, I will not be glad to see the back of him any time soon. As you say, he is charming as a hound pup, or a child—but he loves like a man. I vowed, after murdering my last husband, I would never take up with another, yet I now find myself content."

Catherine lowered her sewing and stared. "You murdered your last husband?"

"Do not fash yourself. He deserved it," Meg said breezily.

"And Lachlan knows of this?"

Meg smiled. "I told you he is a fool."

For Isobel, the day dragged on. She paced the solar and, when her companions continued to complain, the hallways, where drafts of cold air made her shiver. She was one of the first to hear the pounding at the front door.

Could it be Dougal, returned? But no—surely not

so soon.

Two of the household guards, one the estimable Rab, ran to the door, Rab with his sword drawn. But when the door was drawn open, Isobel saw her husband's own warriors in a cluster and bearing a rough litter constructed of cloaks and pine poles.

The men spoke together, quick and fierce, their accents blurring the words. Isobel ran forward to see a man on the litter, covered in blood—Lachlan. He looked dead.

She gasped, and Rab roughly pushed her out of the way. "Lady, let us get him in!"

"What happened?" Isobel asked. "Does he yet live?"

One of the men bearing the litter answered her, though she caught perhaps one word in ten. They had come under attack by a large number of MacNab's warriors under the leadership of Bertram MacNab. Lachlan had fought valiantly, as had they all, but once he fell it became a battle on the part of the others to get him away.

"They came like an army," the man told Rab. "They mean to attack while the Devil is awa'."

Isobel's heart clenched in her chest, but she had eyes only for Lachlan.

She lifted her voice and called, "Meg! Meg, come quickly!"

The two women ran from the solar into the ghastly scene. Isobel watched the color drain from Meg's face.

Meg wasted no time with questions and instead gestured to the men. "Bring him into the solar, where 'tis warm. Carefully, now!"

"How sore hurt is he?" Isobel asked her sister-in-law. "Can you save him?"

Meg shook her head. "Who can say? There is healing in these hands, as well as harm. I cannot tell if 'twill be enough."

The men bore Lachlan off, and Isobel turned to Rab. "If MacNab attacks the keep, it will hold, yes? Can he breach the defenses?"

Rab shrugged and his gaze turned uneasy. "We will fight to the man to protect you, Lady—and die if need be." He grimaced. "Better death by the sword, I am thinking, than to face the ire of the Devil Black."

Chapter Thirty-Three

"So, that is the King of all England and Scotland," Thomas said wonderingly, and not for the first time. "He was in a right foul mood for himself, was he not?"

"As vile as this weather," Dougal replied. The two men, with their escort of warriors, traveled home following an audience with the King during which Dougal had his knuckles slapped quite sharply. He knew he should be grateful—he might have received far more than chastisement. And he was aware much of the credit for it might be laid at the feet of the man who rode beside him.

Thomas had proved quite forthright and eloquent in his explanations and defense of Dougal, managing to convince James that Dougal had not, in fact, abducted Bertram MacNab's betrothed since she had never traveled north from Yorkshire and had, at the time, been wed to Thomas himself.

The King, with a written complaint from Gerald Maitland in his hands—Isobel's father had not been present—listened and lost a shade of his bad humor.

"All for the sake of love, was it?" he asked. "Who can fault that? It does not mean, Master MacRae, you can go about snatching women from carriages."

"I rescued her from the wreck of a carriage, your highness."

James did not swallow it. "You, sir, have a

reputation that precedes you. Your neighbors complain ceaselessly of your activities. We tire of listening."

"I assure you, Sire, I am mending my ways and have wed just as you, yourself, instructed. I hope for a family soon and mean to devote myself to tending my children and my lands."

James grunted, "Do not let us see you here on any future complaint, or it will go badly for you. You have been warned. Now, waste no more of our time."

Recalling it now, Dougal narrowed his eyes. "Aye, Thomas—that is the very man who wields the power of life or death over us. This time, thanks to you, he proved lenient. You have a place wi' me so long as you need it."

"Thank you, MacRae. I promise to serve you as bailiff, faithfully." Thomas gave Dougal a quick smile. "And perhaps I can help you keep your nose clean, eh?"

Not while either Randal or Bertram MacNab draws breath, Dougal thought bitterly. Oh, aye, he would act the part of the responsible landowner to the best of his ability, if only for Isobel's sake. But there were still a number of scores to be settled, and the anger inside him would find no rest until it knew revenge.

Right now, however, he just wanted to get home, to reach journey's end and be with his wife. It astonished him how much he longed for that moment and how he ached to see Isobel, hold her, crawl into bed and avail himself of her warmth.

That desire sustained him through the many miles from Stirling, through cruel wind and driving sleet. Weary, he and his party reached their own lands just at nightfall, and Dougal knew from crossing his borders that something was amiss. Instinct told him so, a kind of sixth sense acclimated to the land, as well as the absence of the guard.

He called to his warriors at his back, "Something is very much wrong!" And they pushed their tired mounts hard through the gathering dark.

For all that, when Dougal beheld his own gates he stared in disbelief. They lay in ruins, charred and broken, and beyond them the forecourt of the keep lay in darkness, a yawning black hole.

His heart began to pound as if it would force its way out of his chest. He dismounted just inside the forecourt and began to bellow, "Rab! Lachlan! Here, to me!"

Silence met his ears, but for the sharp wind whistling round the stones. He heard his men mutter to one another and dismount behind him. He stared, transfixed, at his front door.

Battered, broken like the gates, one of the stout panels had fallen, charred, and there on the threshold he saw the stain of blood.

He hollered wordlessly and pushed his way inside, his head feeling as if it would burst. And there, coming to meet him, Meg…

They met in the center of the entry hall, and Dougal wondered at his sister's appearance—hair loose and flying, face pale—she looked as if all the fire had been taken from her and only sorrow and resignation remained.

"What has happened here?" The words tumbled from him. "When—?"

"We fell under attack yesterday. He came with a small army and a ram, fire—I placed a spell of protection round the place and your men fought like badgers, but we could not hold."

"He?"

"Need you ask?" Meg's eyes looked dull, flat like black stones. "Bertram MacNab. They call you the Devil, Brother, but he has earned the name."

Dougal's party entered behind him. He felt them gather, stricken, at his back. He swallowed and asked what he must. "My wife?"

"Taken, along with her sister."

Thomas groaned. "But my wife is with child—"

Meg shot him a hard look. "Then pray for her, if you believe in anything."

Dougal's tongue tripped on. "Rab? Lachlan?"

For the first time emotion showed in Meg's eyes. "Rab is dead, as are most your guard. He fought valiantly and, for a time, held his ground as an army might. They burned him and still he fought. The MacRae blood ran strong in him!"

Dougal felt the color drain from his face. "And Lachlan?"

"He lies dying." Meg's expression betrayed none of her agony, but it filled her voice. "Everyone left alive here, save two maids and myself, is injured unto death. They would not take me, for they feared my magic. Yet it was no' strong enough to save anyone."

Isobel. Lachlan. Dougal's mind stuttered over their names, painful as a raw nerve. He knew, then, the complaint to the King has been a ruse, yet another distraction to remove him from the place so the attack could be carried out. MacNab had taken everything he cared for—once again—and left him nothing with which to fight.

"My wife," said Thomas, and touched Dougal's

arm. "Somehow, we must get them back—"

"How?" Dougal asked, looking into the man's eyes which burned with cold fury. "He has slaughtered my warriors, all but these who ride with me."

Thomas said, "We will return to the King, ask him for justice. It will surely be forthcoming—"

Dougal laughed harshly. "Aye? When? Our women are in that bastard's hands and, I assure you, one day is too many. You know not what he is." And I understand him, Dougal thought. I never should have left Isobel here, should have taken her with me as she begged.

"We must do something!" Thomas protested, heated now. "My wife—"

"And mine." Dougal turned to Meg. "Lachlan. Take me to him. The rest of you, check our defenses, what is left of them."

Lachlan lay in the solar on a makeshift bed constructed of bloodied cloaks. Meg began to speak as she led Dougal in, as if the words were compelled from her.

"He was very brave. You know, for years I thought him naught but a pretty boy, but he has proved me wrong—aye, proved me wrong! They injured him in an attack the day before yesterday when he was out with the guard. Our warriors managed to bring him home. He was so sore hurt—yet when MacNab brought the attack here yesterday at dawn, he got up somehow and fought. He fought!"

The solar, usually the most charming room in the keep, lay in disarray and smelled of blood and sickness. Casting one cursory look about, Dougal saw at least some of the battle had taken place here.

He went forward and knelt at Lachlan's side, the

sword he wore clanking. "Lachy?" To his dismay, his voice broke. A shocking thing, since he supposed he had conquered all emotion years ago.

Lachlan's eyelids fluttered, but he did not otherwise respond.

Meg sank to her knees beside Lachlan and touched his brow. "I worked over him all night after they brought him in—he and a troop of warriors had been riding the borders when they encountered MacNab attempting to steal back his own cattle. There was a sharp, short battle, the men said. I thought I should lose Lachy. I poured all my magic into him. I have little left, now."

Dougal asked, his voice hoarse, "Tell me what transpired when MacNab attacked yesterday."

Meg shuddered. "We three women were together here in this room, I keeping watch over Lachlan. Rab, who had gone out on patrol, returned soon after dawn. I think he had an instinct and wanted to be here defending the gates."

"The best warriors are all about instinct," Dougal said, grief gripping his heart.

"Our men reached the forecourt just before Bertram MacNab and his men attacked. Many of our warriors fell at the outer gates—dragging our dead, they withdrew to the doors of the keep and fought on. When the doors broke, and Rab fell, that is when Lachy pulled himself up. He stood in that doorway and held off MacNab's men as long as he could. When they at last took him down, I believed him dead."

She paused and sucked in a breath. "It felt like my heart tore from my chest. I did not want to love him! I swore I would never again be so weak."

To Dougal's horror, she began to weep broken, ragged sobs into her hands. Dougal experienced one moment's pure identification with his sister: he knew in full her pain, her dismay, her belief that she had protected herself. He too had grown a shell woven of darkness and hurt, fancying himself untouchable.

Isobel…

Yet, he did not love his wife… He feared for her, aye, he desired her, he longed to protect her. But unlike Meg, he was incapable of love.

And he had little comfort for his sister, now. He did not attempt to take her into his arms. Instead he looked at his friend—his one friend in the world.

"What are his injuries? His arm, you say?"

"The original wound was a grievous blow to his chest. His right arm is cut to the bone in two places—I do not know how he held a sword. So many other wounds, I lost count of them." Meg flipped back the cloak that covered Lachlan. Beneath it he lay naked, a maze of slashes and contusions.

Dougal winced and raised one hand to the deep scar on his own cheek.

"He may lose the arm," Meg went on, "if he lives. I have done all I can, all I know. The fever may defeat me."

"Never say that," Dougal whispered. "He is strong." And, what would life be without Lachlan at his side, rueful and light of spirit, his humor always matching Dougal's own and game for any endeavor? "His own courage will save him."

Meg turned her head and looked her brother full in the eyes. "I only wish you had possessed such courage when Aisla needed you. It might have prevented all this."

Dougal did not duck the accusation in her eyes. "Do you not think I have blamed myself a thousand times?"

Her lips twisted. "Much good that does us now. Much help to Isobel and Catherine—you know what MacNab will do to them."

"You think I will not fight to rescue Isobel?"

"Will you? As you fought for Aisla?"

Aye, Dougal thought desperately, passionately, though no word passed his lips. I did the best I could. I failed—I was little more than a lad, and I failed. It shall not end so, this time.

"Tell me how they left Lachy alive," he begged.

"They thought him dead, as did I. MacNab took the women and would have taken me, also, but I threatened him with a curse. I stood over Lachy's body—I stood, Brother, and defied them. A lesson you might well learn."

Dougal nodded, again not dodging the missile of her hate.

"What will you do?" Meg challenged with a sneer.

"Give MacNab what he wants—what he has always wanted."

Meg lifted a brow. "And, what is that?"

"Me," Dougal replied. "I mean to place myself squarely in his hands."

## Chapter Thirty-Four

"Courage, Catherine," Isobel said to her sister with assurance she did not truly feel. "You must be brave for the sake of your child, if for no other reason."

Catherine made no reply. She had been ill, shivering and vomiting, since they arrived at MacNab's keep, and that worried Isobel sorely. Truly, Isobel fretted for the babe her sister carried, more than for her own safety.

At least they were together, she thought now, and at least Bertram MacNab had not put them in the vile chamber where Isobel had last been held—that where Aisla had been imprisoned and had doubtless died. The bedposts in this bedchamber held no scars, and Isobel would take reassurance wherever she could find it.

She stroked her sister's hair, a gesture she had often employed since their mother's death. Back then, Catherine had clung to her and wept. As the elder, Isobel strove to hide her own grief, even as she hid her terror now.

"Only think on our Viking ancestors," she said, "or, indeed, the Scottish ones. Would those brave women weep and moan?"

"I am not weeping," Catherine protested, sounding more herself. "I am trying very hard not to be sick. What do you think they will do with us?"

Isobel dared not answer that truthfully. Her first

visit had acquainted her all too well with Bertram MacNab's depravities. She could only hope to direct his attentions to herself, and so spare Catherine.

"Thomas will come for me," Catherine said when Isobel did not answer, holding fiercely to the belief.

Would he? What would Dougal do when he returned home from Stirling—if he returned home—to find his wife gone? Isobel thought back to the scene at MacRae's keep when she and Catherine had been dragged away. So many of Dougal's warriors dead—even poor Lachlan. She remembered Meg standing over her lover's corpse, fierce and defiant. Could she even imagine Dougal feeling that way toward her?

And Thomas, she thought, though she did not say, possessed no means to rescue his wife, just as Dougal now possessed no might. Means and might—were both not vital to the kind of battle that would be required?

She whispered, almost to herself, "Thomas and Dougal are away with the King."

"They will return, and soon."

Catherine's assertion made Isobel's stomach turn over. She knew Dougal might not return. The King might, rather, decide to punish him for past crimes, and even to sentence him to death. If so, did that mean her future lay here, a grim span of days filled with grief for him, pain and endurance? Could she even live without the man she loved? She might well survive, but it would not be living.

"Thomas will come." Catherine repeated it like a prayer. "He will come for me and his child."

Thomas, a bailiff's son, not even a bailiff in his own right… He might well throw himself against the stones of Randal MacNab's stronghold. He might also die there.

Isobel knew their only hope was Dougal MacRae, her husband, the man she would follow anywhere—the man who loved her not.

He had loved Aisla and loved her still, but he had let Aisla die here, in the precise place where Isobel now stood.

"What—?" Catherine began, only to be interrupted by a commotion at the chamber door: harsh voices, an exchange with the guard posted outside, and then the scrape of the bar lifting.

Isobel, never very devout, began to pray. *Please, not Bertram, anyone but Bertram. Please!*

The door swung open, revealing not Bertram MacNab but his father, Randal. Isobel had no way to know which way Randal's depravities might lie—to cruelty, surely, and the ruthless use of power. But would he carry out the threats his son had made?

Somehow, Isobel got to her feet, her arm curled protectively around her sister's shoulders.

"Sir," she began before Randal MacNab could speak, "this is an outrage! My sister is ill, and as you can see, she is with child. I demand you release her at once."

"You demand, do you?" Randal's mud-colored eyes, so like his son's, inspected the two of them with disparagement. "And, wench, why should I do that? My good friend your father asked us to recover his daughter. Shall he not be doubly pleased with both?"

A spark of hope lit Isobel's heart. "Is my father here? Or on his way?"

"No." MacNab smiled grimly. "But I am empowered to act as his agent in this matter."

Isobel thought swiftly. "Fine. Well, send Catherine home to him."

"Send the both of us," Catherine said.

Randal shook his head. "And then what would I have with which to bargain? Mistress MacRae, I have a score to settle with your husband."

"What score?"

MacNab tossed his head. "A thousand injuries, over any number of generations. Blood for blood—'tis how we do it here. Or, coin for coin."

"Coin?" Isobel repeated, foundering.

"I mean to ransom you," Randal said, "and the price will be high."

Isobel drew a breath. "Ransom me, if you will. Let my sister go. She means nothing to Dougal." *And I, too, mean little enough to him. Yet, it matters not what happens to me—I will pay any price for Catherine's sake.*

"I shall think on that," Randal said, and Isobel knew he lied. She had just shown him her weakness and he would use it against her any way he could.

"When your husband arrives," he went on, "I shall permit you to observe the negotiations."

Again, Isobel's heart clenched. "He has journeyed to see the King."

"Aye, and he has returned again, curse his black heart! Och, well, if James is too lily-livered to do the job for me, I shall take care of it myself." He waved a hand at the room. "Meanwhile, enjoy your accommodations. As you see, there are no windows through which you might climb." He bared his teeth. "In fact, there is no way out at all."

He went out, and Isobel heard the bar slam down

across the door, outside.

Catherine began, "Well, if he means to ransom us—"

"He does not," Isobel said with certainty, "at least, not at once. He will inflict hurt any way he can."

Catherine stared at her. "But he said—"

"Trust no lie coming from that monster's mouth. What he says matters not at all."

Isobel paced the chamber for what felt like hours. Catherine, exhausted, dozed fitfully. The room, cold and bleak, offered no way to tell day from night, but Isobel counted the moments and Bertram did not come to tie her or Catherine to the bed and unleash his vile appetites. She tried to be grateful for that.

Weariness nibbled at her before she once more heard someone at the door. Her heart dropped, and Catherine, who had at last slept soundly, lifted her head.

"What is it?"

Isobel shook her head and curled her fingers into fists as the door opened. She would fight as hard as she could, and for as long as she could.

Bertram MacNab stood in the doorway, a leer on his face and two guards at his back. Hate seared through Isobel, so fierce it made her lightheaded. She moved and put herself between Catherine and the monster. *You shall not touch her.*

Bertram gestured at her. "We need one of you. You choose."

Catherine scrambled to her feet to stand beside Isobel. Isobel felt her sister's fingers catch hers, and hold. *Courage...*

"Why?" Catherine asked. "What do you—"

"I will go," Isobel cut her off. She did not know

what MacNab intended, but better her than Catherine, who had a babe to protect.

"No!" Catherine cried. "I demand you leave us together! I—"

Calmly, Bertram stepped forward and slapped Catherine across the face so hard she fell down. When Isobel stooped to lift her, she saw blood at the corner of Catherine's mouth.

"Sister?"

Catherine, bless her, looked angry rather than cowed. Rage glinted in her eyes.

"Let me go," Isobel begged. "I will return."

"No!"

"Catherine, please!"

Unhappy, Catherine subsided. Isobel turned to Bertram. "Take me."

His leer widened, and his eyes inspected her with what she very much feared was anticipation. Would these three haul her back to her previous prison, tie her to that bed where Aisla had no doubt died, be the first three to rape her?

Again she whispered a prayer in her mind, not, strangely enough, to any deity, but to the devil, Devil Black MacRae. *Please, please, please...*

"Come," MacNab growled.

She went with her head high, but her treacherous legs threatened to go out from under her. Down the corridor they went, past the chamber where Isobel had been confined before, down the stairs to the great hall, where Randal MacNab stood waiting with another man.

Isobel saw it was dark outside the windows—night. Had she and Catherine been here so long? Dawn had just been breaking through the filthy storm when they were dragged in.

She tried to focus on Randal. The man beside him, squat and ginger-haired, looked nervous. He had a roll of fabric tucked under his arm.

Randal addressed Isobel abruptly, while still her senses swam. "What part of you will your husband recognize?"

"Eh?"

"We need a token to show him, to prove our intentions when he comes."

"If he comes," Bertram put in. "The Devil Black likes to play the dangerous villain, but we all know his heart is white."

"He will come," Randal told his son. "'Twill be a point of pride with him. So, Mistress, what will your husband recognize? This man, here, is a surgeon." He grimaced. "Well, so, he is a barber, which is nearly the same thing."

Isobel gasped, and for an instant the room went dark around her. They could not mean what they said!

The ginger-haired man unfurled his roll of fabric; it contained an array of knives arranged small to large.

"Come now," Randal told Isobel. "What token?"

"You are mad!"

Bertram laughed, a strange, high-pitched giggle.

The ginger-haired barber looked at Isobel uneasily. "Her hair?" he suggested. "'Tis bonny hair. Surely her husband will recognize—"

"Yes," Isobel said through a throat constricted by terror.

"Na, na!" Randal waved a hand. "Perhaps a finger."

"A strip of flesh off her arse," Bertram suggested,

"or a nipple. Sure, he will know her nipple."

Isobel's legs failed her, and she sank to the floor. "No," she mumbled.

Bertram nodded to the guards. "Bring the other wench. I told you, Father, the best message we can present to them, when they arrive, is the babe cut from her womb."

"No!" Isobel struggled to her feet. "You shall not harm her! Use me!"

Randal MacNab nodded at the barber. "Take a finger. No doubt her pretty hands have been all over him."

"A lock o' hair—" the barber suggested again.

Randal glared at him. "You will do as you are told, man, if you wish to keep that wee bit cottage over your eight—is it eight?—squealing children's heads. And that wife o' yours—she is ill, is she no'? A shame to force her out into the winter snow."

The barber, avoiding Isobel's eyes, reached among his knives and selected one. "Hold her."

In the end it took four strong men to hold Isobel and another to stretch her hand on the hearth stones and pin it there. She struggled and fought with every drop of her strength, but they bore her down until she could only watch the barber move, like something in a dream, slow and deliberate.

She did not want to scream, but the sound tore from her—not when the barber's knife severed the smallest finger on her left hand, but when he pulled an iron from the fire and cauterized the bleeding stump.

Then, even before her eyes rolled back in her head, she bellowed like a banshee, "You shall pay for this! He will come! I tell you, the Devil Black will come!"

Chapter Thirty-Five

"Open the gates, MacNab!" bellowed Dougal MacRae. "Open to me! You have something that is mine!"

The filthy weather had cleared at last, and a weak sun had now sunk into the horizon, stealing all light. In the dense gloom, the stones of MacNab's stronghold looked dark and forbidding. Surrounded by the handful of men left to him, Dougal knew himself to be utterly vulnerable. If MacRae let him in—and he would—there existed a good chance Dougal would never ride out again.

At his side, Thomas sat his horse, looking grim and uneasy. No fool, he. The man knew the odds. Yet he had been the first to declare himself ready to ride into the monster's lair.

"I am no warrior," he said, "but I am willing to die for the woman I love. My life is nothing without her anyway."

Those words hung in Dougal's mind and played over and over again. Aisla, the woman he had always loved, had died here in MacNab's hands. Dougal could no longer say what he felt for Isobel. He still believed himself incapable of the fine emotion called love, but the idea of failing her made him go cold and hollow inside.

He could not fail her, but curse him if he knew how

he could win.

The gates opened like the doors to hell and he and his small party rode inside. MacNab's warriors ringed the forecourt, all armed. Dougal knew Rab and his warriors had slain more than a few during the assault on his keep, yet these put on an impressive display.

Hate burned in his heart; it brightened when he saw Randal MacNab strut toward him.

"Welcome, neighbor," MacNab said. "Kind in you to call."

"Curse you, MacNab. I am in no mood for games. I ha' come for my wife."

"Your wife? Have you lost her, then? And what makes you think I have her? Och, wait. Would that be the lustful, red-haired wench who has been entertaining my warriors? Or her sister, with the swollen belly?"

Beside Dougal, Thomas grunted. Dougal hoped he would not lose his head, and his life. This was Dougal's battle to fight.

"What do you want?" he asked, looking Randal in the eye. "What price have you set on them?"

"What will you pay? Perhaps you should come in, and we will talk it over." Randal smiled, a terrible thing to see. "And, lest you have any doubt your wife is the wench in question, I ha' something inside to show you."

"I demand to see her!"

"I think not. Part of her, perhaps."

Dougal's stomach plummeted. He exchanged looks with Thomas as they dismounted, cautioning the man to contain his ire. If only Dougal could manage the same.

"Leave your army here," Randal sneered, eyeing the small group of warriors at Dougal's back. "You will not need them."

Dougal nodded at his men and, with Thomas at his side, entered his enemy's walls. The air inside smelled dusky and singed, the way he imagined it might in Hades. Randal led them to the great hall, where the bastard Bertram waited. The man stood in front of the fire, juggling a small object in his hands.

"Ah!" said Bertram with a ghastly grin, "our erstwhile neighbor. Pray tell, MacRae, how went your audience with the King?"

Dougal did not deign to answer Bertram. "Where is my wife—our wives?" he amended with a glance at the silent Thomas. He spoke to Randal, his anger a banked fire. "If you have harmed either of them—"

"Define 'harm,' " Bertram commanded. "It can encompass so much; there are so many ways to inflict pain."

Thomas gave a strangled growl and started forward. Dougal seized his forearm in a grip of iron. His own anger barely under control, he said, "You cannot just seize a man's wife. There are laws in this land."

Randal threw back his head and laughed. "You, to cite the law to me? 'Tis a crime to steal a man's wife? But no crime to steal his betrothed?" The older man's face grew hard. "You cost us a fine estate that would have come to my son on the death of the wench's father. Now you shall make up for it."

"How?" Dougal's heart sank. Half distracted, still trying to identify the object with which Bertram played, he scowled at Randal.

Randal smiled again, and this time it looked cold as the north wind. "I am a kind man at heart, MacRae. I will let you ransom your women, and let bygones be bygones. Forget the sins of the past."

Dougal gritted his teeth. Some things could never be forgotten, yet his heart told him now was no time to assert that truth. He needed Isobel back again. "Name your price."

MacNab pretended to think about it. He exchanged a look with his son and feigned indecision, even though Dougal knew this scene had been planned weeks ago.

"The price I require is: the whole of your lands."

Dougal's mouth went dry and his heart clenched so hard he thought he must fall down.

"Do it," said Thomas, beside him. "Agree. Get them out of here."

Aye, it seemed the canny response. But Dougal said, "Wait! Those lands have been in my family for generations. My ancestors bled for them. They are not mine to give."

"They are." No uncertainty tainted Thomas's voice. "Just agree." Softly, for Dougal's ears alone, he added, "These men have no honor. You can break the agreement later and fight it out."

Fight with what? A handful of warriors and no legal right? The old snake would make him sign a paper. That he did not doubt.

"No time to waste," said Bertram, his eyes gleaming. "Perhaps this will persuade you."

He tossed the object he had been juggling so playfully. By instinct, Dougal caught it and cradled it in the palm of hand. A curious thing—small, narrow and tapered, with a bloody stump at one end and a delicate nail at the other. In dawning horror he realized it was a finger.

Dougal's world tilted around him, sickeningly, and went dark for an instant.

"I am sure you recognize that," Bertram leered. "No doubt you ha' seen it often enough, wrapped round your cock. Do you doubt it belongs to your wife?"

Dougal launched himself at the grinning face, his control snapping abruptly. What had they done to her—the bastards, the bastards! He would kill Bertram MacNab slowly and then feed his heart to his misbegotten sire…

He managed three damaging blows before he was hauled away by a number of MacNab's guards who stepped forward from the shadows. Too late now to feign indifference or disbelief. When they released him, he stood trembling with rage so powerful he had to consciously fight it down. Nay, he did not doubt from whence they had taken the grisly trophy. Had he not marveled a score of times, as she caressed him, that such a slender being could contain so much fire and courage? Isobel! All at once his longing for her had a power that should have moved mountains.

Randal shot his son a look. "Bring her. Her husband should harbor no doubt. And she should witness what he does or does no' think of her, and his lack of honor."

Bertram, now trickling blood from one corner of his mouth, went, and Dougal retrieved the grisly treasure from the stones, where it had flown. A treasure it was. They had taken this from her by force, in terror and pain. How his Isobel must have felt—the same hurt and loneliness Aisla had endured.

He had failed Aisla. He could not fail Isobel now, not at any cost.

Had he believed in anything, he might have prayed; he would call upon the devil, if he thought Satan might respond. Beside him Thomas, dead pale, stood like a rock.

And then she was there, hauled in through the far doorway by the vile Bertram, her feet dragging on the ground. She looked twice as pale as Thomas, near to fainting, her clothes in disarray and her hair streaming down, a bright curtain. But her eyes found Dougal's and held, burning with will and another emotion Dougal identified with a sudden rush of humility.

"Take your hands from her!" he barked, and started forward to free her from Bertram's grasp. To his surprise, Bertram released her. She half fell into Dougal's arms; his eyes and hands both searched her avidly. He found her hand and lifted it in his own.

They had not even bandaged her wound, the scunners. It showed as a blackened blight, doubly marred by cauterization, and he felt his gorge rise.

"What ha' they done to you?" He brought her hand to his lips and kissed it reverently. Tears flooded her eyes, but she did not speak.

"You agree," Randal MacNab said smoothly, "this is, indeed, your wife?"

Dougal rounded on him. "You will pay for this—in hell, if not sooner to me!"

"No doubt. But you will pay first. Agree to my demands, and you can take your wife and her sister home."

"Demands?" Isobel whispered. Dougal heard it in her voice—she was spent, her courage unraveling. But it held her still.

Randal ignored her. "I have a scribe standing by—

a lawyer, in fact. We shall make this legal, aye, so there can be no question later—no reneging by you, black devil that you are."

"You would ransom me?" Isobel questioned, her eyes clinging to Dougal's. "What does he ask?"

"Your husband will sign over to me and my descendants all his lands in exchange for your freedom and that of your sister."

"No!" Isobel cried before anyone else could speak. She straightened her spine and drew away from Dougal. "Go to the King, Husband. Make complaint. It is illegal, what he does here."

Dougal's lips twisted. "He has destroyed my credibility with the King. Besides," he swallowed hard, "how long would that take?" How could he leave her and Catherine in these monsters' hands the while? What condition would she be in, if he did manage to get her away through legal means?

"But your lands..." she whispered, eyes still holding his, "they mean everything to you. Everything."

"Aye." The blessed land, the waters, the sky above both, remained as vital to him as breath, blood of his blood and bone of his bone.

But, he realized with an impact that shook him, this woman might well be just as vital to him.

He refused to fail her.

He never knew, later, what Isobel saw in his eyes, but it caused her to catch her breath and round on MacNab. "I demand a few moments with my husband, alone."

"You demand?" Randal sneered.

"And that my sister be permitted to see her husband before any agreements are made—or signed."

"What right have you, wench, to ask for anything?"

Isobel's chin came up. "You will grant my request," she pronounced, "or I shall bid my husband leave me here. And then, sir, what will you have?"

## Chapter Thirty-Six

"Listen to me," Dougal said, "we do not have much time."

They huddled close beside the fire in MacNab's great hall, the four of them alone, as private as a room under guard could be. MacNab had ordered Catherine brought down from her imprisonment to join Isobel, Dougal, and Thomas. Catherine had gone into Thomas's arms and not come out again; the two of them spoke in murmurs, oblivious of their companions.

Isobel, standing beside her own husband, shot a half envious look at her sister. Of course she was glad Catherine and Thomas were together, however briefly, and she wanted Catherine to be happy. She had done much and gone far since their mother's death to assure just that. Yet at this moment she felt inclined to weep for the fact that she, herself, could not burrow into Dougal's arms where she so longed to be.

She lifted her eyes and searched those of her husband. What she saw there made her throat tighten: banked rage, determination, and concern for her. Concern. That was all. She must have been mistaken when, a few moments ago, she thought she had glimpsed love.

"Your hand—" he began.

"You are right," she interrupted him. "We have no time now to speak of that."

"Have they hurt you in any other way?" He tipped her chin up, his eyes plundering hers for the truth. "Bertram did not—?"

Isobel shook her head. "Not yet. So far we have been kept together. There is no way out of our prison. I have looked. But that is not why I asked to see you alone. Dougal—"

Passionately, he broke in, "I will no' fail you, Isobel, I swear it. I will win you free from here somehow, so I do vow!"

His earnestness made tears flood Isobel's eyes. She seized hold of him with her good hand; the other was paralyzed by pain. "Yes, but you cannot surrender your lands. That is what I wanted a chance to tell you, Husband. I know what they mean to you, how dear to your heart!" Indeed, were his lands not the sole occupant of that fiercely-guarded chamber? "There must be another way."

Slowly, he shook his head. "I have thought on it, on naught else. MacNab is a clever bastard and has long plotted to have my lands—do you no' see? Had the King condemned me to death, who but the King's good friend would have been awarded stewardship over my confiscated holdings? The greedy lout will have them one way or another."

Isobel said, as steadily as she could manage, "But you cannot sign away all you own, all your ancestors held—not for me."

"I will not leave you here."

"You are thinking of Aisla, are you not?" Isobel challenged. "You think on how she died here, in his hands. You regret—"

"Regret does not begin to describe it."

"So," Isobel drew a breath, "you act, still, for her and not for me."

"You are wrong." He reached out and his fingers touched her face softly, like the brush of feathers. Again, she saw something stir in the smoky depths of his eyes. "I care for you, Isobel, and 'twould murder me to leave you now. I care as much as I am able—"

"There must be another way." Thomas repeated Isobel's own words. He stepped to their sides with Catherine tucked into his arm. "What about a challenge?"

Dougal turned guarded eyes on him, with no reply.

Thomas spoke on, "My father used to tell us tales of the old times, as he called them, here in Scotland and sometimes, in Viking days, in Yorkshire as well. Great matters were known to be settled by single combat—one warrior pitted against another. If you challenge yon monster's son, Bertram, honor will not let them refuse."

"Honor?" Dougal repeated the word as if foreign to him. "Did you not say, yourself, these men know nothing of it?" He lifted his hand and touched the deep scar on his cheek.

"It gives us a better chance, surely," Thomas urged, "than signing away your lands? Even if you do that, how do we know MacNab will release our wives?"

"I agree," Isobel cried. "You are a fierce warrior. I know you will win—"

Catherine, reading Dougal's expression, spoke up unexpectedly. "He would win, did MacNab give him a fair chance. It is what you fear, is it not, Brother-in-law? An unfair contest?"

The room went suddenly still. Isobel, caught by the look in her husband's eyes, felt some of the pieces of the past fall into place.

"It is what happened before, is it not?" she hazarded. "This would not be the first time you fought Bertram MacNab. Last time was for Aisla?"

"Aisla?" Thomas questioned.

Isobel glanced at Thomas and Catherine while Dougal stood as if carved from wood. "Bertram MacNab's first wife, and the woman Dougal loved— loves still."

Dougal stirred slowly, like a man moving through molasses. "I was but a lad of twenty then," he growled, "and a fool who believed in such things as honor and right. I came here, aye, after Meg received that letter from Aisla. I told no one, not Meg and not Lachlan, not then nor afterwards. I challenged Bertram MacNab to combat for her."

Again he touched the scar on his face, and Isobel felt her stomach clench. "What happened?"

"Bertram told me he would accept my challenge, aye, but since Aisla was his wife under law, I should need to earn my right to face him in single combat."

"How?" asked Isobel, trying to picture her husband at twenty, determined and idealistic.

"He said I must work my way up to him by first facing the members of his personal guard in succession, one on one, seasoned warriors all, and avid for it. I see now he wished only to humiliate me. In that he succeeded all too well.

"It took place here in the forecourt, myself surrounded by the pack of them, yelping like wolves. I loved her so much—" He closed his eyes for an instant, as if at a surge of pain. "I thought I could overcome anything. I asked him for but one thing, that he might tell Aisla I was there. I wanted her to know I had come for her, however it ended. He refused. So she never knew. She never even knew."

Thomas swore softly, and Isobel bit her tongue so hard she drew blood. So, this made the wound not yet healed. She did not want to hear the rest of it but knew she must listen.

Thomas spoke again. "How many did you face?"

"Sixteen," Dougal said bitterly, "with Bertram himself the last. By then I was covered in wounds and could barely stand. The mind may remain willing, but the body gives out. At least, mine did that day. Bertram took me down on the stones and cut my face—deep—with his sword, giving me something to remember. As if I could ever forget!"

"What happened then?" Thomas asked softly.

"They hauled me up, half dead and bleeding, dragged me out, and dumped me beside the burn on the border of my land. I made my way home somehow and never spoke of it—not to anyone. I was too sore ashamed. Next morning, early, I told my servant I was off hunting. I took myself away to the wood, meaning to wait for my wounds to heal. And while there alone, I felt Aisla leave this world—believe that as you may. I returned home only to have Meg shout at me. Word had come that Aisla was dead. Meg called me a coward and blamed me for it. She has never stopped. Nor have I."

"By God!" Catherine exclaimed.

And Thomas added, "But you cannot blame yourself, man!"

"Och, I do."

"It was not a fair fight!"

"And that is what I should have known. That is

what I have learned. MacNab does not play fair. I wasted my one chance, and Aisla died for it. How can I ever put that aside?"

Isobel caught her husband's hand and, trying to speak round the emotion that clogged her throat, said, "The courage you showed on Aisla's behalf surpasses what she could ever have asked. She would have forgiven you, had she known what you endured that night."

"You do not know that."

"Yes! If she loved you, she would forgive. Yet you have continued to punish yourself all these years and allowed Meg to punish you with her hate. Why did you never tell her? How did you hide your wounds, your scars, when you did return from the wood?"

Dougal laughed bitterly. "A many nights' drunken stupor and a number of brawls can disguise many things. Aye, and I would have crawled inside my flask then. But as I have learned, there is no escape, even in the drink." His eyes met Isobel's. "I could not tell Meg, or anyone, and admit my shame."

"There was no shame," Thomas insisted, "for you were cheated."

"Yes," Catherine agreed, "and it will not end so, this time."

Dougal rounded on her. "What makes you think I can trust them now, any more than then?"

"You are no child now," Thomas said. "You have many witnesses, and you can insist Bertram face you fairly. Unless he is a coward, he must agree."

"Must he?" Dougal grimaced. "Tell that to him."

"I will, and gladly."

"This decision," said Isobel, speaking from her

heart, "cannot be ours, Thomas, Dougal alone can decide."

"There you are wrong." Once more, Dougal touched her face tenderly. "'Tis yourself and your sister, Wife, who will pay the price, should I fail."

"You will not fail," Isobel said fiercely, her eyes holding his.

"I did, last time. You have no right to have such faith in me."

"I have every faith in you. I entrust you with my life. Yet, I would not have you do anything in which you do not believe—"

"You know what will happen to you if I leave here without you, Isobel. Even if I go straight to Stirling to plead our case—against James's loyal subject and friend, no less—'twill take too long. Once I am gone, MacNab will unleash his every perversion..."

"I know." Isobel thought of that terrible room— Aisla's prison and death place—the ropes on the bedposts, the threatened wave of warriors. Could she endure it? Maybe not, but neither could she endure costing this man, whom she loved, the one remaining occupant of his heart. "Yet surrendering your lands will beggar you. I cannot send you—send all of us— penniless into the world!"

"We shall not leave you here." Thomas spoke. "I shall offer to fight the bastard myself, if need be."

Dougal looked hard at Thomas before giving a tight smile. "You, the son of a bailiff, when here stand I, descendent of chieftains? I would fight the bastard in a heartbeat, man, if I thought we had a fair chance."

"Then let us put our heads together," Thomas growled, "and see how we can assure it."

Chapter Thirty-Seven

"So that is our offer—our only offer!" Dougal roared into his opponents' faces. "Combat, single combat, one on one between myself and Bertram. When I win, you will release all of us—myself, this man, Thomas Hewett, and both our wives."

Randal MacNab smiled into Dougal's face. "We have been here before, I think," he tossed back at Dougal with satisfaction. "I remember you lying in a bloodied heap on the stones of my forecourt. You were taught a lesson then, MacRae. Have you truly forgotten?"

Dougal felt rage rise to his head, so strong it barely left room for thought, and fought it down. Now, of all times, he needed a clear head.

"We ha' not been here before," he shouted. "This time it shall be done fairly—one on one, I say, and with honor, if you can muster any."

Bertram spoke. "Och, and listen to him whinge and whine. Your combat last time was one on one, was it not, man? You faced but one opponent at a time."

Dougal stiffened in ire. He wanted to strangle Bertram, the bastard, with his bare hands, wanted it so badly the desire felt like fire in his blood. He wanted to leap upon the man now, but he felt Isobel, at his side, reach out and touch his arm.

"This time," he told Bertram through his teeth, "if

you have the balls for it, I will face you and only you, not the master of your guards, nor so many of your warriors I lose count. Two men only, yourself and me, with two swords—to the death, if need be."

Bertram and his father exchanged glances.

"And," said MacNab the Senior, "should my son prove victorious again?"

Stony-faced, Dougal replied, "I sign away my lands to you—this night—all MacRae holdings in Lothian."

"And the women?" Randal's eyes narrowed.

"They go free, either way. You can keep me if you wish—"

"You," said Bertram flatly, "will be dead."

"Na, na," Randal objected, "I canno' see that. One of these women will, one day, inherit a fine holding in Yorkshire, after their father dies. 'Tis what you are thinking, MacRae, is it not? Surrender your lands here, crawl away on your belly, and take up the lands of your wife's father?"

"He will crawl nowhere," Bertram put in, fingering the hilt of his sword. "He will lie leaking his life's blood."

"Aye, so," Randal mused, "yet I am a man who likes assurances. What of this, MacRae—if you lose, I keep the women and your lands. Let us make the stakes high and the contest interesting."

Dougal shook his head. He had to bargain cannily, now, and get this thing right. "No, we fight for the lands only. The women will leave here first, under the protection of my wife's brother-in-law."

He shot Thomas a look. The bailiff's son stood strong and steady. Thomas had his instructions and

Dougal felt a bit surprised to realize he trusted the man to carry them out.

MacNab laughed. "I begin to think you as innocent as you were all those years ago. Do you take me for a fool? The women stay."

Dougal looked at Catherine, who stood clutching Isobel's hand. "At least let my wife's sister accompany her husband away. She is with child and thus no good to you. Her father will never believe she took your son in marriage."

Randal appeared to ponder it. He, too, eyed Catherine and then said, "Hewett leaves before the fight?"

"Before the fight," Dougal insisted. "He is my assurance, you see, that you shall play fair this time. He shall travel directly to Stirling and await word from me."

"And if you fall?" Bertram demanded avidly. "If you die?"

"Then he awaits word from my wife."

"No." Randal balked at it. "She stays with us."

"There is no one else here free from your influence," Dougal pointed out, trying not to reveal his desperation. "How are we to assure the contest is fair?"

"I shall assure it." Unexpectedly, the scribe stepped forward. "My name is William Campbell, and I become interested in this."

"Trust a Campbell?" Dougal sneered inwardly. "And how do I know, sir, you are not also under his influence? He is the one who brought you here as witness to all this."

"I shall write the terms out in a letter," Campbell said, "which your man, Hewett, will carry with him."

Dougal looked at Randal and quirked a brow.

"Aye, agreed," Randal growled. "But both women stay. That is my assurance."

Catherine lifted her head. "Stay I shall. I am not afraid. I know, Master MacRae, you will prove victorious."

If only, thought Dougal, he himself felt half so confident.

**** 

The flames from the torches on the wall danced in a draft of air as the company sorted itself, the warriors muttering in anticipation, the two women standing close, still with clasped hands. The men had formed a rough ring in the forecourt, site of Dougal's previous defeat, as he remembered all too well. Randal MacNab, looking every bit the proud laird, stood at one side, the scribe at the other, where he could, presumably, witness fair play.

Bertram MacNab and Dougal had both stripped down to kilts and leggings, assuring their only weapons were the swords in their hands. But Dougal did not feel the cold wind. His entire being focused on the man in front of him. Stripped down, Bertram looked massive, bulky with muscle and ugly as a boar. Rage touched Dougal again at the thought of Aisla, so delicate and beautiful, in this brute's hands, but he knew he had to manage his anger, channel it. He would need every advantage at his disposal.

He glanced at Isobel, who stood straight and tall, and her eyes met his and caught. His heart clenched painfully at what he saw there, for it seemed she offered to him, at that moment, all her faith, all her strength— all her love.

By God—if, indeed, such a being existed—did he deserve such a woman? Curse his black heart, he felt sure he did not. But perhaps, just now, for one moment in time, he could earn such love.

And, return it? The idea, pure and golden as flame, blossomed in his mind. Did he love Isobel? Suddenly, it seemed impossible he should not. But his feelings for her were so different from what he had felt for Aisla, gentle Aisla, like a dream. For Isobel, he felt passion, admiration...aye, respect. And he would gladly give his life for her now, to pay for her safety and happiness.

Was that love?

"Fight to first blood, for the sake of honor?" Campbell asked Randal MacNab.

Bertram laughed. "First blood? What coward chooses that? 'Twill be last blood or none at all."

Dougal nodded, tore his gaze from his wife's, and shut down all distractions. There existed, in all the world, naught but himself and this bastard, the man he must kill.

His sword felt good in his hand; he felt good withal, strong and undefeatable. And so he must prove.

Bertram came at him like a charging bull, with a snarl that rose to the chill night sky. Using the brute's own impetus against him, Dougal stepped aside at the moment of impact and raised his sword to slash Bertram's legs. *Aye, and I am no' the lad you brought to his knees last time.*

Bertram might be cruel and merciless, but he was not stupid and learned caution swiftly. He rounded on Dougal, blood streaming from his knees, and narrowed his eyes.

*How patient are you? How canny?* Dougal

watched to see.

Not very. Bertram's next charge came in a forward sweep of sword and muscle. Dougal, more agile, ducked beneath it and just missed landing a slice to MacNab's belly. The man moved quickly for a great lout. This time, Dougal rounded and slashed him from behind. His sword just caught Bertram's shoulder before Bertram turned, and the big man howled in what sounded like outrage. The watching warriors began to mutter again, and Dougal strove to shut them out.

*Concentrate. It may mean your life, and Isobel's.*

Bertram swung round and faced Dougal again, rage in his eyes, and deadly intent. The next rush came in a flurry—Bertram was learning, and this time Dougal was not quick enough. He felt Bertram's blade tear the flesh over his left bicep, but felt no pain.

*I must bleed him, and tire him. I shall, aye, give no quarter...*

There began, then, a deadly dance. The wind rose above their heads, and the clouds cleared to reveal the stars. It might, Dougal reflected, have been a contest taking place at any time, anywhere in Scotland. The blood knew, the blood remembered.

And he, he fought for her. As his breath grew short and his muscles began to scream in pain, as he took and inflicted wound after wound, his heart continued to cry her name.

Bertram MacNab's face became a snarling mask before Dougal's eyes, and all he saw. Move, duck, slash, parry, round, and struggle for breath, let a bit more blood, and do it all again. Almost imperceptibly, Bertram began to tire, and Dougal bared his teeth in a grim smile. He, himself, now had half a score of wounds, but none of them was potentially fatal. They stung and burned, no more. And he knew he had touched Bertram gravely at least twice—a slash to the left thigh and one on the right arm that felt as if his blade had penetrated to the bone. That being Bertram's sword arm, it had now begun to hamper him visibly.

They turned again in a dreadful parody of grace, boots shuffling in time, and Dougal caught a glimpse of Isobel's face: milk white, eyes stretched wide. The breath seared his lungs. He must be more tired than he thought.

He shook the hair out of his eyes and adjusted his grip on his sword; the hilt felt sticky with blood. In that instant of distraction, Bertram made his move, launched himself in a rush of clumsy energy, screaming.

Bertram's sword struck Dougal a glancing blow in the center of his chest and they both went flying, Dougal over backward and Bertram, losing his footing, atop him, a tremendous weight.

Dougal felt what little breath he possessed leave him as he hit the stones. He struggled to determine the location of Bertram's weapon—if he did not, he might well lose his head. His own sword remained, miraculously, in his hand.

Bertram's face, covered in gore, hovered just a breath above his. Bertram grinned, his eyes wild, and growled, "Bastard! Are you ready to die? Get you to hell where you belong!"

Not quite yet, Dougal thought, and struggled, using every muscle, to buck the man off. His sword arm felt numb, yet his fingers still gripped the hilt.

"Will you die for her?" Bertram spat. "Even as you would for the other, weak bitch that she was? I enjoyed her, MacRae—liked breaking her, but she broke too easily. This one, I think, will last longer."

Hatred sent a spear of pure energy through Dougal's veins and limbs. He brought his feet up, used them to kick at the bastard's legs, and must have got in a lucky blow to the injured thigh. Bertram howled and, in one motion, Dougal brought up his sword, struck the side of the man's head, and heaved him off.

Somehow, he got to his feet.

Bertram lay on his back, on the stones, a new ribbon of gore leaking from one ear.

The ring of warriors had now closed in so tight they virtually breathed down Dougal's neck.

"Back!" He swung his sword in a wide arc, chasing them, then nudged Bertram with one foot.

"Is he dead?" The words came from Isobel in a rough croak.

Bertram's eyes stared upward like those of a dead man, but his chest still rose and fell. Dougal leveled the point of his sword at the fallen man's throat.

And Bertram erupted. With another of those bovine bellows he rose, disregarding Dougal's blade as it sliced into the skin from neck to shoulder.

Bertram had lost his sword yet, maddened, he came at Dougal with his bare hands. A woman screamed and all the warriors yelled. Dougal felt Bertram's hands close on his throat. He kicked out—once, twice, landing solid thumps. But the eyes now staring into his were utterly mad. Dougal, no longer sure Bertram could even feel pain and rapidly running out of air, drew back his sword and used it to thrust upward, a short, brutal blow. Bertram sank, slowly.

"That is for Aisla," he said, his voice roughened

and yet so full of rage it rang against the stones. He bent over his opponent and once more brought the point of his sword to Bertram's throat. "And this, for Isobel—"

Isobel! He fought for another breath and shook his hair back, thinking for once beyond the anger and the desire to mete out what was deserved. He wanted so badly to press the blade home, to end this cur's life, yet he trusted in Randal MacNab's honor not at all and they had yet to get free of this place.

"Get up!" he rasped at Bertram. "Up!"

"Finish it," Bertram told him.

"Och, I will. Just not yet." Using strength he did not know he possessed, he hauled Bertram up by the remnants of his kilt and held the sword to his throat. He looked round, saw Randal MacNab staring like a man struck, and found the scribe.

"Campbell! You saw it all? You wrote it down?"

"I did, Laird." Campbell glanced at Randal MacNab uncertainly. "I will so testify. But I pray you take me with you."

"No fear. MacNab, your son comes with us also. If you want him to live, you will give the four of us safe passage away from here."

"'Twas not in the agreement," Randal began to bluster, "that you should take Bertram with you."

"A temporary hostage only, to assure our safety. Whether he lives or not, once we are away from here, depends on how quickly you move."

"Bring their horses," Randal commanded, his expression sour. "And, aye, open the gates."

Chapter Thirty-Eight

"This is not over," Dougal said as the five of them rode away through the windy darkness. Bertram MacNab—well-bound and still streaming blood—rode double with Dougal, so Dougal could keep his blade at Bertram's throat. "I have still to decide the fate of our captive."

Isobel, riding alongside the two men, blinked at her husband—this stranger with the wild, black hair, bloodied face, and seeping wounds. In the light cast by the stars and a half moon, with the blade glittering silver in his grasp, he might have been a savage conjured from the past.

She knew Dougal MacRae as harsh, unbending, and ruthless. He had earned the name of Devil Black full well. Yet always, in her experience, had he held his emotions in check. Even when they lay together and their passions ran high, she sensed a part of him kept back as if he guarded himself.

But the battle she had just witnessed defied all that, made a mockery of restraint and any civilized veneer he had ever worn. Life and death had balanced on his blade, and did yet.

"No one pursues us," said the scribe, looking over his shoulder, and not for the first time. He seemed nervous about the choices he had recently made and how he had cast his lot.

"They will not come," Dougal growled from between clenched teeth. "Not unless they want this bastard to die."

He jerked Bertram by the rope that encircled his throat, and Bertram made a sound like a trapped animal. Isobel could feel the rage emitting from Dougal. She also felt such a tangle of other emotions—terror, relief, horror, love, and, surprisingly, pride—she could barely contemplate them.

"Do you mean to kill him?" Catherine asked. Isobel glanced at her sister and felt concern; Catherine rode her mount hunched over, as if in pain or as if protecting the babe she carried, but her voice sounded strong.

"I am no' certain," Dougal replied.

"He deserves to die," Isobel shocked herself by saying, and her husband looked at her sharply.

"I know."

Bertram, fool that he was, spat, "You ha' not got the balls to kill me, MacRae! 'Twould mean all-out war and an excuse for the King to end your practices in the district." Beneath his defiance, Isobel heard the pain in his voice, and it gave her satisfaction.

"And what of your practices in the district," she challenged quickly, "terrorizing the women who fall into your hands and, no doubt, the wives and daughters of your clansfolk and tenants. Should that not be ended? Would the world not be a better place without you?"

With difficulty, Bertram turned his head to stare at her. "By God, what kind of woman are you?"

Dougal laughed joyously. "She is the daughter of Celts and Vikings—a fearful combination! Trust me, MacNab, the only thing keeping you alive is my need to get these women safe off your lands. When we reach my border, we shall think again." Cruelly, he drew Bertram's head back. "You recall the boundary where you left me some eight years ago?"

"Still no one coming," said Campbell.

Ahead, a shallow burn marked the boundary of MacNab's holding. On the far side of it waited Dougal's small troop of warriors, all mounted. They gave a shout when they identified the approaching riders, and lowered their swords.

"Go," said Dougal to Isobel. "Take your sister across."

"What will you—?" Isobel began, trying to look into his eyes.

He lowered his lashes. "Go." He told the scribe, "You stay. I need a witness."

Campbell, looking unhappy and a bit ill, obeyed. Isobel splashed her mount through the water to the opposite bank, with Catherine behind her.

One of the warriors called to Dougal, "Your man Hewett is awa' with your letter to the King."

"It is well. You hear that, MacNab? What do you think the King will make o' this night's work?"

Bertram sneered, "He will have your head, MacRae. James is in my father's pocket."

"You think so? For, I am thinking 'tis you who may hang, instead of me. Get down."

Swiftly, Dougal dismounted and hauled Bertram after him. Isobel, watching from the far bank, thought it a scene out of some dark dream, lit only by the cold stars and the half moon.

Bertram wobbled when his feet hit the ground; the wound in his thigh, grave and deep, had cost him a lot of blood. Dougal leveled the sword, already stained, at his throat.

"On your knees," Dougal ordered. "I want to hear you beg for your life."

"I will be damned!"

"Aye, no doubt, but that will come later. This is my time of justice. On your knees, or you die where you stand."

Slowly and with a glance at the scribe, Bertram sank down onto his knees.

"Now," Dougal told him, "we will have a confession. You will recite all your sins—well, I doubt we ha' time for that, but give us the major ones. Start with what you did to Aisla."

"That craven bitch," MacNab said.

Dougal struck him, a sweeping, openhanded wallop that knocked him over, and then hauled him up again by the rope that encircled his neck.

"You will tell what you did to her, and fairly. How she suffered and died. These folk," he swung his sword at the listeners on both sides of the burn, "are your council who will help decide your fate."

Bertram said nothing.

"Come, man! Is that not justice?" Dougal shouted at him. "I want to kill you now, my blade thirsts for it, but I give you, here before witnesses, the chance you did not give her."

"She was weak," Bertram said. "From the moment I took her, she wept and moaned. She did not deserve to live—only the strong deserve to live."

"She was a child," Dougal cried, "a lass of sixteen when you took her. What need had you to torture her?"

"I shall tell you, MacRae, why I treated that bitch

the way I did, if that is what you want to hear," Bertram spat up at Dougal. "'Twas because she loved you. And once, when I rutted with her, she was foolish enough to call your name!"

Dougal sagged where he stood. Isobel, watching, saw the strength go out of him, precisely as if he had been stabbed to the heart. But his blade remained steady at Bertram's throat.

"And then you came to save her," MacNab went on, "fancying yourself the great hero. I could no' let you have her, could I? Nay, I wanted your shame! And do you know, MacRae, she died soon after—still with your name on her lips?"

"Kill him," said Catherine in a harsh voice, making Isobel jump.

"Aye, kill him," agreed one of Dougal's warriors, beginning a chorus. "He deserves it!"

Dougal's blade trembled visibly at MacNab's throat—with eagerness, Isobel fancied.

"Kill him," said the scribe, Campbell.

Dougal raised his head and looked at Isobel. By some trick of the moonlight, she could see all of what filled his eyes—blinding pain, the lust for revenge, and a question.

"Leave him live," she voted after a moment's deliberation. "But make certain he never finds pleasure in raping another woman—anywhere or at any time."

Slowly, Dougal grinned. At that moment he looked so like a devil Isobel shivered. But at the same time something within her responded to that look and gloried in it.

"My wife has spoken, MacNab," he cried. "And despite all you ha' done to her, she chooses mercy."

"No!" MacNab howled.

"I think you should kiss the ground in gratitude to her. Kiss the ground, MacNab!"

He struck Bertram again, a thunderous blow that sent him tumbling sideways in an awkward sprawl. Bertram's bound hands moved to protect his genitals, but Dougal's blade moved more quickly still and laid the grievous wound. Bertram howled, like a pig at the slaughter, into the night sky.

"You should have killed him," said the scribe mildly. "Now he will hate you twice as much."

"There is still time for him to bleed to death," Dougal said levelly. "Just you be sure, Campbell, you write down the fact that I granted him mercy, and left him alive."

Campbell looked round at the assembled company and gave a tight smile. "Aye, so—left him here beside the burn, bound and in the same condition he left his stronghold. I do no' know how he came by that last crippling injury."

"His word against ours, and yours—I like that, fine!" Dougal grinned again, turned, and sprang back onto his horse. Bertram had ceased writhing and lay motionless on the ground.

Isobel looked again at her husband—wild-haired, calm-eyed, and with an ease about him that argued he had shrugged the weight of the world from his shoulders.

He splashed his horse across the burn and held out his hand to her. "Let us, Wife, go home."

Chapter Thirty-Nine

"Bertram MacNab has been taken into custody by the King's guard," said Dougal, paused in the doorway of his wife's bedchamber. "They say he languishes even now in a dank cell."

Isobel looked up. Dougal had caught her at her morning ablutions. Bright sunlight poured through the slit windows of the chamber and turned her hair to flame. Barely a week had passed since the rescue, but the grey weather seemed to have cleared as miraculously as the cloud of despair on Dougal's heart.

"How is Lachy?" Isobel asked.

"Definitely on the mend—Meg even believes he will keep his arm. Lachy must be nearly well, for he insists on sending for O'Rourke, to perform for him a marriage service."

"O'Rourke does perform a very fine marriage. To that I can attest." Isobel raised one eyebrow. "But has Meg agreed to wed with Lachlan?"

"Not yet, though I canna' think she clawed him back from the very edge of death only to reject him now."

Isobel did not reply. Dougal watched as a single drop of water trickled down her neck, caressed her throat and headed toward still more interesting regions. By the devil's horns, how bonny she looked with that red hair all loose, flowing over her shoulders, and wearing but a thin sleeping gown that revealed the tantalizing shape of breast and thigh.

He had not yet attempted to share her bed since their return from MacNab's stronghold. He had told himself he might yet be arrested if Randal MacNab complained loudly enough to the King, and that Isobel needed time to recover from her ordeal. Aye, he had made all kinds of excuses, dodging the truth, which was that there were things needing to be said between them, and a ghost still to be laid.

Now she lifted her chin and her clear eyes met his steadily. At that look, he felt his blood stir.

"And so Bertram MacNab did not succumb to his injuries, either?"

Dougal leaned against the doorway. "He did not. The man is strong as a bull."

"And evil as a demon. Husband, will you not come in?" She added carefully, "You might tell me the rest of your news."

Dougal sauntered in and closed the door behind him. "As you wish." He sat on the bench in front of the fire, where he had a good view of her, bending to her basin. "Word has it the King, tiring of the cold and damp, has left Stirling and returned to London. It may be Bertram will rot in his cell a long time."

"So then Randal MacNab will be unable to bend the King's ear?"

"He will not. But only listen to this—it turns out the estimable scribe William Campbell is himself right close to the King and went to him directly with his account of MacNab's sins. Who would have thought?"

Isobel stared. "Certainly not I."

"Nor I." Dougal stretched comfortably. "The man

from whom I got the news says 'tis largely why Bertram was arrested in the first place."

She raised an eyebrow. "The man from whom you got the news?"

"Campbell, himself." Dougal grinned. "He stopped by here late last night on his way from Stirling, while you slept. He is away again now, on the King's business."

Carefully, Isobel laid aside her cloth and hand towel; he saw her breasts rise as she drew a breath. "Does this mean it is over—truly over?"

"I suspect so. Campbell says Bertram is a broken man who does not wish to live. Apparently that last wound he took refuses to heal."

Isobel shuddered, but said, "He has what he deserves. And what of his father?"

"Now, there is an interesting thing. When Campbell recited to James a full account of what had taken place, and the things he heard Randal say, the King became so incensed he confiscated all MacNab lands in Lothian. The King does not take well to being a pawn to another man's ambition. It makes a fine justice, does it not?"

Isobel nodded, still watching him.

"Campbell has recommended a steward—someone local, you understand—to oversee MacNab's former holdings. He is a man you know right well, who has vowed most sincerely to settle down and live the balance of his life for his lands—and his family."

"Has he, indeed, so vowed?"

Gravely, Dougal nodded. "So as for whether the thing is over and done—in part that rests with you, Wife, does it not? Can you put what happened behind you? Can your wounds heal?"

She met his gaze, fearless and challenging. "Can yours? They are far deeper than my own."

He lifted a hand and touched the scar on his cheek. Then he rose and approached her, his thoughts rampant in his mind. Of all the things he needed to say to her, one reigned supreme, and his native honesty would not let him dodge it now.

"I suspect my wounds will scab over now that they have been cleansed," he said. "Perhaps that is the best for which I can hope." He reached out softly and touched her face, brow, and chin. "I need to tell you, Wife, I will always love Aisla and will never love any other as I did love her."

"You think I do not know that?" Gently, she withdrew from his touch, her eyes still holding his.

"'Twas a first love, and with something innocent in it. I suppose 'tis hard for you to imagine me innocent."

She shook her head.

He smiled sadly. "Do you know, she and I never even lay together? I feared hurting her. I kissed her, aye, and dreamed. I made promises—too many promises—but she was taken from me before I could taste her, in truth."

"And so she will always be pure to you, no matter what happened after. She will always," Isobel added bitterly, "be beautiful and young."

"Aye." He went on heavily, "But I, for my sins, have changed a great deal. I am no' the lad I was then, but a man, with a man's needs. A man's wants. Isobel, I ha' been so unfair to you, forcing you into this marriage, neglecting to value you as I should. You have every right to walk away from me now, return to your father, or go make a life for yourself. If that is what you want, I tell you fairly I will not hold you, and I will settle a sum of money on you so you might have what I suspect you prize most—independence."

Isobel's eyes widened and she got slowly to her feet. "You would grant me that?"

"Someone should. You are strong and courageous, and graced with the brains to make your own way."

"Oh!" she said.

"Thomas Hewett has agreed to stay here, however," Dougal went on, not at all steadily now, "to act as my bailiff, and your sister, of course, with him. I did hope you might choose to remain here with her."

"You are saying I should stay for Catherine?"

"No." Dougal closed his eyes for an instant and called upon a deity all too often denied, before he sank to his knees at her feet in unthinking humility. "Stay, Isobel, please? Stay wi' me."

She caught her breath, and one hand flew to her throat. He captured the other, still damp, and brought it to his lips to kiss, not the back of it but the palm.

She said, "I can imagine very little worse than living my life with a man I love but who loves me not."

"Nor I," he agreed, searching his mind, his heart for words—the right words—those he needed to make her understand. "I do not deserve you. I know that fine. But by God, I want you. No—not just in my bed but in my life. I want you to fill my days, my dreams, share with me your laughter and the beauty of your spirit. Isobel, I thought my heart crippled and blighted, and it was, aye, it was—until you poured your light upon it. I thought I could never love again—I was wrong!"

Isobel trembled where she stood, but she did not

bend. "Aisla will always come between us."

Dougal felt the incipient blow of her imminent refusal, but he held strong. "I see now Aisla was a lass loved by a lad, as a lad loves. He gave her all his heart, everything he had to give. My heart, now, is a far uglier thing—scarred, torn, and battered. But 'tis a man's heart, and for what it is worth, I offer it to you. 'Tis true, Isobel, the lad I was will always love that lass who was Aisla. But the man I am will always love you."

Tears flooded Isobel's eyes. She clasped his hand between both of hers and drew him up until they stood close, so close even the sunlight could not part them.

"Is it enough?" he whispered. "Dare I hope?"

"I find your heart—battered, scarred, and ever-true—a fair prize. And one I think I must accept."

His arms closed around her, and the last of the hurt inside him eased. "Ah," he said, "and I promise you will never regret—"

She laughed, the sound slightly breathless, and slightly wicked. "That I very much doubt, Husband. There will be regrets in plenty, rues and quarrels, hurt feelings and fallings out. But what I promise you in turn is none of that will ever part us, nor ever make me stop loving you."

Dougal felt his heart rise on a surge of feeling that buoyed and lifted him, so unfamiliar he barely recognized it as happiness.

"It is a good promise, and one I make also," he said devoutly. "But how can I show you my gratitude, scoundrel that I am?"

"I can think of but one way," Isobel said, and led him softly to the bed.

### A word about the author...

Born and raised in Western New York, Laura Strickland has been an avid reader and writer since childhood. Embracing her mother's heritage, she pursued a lifelong interest in Celtic lore, legend, and music, all reflected in her writing.

She has made pilgrimages to both Newfoundland and Scotland in the company of her daughter, but is usually happiest at home not far from Lake Ontario, with her husband and her "fur" child, a rescue dog. She practices gratitude every day.